BRIAN
THE SWING

BRIAN FLYNN was born in 1885 in Leyton, Essex. He won a scholarship to the City Of London School, and from there went into the civil service. In World War I he served as Special Constable on the Home Front, also teaching "Accountancy, Languages, Maths and Elocution to men, women, boys and girls" in the evenings, and acting in his spare time.

It was a seaside family holiday that inspired Brian Flynn to turn his hand to writing in the mid-twenties. Finding most mystery novels of the time "mediocre in the extreme", he decided to compose his own. Edith, the author's wife, encouraged its completion, and after a protracted period finding a publisher, it was eventually released in 1927 by John Hamilton in the UK and Macrae Smith in the U.S. as *The Billiard-Room Mystery*.

The author died in 1958. In all, he wrote and published 57 mysteries, the vast majority featuring the super-sleuth Antony Bathurst.

BRIAN FLYNN

THE SWINGING DEATH

With an introduction by
Steve Barge

DEAN STREET PRESS

Published by Dean Street Press 2022

Copyright © 1947 Brian Flynn

Introduction © 2022 Steve Barge

All Rights Reserved

The right of Brian Flynn to be identified as the Author of the Work has been asserted by his estate in accordance with the Copyright, Designs and Patents Act 1988.

First published in 1947 by John Long

Cover by DSP

ISBN 978 1 915393 40 1

www.deanstreetpress.co.uk

INTRODUCTION

"I let my books write themselves. That is to say, having once constructed my own plot, I sit down to write and permit the puppets to do their own dancing."

DURING the war, Brian Flynn was trying some experiments with his crime writing. His earlier books are all traditional mystery novels, all with a strong whodunit element to them, but starting with *Black Edged* in 1939, Brian seemed to want to branch out in his writing style. *Black Edged* (1939) tells the tale of the pursuit of a known killer from both sides of the chase. While there is a twist in the tale, this is far from a traditional mystery, and Brian returned to the inverted format once again with *Such Bright Disguises* (1941). There was also an increasing darkness in some of his villains – the plot of *They Never Came Back* (1940), the story of disappearing boxers, has a sadistic antagonist and *The Grim Maiden* (1942) was a straight thriller with a similarly twisted adversary. However, following this, perhaps due in part to a family tragedy during the Second World War, there was a notable change in Brian's writing style. The style of the books from *The Sharp Quillet* (1947) onwards switched back to a far more traditional whodunnit format, while he also adopted a pseudonym in attempt to try something new.

The three Charles Wogan books – *The Hangman's Hands* (1947), *The Horror At Warden Hall* (1948) and *Cyanide For The Chorister* (1950) – are an interesting diversion for Brian, as while they feature a new sleuth, they aren't particularly different structurally to the Anthony Bathurst books. You could make a case that they were an attempt to go back to a sleuth who mirrored Sherlock Holmes, as Bathurst at this point seems to have moved away from the Great Detective, notably through the lack of a Watson character. The early Bathurst books mostly had the sleuth with a sidekick, a different character in most books, often narrating the books, but as the series progresses, we see Bathurst operating more and more by himself, with his thoughts being the focus of the text. The Charles Wogans, on the other hand, are all narrated by Piers Deverson, relating his adventures with Sebastian Stole who was, as per the cover of *The*

Hangman's Hands (1947), *"A Detective Who Might Have Been A King"* – he was the Crown Prince of Calorania who had to flee the palace during an uprising.

While the short Wogan series is distinct from the Bathurst mysteries, they have a lot in common. Both were published by John Long for the library market, both have a sleuth who takes on his first case because it seems like something interesting to do and both have a potentially odd speaking habit. While Bathurst is willing to pepper his speech with classical idioms and obscure quotations, Stole, being the ex-Prince of the European country of Calorania, has a habit of mangling the English language. To give an example, when a character refers to his forbears, Stole replies that *"I have heard of them, and also of Goldilocks."* I leave it to the reader to decide whether this is funny or painful, but be warned, should you decide to try and track these books down, this is only one example and some of them are even worse.

Stole has some differences from Bathurst, notably that he seems to have unlimited wealth despite fleeing Calorania in the middle of the night – he inveigles himself into his first investigation by buying the house where the murder was committed! By the third book, however, it seems as if Brian realised that there were only surface differences between Stole and Bathurst and returned to writing books exclusively about his original sleuth. This didn't however stop a literary agent, when interviewed by Bathurst in *Men For Pieces* (1949), praising the new author Charles Wogan . . .

At this stage in his investigative career, Bathurst is clearly significantly older than when he first appeared in *The Billiard Room Mystery* (1927). There, he was a Bright Young Thing, displaying his sporting prowess and diving headfirst into a murder investigation simply because he thought it would be entertaining. At the start of *The Case of Elymas the Sorcerer* (1945), we see him recovering from "muscular rheumatism", taking the sea-air at the village of St Mead (not St Mary Mead), before the local constabulary drag him into the investigation of a local murder.

The book itself is very typical of Brian's work. First, the initial mystery has a strange element about it, namely that someone has stripped the body, left it in a field and, for some reason, shaved the body's moustache off. Soon a second body is found, along with a mentally-challenged young man whispering about "gold". In common with a number of Brian's books, such as *The Mystery of The Peacock's Eye* (1928) and *The Running Nun* (1952), the reason for the title only becomes apparent very late in the day – this is not a story about magicians and wizards. One other title, which I won't name for obvious reasons, is actually a clue to what is going on in that book.

Following this, we come to *Conspiracy at Angel* (1947), a book that may well have been responsible for delaying the rediscovery of Brian's work. When Jacques Barzun and Wendell Hertig Taylor wrote *A Catalogue Of Crime* (1971), a reference book intended to cover as many crime writers as possible, they included Brian Flynn – they omitted E. & M.A. Radford, Ianthe Jerrold and Molly Thynne to name but a few great "lost" crime writers – but their opinion of Brian's work was based entirely on this one atypical novel. That opinion was *"Straight tripe and savorless. It is doubtful, on the evidence, if any of the thirty-two others by this author would be different."* This proves, at least, that Barzun and Taylor didn't look beyond the "Also By The Author" page when researching Flynn, and, more seriously, were guilty of making sweeping judgments based on little evidence. To be fair to them, they did have a lot of books to read . . .

It is likely that, post-war, Brian was looking for source material for a book and dug out a play script that he wrote for the Trevalyan Dramatic Club. *Blue Murder* was staged in East Ham Town Hall on 23rd February 1937, with Brian, his daughter and his future son-in-law all taking part. It was perhaps an odd choice, as while it is a crime story, it was also a farce. A lot of the plot of the criminal conspiracy is lifted directly into the novel, but whereas in the play, things go wrong due to the incompetence of a "silly young ass" who gets involved, it is the intervention of Anthony Bathurst in this case that puts paid to the criminal scheme. A fair amount of the farce structure is maintained, in particular in the opening section, and as such, this is a fairly unusual outing for Bathurst. There's also a fascinating snapshot of history when the criminal scheme is revealed. I won't go into details for obvious reasons, but I doubt many readers' knowledge of some specific 1940's technology will be enough to guess what the villains are up to.

Following *Conspiracy at Angel* – and possibly because of it – Brian's work comes full circle with the next few books, returning to the more traditional whodunit of the early Bathurst outings. *The Sharp Quillet* (1947) brings in a classic mystery staple, namely curare, as someone is murdered by a poisoned dart. This is no blow-pipe murder, but an actual dartboard dart – and the victim was taking part in a horse race at the time. The reader may think that the horse race, an annual event for members of the Inns of Court to take place in, is an invention of Brian's, but it did exist. Indeed, it still does, run by The Pegasus Club. This is the only one of Brian's novels to mention the Second World War overtly, with the prologue of the book, set ten years previously, involving an air-raid.

Exit Sir John (1947) – not to be confused with Clemence Dane and Helen Simpson's *Enter Sir John* (1928) – concerns the death of Sir John Wynward at Christmas. All signs point to natural causes, but it is far from the perfect murder (if indeed it is murder) due to the deaths of his chauffeur and his solicitor. For reasons that I cannot fathom, *The Sharp Quillet* and *Exit Sir John* of all of Brian's work, are the most obtainable in their original form. I have seen a number of copies for sale, complete with dustjacket, whereas for most of his other books, there have been, on average, less than one copy for sale over the past five years. I have no explanation for this, but they are both good examples of Brian's work, as is the following title *The Swinging Death* (1949).

A much more elusive title, *The Swinging Death* has a very typical Brian Flynn set-up, along with the third naked body in five books. Rather than being left in a field like the two in *The Case of Elymas the Sorcerer*, this one is hanging from a church porch. Why Dr Julian Field got off his train at the wrong stop, and how he went from there to being murdered in the church, falls to Bathurst to explain, along with why half of Field's clothes are in the church font – and the other half are in the font of a different church?

Brian's books are always full of his love for sport, but *The Swinging Death* shows where Brian's specific interests lie. While rugby has always been Bathurst's winter sport, there is a delightful scene in this book where Chief Inspector MacMorran vehemently champions football (or soccer if you really must) as being the superior sport. One can almost hear Brian's own voice finally being able to talk about a sport that Anthony Bathurst would not give much consideration to.

Brian was pleased with *The Swinging Death*, writing in *Crime Book Magazine* in 1949 that "I hope that I am not being unduly optimistic if I place *The Swinging Death* certainly among the best of my humbler contributions to mystery fiction. I hope that those who come to read it will find themselves in agreement with me in this assessment." It is certainly a sign that over halfway through his writing career, Brian was still going strong and I too hope that you agree with him on this.

Steve Barge

PROLOGUE

1

DR. JULIAN Field stepped from the train on to the platform at Stoke Pelly, looked round for a moment or two, uncertainly, and then made his way to the door which opened into the booking office and on to the street. The collector took his ticket and the doctor walked towards the open air. His eyes brightened. A car stood by the kerb. A tall, ruddy-faced man stood beside it. He half-moved towards Doctor Field.

"Mr. Stanhope," exclaimed the doctor with pleasure in his voice—"how are you?"

The two men shook hands. "I'm very well, doctor—thank you. As I told you when you were here in September—I don't ail much, thank God. Your profession would never wax very fat on what they got out of me."

Philip Stanhope laughed as he spoke and the doctor joined him.

"Get in, doctor, and make yourself comfortable. I suppose I ought to have inquired after your health as well? Take it as read."

Field fingered his dark, neatly trimmed beard. "Oh—I'm O.K. My patients can never justifiably hurl at me—'Physician—heal thyself'—but there you are—I'm a comparatively young man. I should keep well."

The car gathered speed. "What is more important," went on the doctor, "how's my patient? Has she got over that little—?"

Stanhope smiled. "Yes. That's all right now. My son Howard, and I have talked her out of that. So you need have no worries. On the whole, I think she seems a trifle better than she was when you came down last month. But you must, of course, judge for yourself. All I know is that I've been terribly anxious about her. Mrs. Stanhope's looks never seem to pity her. Isn't the country lovely in late October?"

Stanhope nodded to his right. "Just look at the beautiful browns and greens over there."

"Beautiful indeed," agreed Doctor Field.

"What train would you like to return by?" asked Stanhope—"the same train as you caught before?"

"I think so, Mr. Stanhope. I more or less let my wife understand that when I came away this afternoon. It leaves Stoke Pelly just after seven—doesn't it?"

Stanhope nodded. "That's right. 7.3 to be precise. They don't all stop at King's Winkworth—but the 7.3 does. As you know."

The car was approaching Stanhope's house. Stanhope swung the car to the left and pulled up. "Here we are, doctor. And you'll stay to tea, of course?"

Field smiled. "I shan't say no—remembering the excellence of your former hospitality. By George—your garden's really marvellous for the time of the year. Those roses!"

"Yes. They're pretty good for the last week in October. Now come along in and see Mrs. Stanhope. And heaven send your news good!"

The doctor followed Philip Stanhope into the house. "Don't worry about your wife," he said—"no good ever came from worry. Besides—it's very probable I shall find that you've nothing at all to worry about."

2

Plummer, the stationmaster and general railway factotum at Stoke Pelly station left his office which was situated on the "down" platform and crossed the bridge. The time was five minutes to seven. In his own words the 7.3 "up" had just "got the stick." Plummer came down the steps of the bridge leading to the "up" platform, to prepare to receive the train and "get her away again."

Just as he reached a position on the platform, almost opposite to the doors on the "down" side which opened into the booking office, he heard a car drive up and come to a halt just outside the station. Two men got out from the car, came through the doors, stood by the weighing machine on the down side for a brief moment and walked towards the bridge. They passed under the lights of the station lamps and Plummer saw that the taller man of the two was Philip Stanhope, of "Gifford's" and the farm adjoining—a man whom he had known well—and respected—for many years. Ever since the early days, in fact, of his own appointment to Stoke Pelly station.

The other man, of medium height, and wearing a short, dark, pointed beard, was a stranger to him although the stationmaster had seen him in Stanhope's company earlier on that same afternoon. The two men ascended the steps of the bridge on the down side, crossed the bridge together, and descended the stairs to the "up" platform. They approached Plummer but stopped eventually, about the length of a cricket pitch away from where the Stoke Pelly stationmaster was standing. Stanhope saw Plummer and waved to him. The stationmaster courteously acknowledged the greeting. He could see the headlights of the 7.3 as the train rounded the corner which led to Stoke Pelly station. He began to call out—as he had called out before on thousands of occasions.

"Stopping at Maidenbridge, Four Bridges, Greenhurst and King's Winkworth . . ." Plummer repeated the call.

"What were those names, Mr. Stanhope?" The 7.3 was very close now.

"Quite all right for you, doctor."

Plummer saw, too, that the smaller man was wearing a red rose in the appropriate place of his overcoat.

"Thank you very much, doctor," said Philip Stanhope—"for all you've done. I hope your report, when I receive it, will be as you say you're inclined to think. That will mean a great load off my mind. You are really confident, aren't you?"

"Quite."

The two men shook hands through the open window of the compartment. "How long will it be, do you expect, doctor?"

"Within three days," came the reply, "three days at the most—*and don't worry.*"

Stanhope nodded and backed away as Plummer gave the 7.3 the whistle. Neither the stationmaster nor Stanhope saw the man who slipped into the compartment from which the latter had just turned away. Each had his back to him. Stanhope watched the train move out, crossed the bridge and went back to his car. His son, Howard, was seated inside.

"There's one thing, Howard," he said, "he seems confident enough."

Howard nodded. His face was white and set, "Let's hope his confidence isn't misplaced," he answered.

Philip Stanhope took the driving wheel. The car purred out of the station yard.

The man who had jumped into the compartment just before the train left, threw himself into a corner seat and then noticed that he had a fellow-traveller.

"Near thing that," he said—"my fault—I left it a trifle too close. I say—that's a beautiful specimen you're wearing. For the time of the year. I'm a rose-grower myself. Hugh Dickson—isn't it?"

Chapter I

1

The night of the 27th October was cold and dark, but despite the time of the year, there was no rain. For some few hours, there had been a ground mist in low-lying places, but when eight o'clock passed, a wind began to spring up and there were signs evident, here and there, especially in the higher grounds, that the mist would be dissipated by the freshening wind.

Under these conditions, the Southshire countryside, for those who travelled abroad, was anything but attractive and certainly not inviting. Scattered in the distance were tiny clusters of lights, blurred by the mist. A railway station, a village, a handful of farmsteads to each point of the compass, and now and then, through the trees, on higher ground, the lights of a comfortably sized house.

Mary Whitley, as she made her way down the lane that led to the slope, on the hill of which was Fullafold Parish Church, wished fervently that she had postponed her visit to the cinema in the neighbouring village of Greenhurst and had stayed by the fireside of her father's cottage. The omnibus from Greenhurst—the last that evening—had set her down at the top of Strangler's Lane, and as she walked on she had shivered several times. Somehow or other, she had seemed to shiver from a feeling other than that of mere cold. Strangler's Lane was fat with legend, of course, and as Mary Whitley came to the foot of the slope that led up to the church, she knew that she was being very absurd and that the strangled girl whose body had been found at the spot which she had just reached, had died over a hundred years ago.

5 | THE SWINGING DEATH

The hill, at the summit of which stood Fullafold Church, dedicated to St. Mark, divided the small downland village of Fullafold from the much larger village of Greenhurst and it was to this latter place that the residents of Fullafold had to go in the evenings for the entertainment they desired. Mary Whitley's cottage nestled on the downs on the other side of the church, and as she began to breast the slope she was fervently glad that she had but half a mile to complete her journey.

As she ascended, walking briskly, she left the swirling patches of mist behind and with the wind on her face, the flickering lights of life and habitation which she could see now all around her, gave her a stronger courage and she chided herself for her foolish fears of a few moments ago. But when she had travelled about two-thirds of the distance up the thistle-clad slope, something happened which caused her to stop dead in her stride and made her blood run cold. She heard a low, sinister cough. There was no doubt about it. The wind brought it to her distinctly. And then a strange, murmuring, mumbling voice which seemed as it were, to lift into the wind and suddenly drop again. Mary Whitley began to tremble. There was a man—very near to her—somewhere on the slope!

2

In that split second, Mary Whitley came desperately close to panic. Sheer sickening terror seized her and her first shuddering impulse was to run wildly—anywhere—if only the headlong flight would take her from the circle of menace which the sound of that cough and voice had conjured up for her. Her flesh, however, was unequal to the spirit, and the fear which had flooded over her, paralysed her limbs to inaction and she found that she was half-kneeling and half-lying on the wet-fringed grass.

She heard footsteps—they were coming to her—and then that low, blood-chilling cough again. Mary Whitley held her breath. She knew that she was doomed—in but a few seconds' time, a murderer's hands would be at her throat! There would be no mercy for her—she was certain of that. They would find her body in the morning—when the light came. Very likely it would be her own father who would come to it as he walked to his work in Greenhurst. A tall form came out of the darkness at her . . .

3

When Mary Whitley recovered consciousness, she heard the chimes of a clock away in the distance over the hill. The clock struck twelve. Midnight! She was lying on the grass and now the night was wind-haunted. She knew then that she had fainted. Either the killer had not seen her—or he had spared her. She put her trembling hands to her face and knew that she must get to her home at once. Mary scrambled to her feet. Her clothes were saturated by the wet grass. She stood there unsteadily in the wind. Once through the churchyard and down the slope on the other side, she would be all right.

And then, as she stood there, collecting her thoughts and reassuring herself, the wind bore another sound to her ears. It was a horrible sound. Weird and eldritch. It had a regularly creaking note about it, as though the fingers of a spook were turning something round and round—repeatedly. It came at defined intervals—it never really stopped. And it came from the churchyard—through which she had to pass in order to make her way home. Mary Whitley listened hard. There was somebody in the churchyard—at work there. What business could he have there at this time of night? For some reason which she couldn't have explained, some of her courage, at least, began to return to her. At any rate, the noise wasn't actually threatening her.

Mary pushed open the gate and crept silently between the rows of tombstones. As she did so, her ears told her that she was gradually coming nearer and nearer to the creaking noise which had so frightened her when she had first heard it. She came to the main door of the Church of St. Mark which, as far as she knew, was always open. Her footsteps up the churchyard had made little sound as most of her walking had been on grass. The noise seemed to be coming from the porch of the church. Mary knew that porch so well—she passed it on an average half a dozen times every day. Its stone floor, the large mat in the middle of the floor, the wooden settle-like seats on each side of the porch, set hard against the stone wall, the notices to do with church arrangements on the wall, and then the inner door which opened almost on to the font.

Her senses told her that she was in the presence of a noise only. There was nobody working there—as she had at first surmised. If it weren't so unutterably dark! Mary Whitley came to the door of the church. The noise seemed now to be all round her—to be almost touching her, in fact. Mary caught her breath. The knowledge of what the noise reminded her, had suddenly swept into her mind. A gibbet! She had read of the old-time hanging-posts and of how the corpses dangling from them had swung in the chains and creaked ghoulishly in the wind. This noise which she was hearing now was almost what she had always imagined that to be.

And no sooner had this thought registered itself in her mind than Mary realized something else. There was no light in the church porch! There should be. There always was. The lantern of St. Mark's Church was known to all the neighbouring countryside. It had been the custom for many years for the Church of St. Mark to hold the light of a lantern to help the villagers journeying between Fullafold and Greenhurst during the hours of darkness.

The custom had been originated by a vicar during the seventeenth century and his successors had continued unfailingly to honour the tradition. Many a time, on dark winter nights, when she had been coming home alone, Mary herself had blessed the kindly light shining from the porch lantern of St. Mark's. Where was it to-night? Blown out by the wind? And—strangely enough—she hadn't noticed its defection until now. That showed the state of mind she must have been in.

Mary took two further steps, went through the black doorway and stood under the roof of the porch. As she did so, something cold and clammy brushed against her face. Mary Whitley screamed and many people sleeping in their beds in the village of Fullafold, heard that scream, because it awakened them. Then her eyes, bulging with horror, saw what it was that had brushed her face. On the hook in the roof, which normally held the lantern, hung the nude body of a man! And as it hung, it swung in the wind, and as it swung . . .

4

Mary Whitley ran from the porch of horror. She ran blindly almost, through the churchyard of St. Mark's, down the slope leading to Fullafold and until she reached the door of her parents' cottage. There was a light still showing in the front room and Mary pushed open the cottage door, to fall almost on the chair which always stood close to the door. Her father, a mild, inoffensive man in the late forties, who obviously had been sitting up for her, saw at once that the girl had recently passed through an ordeal of some unusual kind.

"Why, lass," he said, "what's amiss? You've fair put the wind oop me—seein' you're so late and all. Another few minutes and I'd 'ave 'ad my boots on to come out to search for you. It be past midnight."

Mary nodded to her father and stammered out her story. Whitley, who was a sensible man and who knew, too, that his daughter's word could be relied upon, heard her out.

"'Anging in St. Mark's porch?"

"Yes, father. The body touched me—and I screamed! I wonder you didn't hear me."

"I must 'ave dozed off—sittin' by the fire as I've bin. I reckon that's why I never 'eard you."

Whitley reached for his overcoat and hat. "This means only one thing," he said, "it's a matter for police. There's a phone box down there by the crossroads, way over towards Four Bridges. 'Bout ten minutes' walk. I'll get down there at once and phone Greenhurst station. You stay by fire, lass." Whitley walked to the door. At the door of the cottage he turned. "I reckon you've bin in luck's way to-night, lass. And I, for one, thank God for it. If you arsk me, it was only His mercy you wasn't murdered too! You was in murderer's clutches—and slipped out. If you 'adn't—there'd 'ave bin two corpses swingin' from 'ook in church. Won't be over-long."

As her father closed the door behind him and she heard his footsteps resounding down the street, Mary burst into a flood of tears. Her mother came to her . . .

5

Whitley reached the telephone booth, and the police station at Greenhurst had the greatest shock of its official career when it realized the full purport of the message he was sending. It metaphorically rubbed the sleep from its eyes, yawned two or three times and shook off the shackles of its bucolic stupor.

Sergeant Bland was the man called upon to sample the morning air. Eventually he reached the decision to take with him to the scene of the crime a young constable and recent recruit, by the name of Nye. Whitley, not to be deprived of any future publicity that might be attracted to the affair, arranged to meet the two members of the police force at the church. It will be observed the complete measure of confidence with which he invested his daughter's story.

The clock which Mary Whitley had heard strike twelve, now struck two as Whitley heard the two policemen ascending the slope on the Greenhurst side as Mary had climbed it some hours previously. Whitley himself was just on the point of entering the churchyard from the Fullafold direction. He walked to the porch, steeling himself for the sight which he knew must confront him . . . he had already heard the ghastly creaking on the hook, and then after one glance, stood there waiting patiently for the approach of the police.

Sergeant Bland came first. He shone his torch into the porch. The nude body swung—right—left—as its weight played on the rope which the hook held.

"H'm," said Bland—"in his birthday suit—eh? Somebody couldn't have been too fond of him! See if you can see the lantern anywhere, Nye. The one that always hangs here."

The young policeman walked towards the inner door of the church. "Here it be, sergeant. In the corner here, by the door. And the 'ook it usually 'angs on, I should say."

"Oh-ho? So they monkeyed with the hook too, eh?"

Sergeant Bland turned to Whitley. "Tell me again—everything your girl told you."

Whitley told him. Bland nodded several times during the recital. When Whitley had finished, the sergeant eyed him shrewdly.

"You lived round here long?"

"All my life," replied Whitley, "born and bred in Fullafold and my father and grandfather afore me. Why?"

Bland jerked his head towards the swinging corpse. "Ever set eyes on this stiff before? Wait—I'll shine the torch on his 'clock.'"

Sergeant Bland suited the action to the word. The light of the torch showed a sallow-complexioned man, with dark brown eyes and a small pointed beard. A man, so thought the sergeant, in the middle thirties. He was of medium height, average weight and from the condition of his limbs generally, looked to be well nourished.

Bland's trained eye judged him as having belonged to one of the professional classes. His hands and feet alike showed unmistakable signs of care and attention. It is doubtful, though, whether, if Whitley saw these things, he understood their full significance.

He shook his head in reply to the question Bland addressed to him. "Never saw him in my life. Take it from me, sergeant—'e don't belong to these parts."

"My opinion, too," rejoined Bland with curt readiness, "and I've knocked about round here for a year or two. I'll say I have! Constable Nye!"

"Yes, sergeant?"

"Get back to where we left the bikes. Take yours and phone through to Four Bridges. Ask for Inspector Bernays. Give him my compliments and the time of day generally with regard to this ecclesiastical outfit. Ask him to contact Doctor Depard, the Divisional Surgeon. I'll make the necessary arrangements this end. Scram!"

Nye made off down the slope towards Greenhurst. The sergeant spoke to Whitley again.

"I won't detain you, Whitley. You've done all you can do for the time being. You pack off. But expect me at the cottage before the day's much older. I shall require to take a statement from that girl of yours. To my way of thinking she had a lucky escape. According to what you've told me—she seems to have been almost on nodding terms with the fellow that did this job." Whitley nodded gravely. "That's what I think, sergeant."

"No doubt about that. Blimey—it's perishin' cold up here at this hour of the morning. Had to happen this time of the year, of course.

That's the way it goes. Now let me see again—what's that address of yours?"

"Number Five, Victoria Cottages, Slater's Lane. First left from the foot of the slope."

"I'll find it," said Bland—"don't worry."

Whitley walked away. Bland went back inside the porch—to the swinging body.

Chapter II

1

THE body of the man who had swung in the porch of St. Mark's, the parish church of Fullafold, was not identified until half-past seven in the evening. It was then identified as the body of Julian Race Field, aged thirty-three, a doctor of medicine, living at "The Bartons," High Street, King's Winkworth.

King's Winkworth, it may be stated, is a small town on the same railway line as Four Bridges and Greenhurst. The identification was established by the wife of the dead man, who had read of the Fullafold crime in the earlier editions of the evening papers. From the description given and from what she already knew, she travelled at once to the mortuary at Four Bridges and identified the body there shown to her as that of her husband—Julian Race Field.

The widow, a distinctly attractive blonde, gave her name as Claudia Millicent Field and her age as twenty-eight. Claudia Millicent Field told the police at Four Bridges a rather extraordinary story. Inspector Bernays, with Sergeant Bland at his side, listened to it with great interest.

2

The first part of Claudia Field's story dealt with her husband. This is the way it went. Julian Field was in practice as a doctor in the smallish market-town of King's Winkworth. He had purchased the practice three years previously. It had belonged to a Doctor Louis Wolff, a graduate of an Austrian university. Wolff had practised in King's Winkworth for over twenty years and Julian Field had purchased the practice on Wolff's death.

On the previous afternoon to the morning when his body had swung in the church porch, he had left his surgery for a consultation at the house of a patient. This patient, so stated Claudia Field, who by this time was greatly distressed, was a Mrs. Philip Stanhope, who lived at Stoke Pelly, forty-odd miles from King's Winkworth. Her husband, so continued the widow, had caught the 2.22 train from King's Winkworth, which was scheduled by time-table to arrive at Stoke Pelly at nine minutes to four. Here Inspector Bernays intervened.

"Mrs. Field," he said, "there are certain questions which arise out of your statements, which I shall be compelled to ask you. No doubt you fully understand that. But I shan't ask you anything until you have told me the complete story. I think this procedure will make it much easier for you than if I continually broke in with an interrupting question. So please go ahead." Claudia Field nodded her understanding and thanked the inspector. She went on with her narrative.

"According to what my husband told me when he left the house, I was to expect him home about nine o'clock. He intended to return by the train from Stoke Pelly which leaves there just after seven o'clock. So that he should have reached King's Winkworth station about half-past eight. I know all these train times, inspector, because when my husband failed to put in appearance at the anticipated time, I grew worried and checked up the trains in the 'A.B.C.'"

Inspector Bernays nodded sympathetically.

"Well, as you may guess—as time went on—my anxiety increased. I could do nothing, however, but wait. Now I'll come to what is really the second half of my story. At half-past eleven—almost exactly half-past eleven—because I looked at the clock in the lounge when it happened—there came a ring on the telephone. Nothing unusual about that, you'll say, in a doctor's house—but don't forget I was agitated over the non-return of Julian and was more or less waiting for something like a 'phone ring to happen. I fully expected that it was my husband himself who had rung up. To tell me that something had occurred to delay him. But it wasn't. It was a man's voice that addressed me. And it was a common sort of voice. Loud and—

er—aggressive. It wasn't a cultured voice by any means. I remember thinking that when I first heard him speaking to me.

"He asked if he were speaking to Mrs. Field—the wife of Doctor Julian Field. I told him he was—and then to my horror he informed me that he represented the police and that my husband had met with a most serious accident at Friar's Woodburn. Would I please come immediately to the railway station at Friar's Woodburn where my husband was lying and where I would be met by the police. In answer to a question I put to him, he told me that Julian wasn't dead—but 'was pretty bad.' That was the phrase he used."

Claudia Field paused to dab the tears in her blue eyes. Neither Bernays nor Bland made any comment. Claudia Field continued.

"Now please understand that this message, when I thought it over, seemed to me to be entirely genuine."

Again Bernays nodded. This girl—for in appearance—with her fair hair and blue eyes she seemed little more than that—was telling her story well. She spoke clearly and she was easy on the eye.

"It seemed to be trustworthy—and—er—authentic because I knew that Friar's Woodburn was a station between Stoke Pelly and King's Winkworth. It was certainly a place where my husband could reasonably be. Or in other words, the man's phone message fitted—the place was in keeping. Have I made myself clear to you? Do you follow me?"

This time Bland nodded with the inspector. Claudia Field made a helpless sort of gesture with her hands and shoulders.

"I'll tell you what I did," she said simply. "I decided to get the car out and drive straight down to Friar's Woodburn. For one thing—it was late—and the trains back might have been awkward. And the distance wasn't too great. About thirty miles. At that time of night the road was comparatively clear and it wouldn't take me very long."

She stopped again—and then spoke with studied deliberation. "When I reached the railway station at Friar's Woodburn—there was nothing there. There had been no accident, they knew nothing of my husband, or of any message or of any police—or anything at all. Then I thought I might have misheard on the telephone and that I had made a mistake and I should have gone to the police station, perhaps, instead of the railway station. So I drove the car to the little police station. It was no good. There was no help for me there."

Claudia Field paused again. She looked blankly into space. It was here that Bernays made his first real interruption.

"And what did you do then, Mrs. Field?"

She looked at him helplessly. "What could I do? I did what seemed to me to be the only sensible thing to do. I drove the car back to King's Winkworth. When I reached home, hoping against hope, almost, that my husband would have returned home—I ran into my third shock of the evening."

Bernays leaned over to her—his eyes alight with interest. "What was that, Mrs. Field?" he asked—almost gently.

"The house had been entered while I had been away—and my husband's surgery had been turned over."

From the lips of Sergeant Bland, of Greenhurst—there came a low whistle.

3

"I immediately telephoned to the police," went on Claudia Field, "and an officer came round to the house very shortly afterwards. I thought the best thing I could possibly do, in the circumstances, was to tell him the whole story. I mean—about my husband not coming home from Stoke Pelly and about the telephone call I'd had—and—well—everything just as it happened."

"Very sensible of you," commented the inspector—"certainly the wisest course you could possibly have taken. What did the officer do?"

"Well—I think it bewildered him rather. Anyhow—he seemed to give the burglary priority as it were. He said that's what he'd been sent to investigate and that, in all probability, my husband had been delayed in some way and might turn up any time."

"Yes. I can imagine him acting in that way. What was stolen from the house? Money? Or jewellery?"

For the first time, Claudia Field showed signs of hesitancy. Bernays watched her closely and wondered why it was. When she replied, the manner of her answer surprised him.

"Frankly, inspector, I couldn't tell you yet what has been stolen. Personally, I can't trace that I have actually lost anything. I may have done—but I shall need time in order to find out for sure. But it's a certainty that my husband's papers have all been turned over, because of the confusion. If anything has been taken it belonged to my husband—and now that this dreadful thing has happened . . . ."

Mrs. Field broke off abruptly and burst into convulsive sobbing. Inspector Bernays waited until this emotional outburst was under control. When he considered the lady had sufficiently recovered he said to her: "Now for one or two questions, Mrs. Field. Don't distress yourself unduly—just answer them quietly and take them in your stride to the best of your ability."

Mrs. Field looked at him through her tear-dimmed eyes and nodded. "I'll do my best, inspector."

"Thank you, Mrs. Field. First of all, this patient of your late husband's? A Mrs. Philip Stanhope was the name you mentioned, I think."

"That is so."

"Can you supply me with the full address of this lady?"

"Yes. When my husband failed to return at the time I expected him, I looked up the address of Mrs. Stanhope in his address book. It is Mrs. Philip Stanhope, 'Gifford's,' Stoke Pelly. His consultation was timed tor 4.15 p.m."

"Thank you." Bernays made certain notes. "Was this Mrs. Stanhope a regular patient of your husband's, do you know?"

"She was on my husband's books. Otherwise I shouldn't have been able to find the address. Because he had visited her before. I remember him going. He caught the same train—2.22 from King's Winkworth. Somewhere about a month ago, I should think."

"I see. We can take it then, I think, that there was nothing in any way abnormal with regard to this consultation of Mrs. Stanhope's."

"I think you can, inspector—certainly."

The inspector tapped his teeth with the butt of his fountain pen. "Is Mrs. Stanhope a widow—do you know—or is there a Mr. Stanhope at Stoke Pelly?"

"That I can't tell you, inspector. I never discussed my husband's patients with him—the result is that I know but little about any of them."

"I see. Now try to help me a little with regard to Doctor Field's own personal background, if you can. It may prove distressing to you—but you understand, I am sure, that I'm compelled to ask these questions. How long have you been married?"

"Just over a year."

"Is that all? Well, I'll put the question that was really in my mind in another form. How long have you known your husband?"

Mrs. Field smiled a sad sort of smile. "Not very much longer, inspector. About seventeen months—to be exact. I happened to be staying in King's Winkworth for a holiday. In the spring of last year. I have cousins living there. They are King's Winkworth people. During that holiday I met Doctor Field and some little time later, he asked me to marry him."

The lady began to cry again. Bernays waited patiently.

"You don't know," he said eventually, "of any enemies that he had? You've no idea if—"

"Oh—no, inspector. I know nobody. I find it difficult, even now, to realize that he is dead. I just can't believe it possible. Because I can't think *why anybody* should want to kill him. That's the only answer I can possibly give to that question you asked me."

"He has shown no anxiety then—lately—concerning anything? No worries? Debts? Professional matters?"

"None at all, inspector. You can dismiss anything of that kind from your mind at once. When Julian left me yesterday afternoon, he couldn't possibly have been in better spirits."

"Thank you, Mrs. Field. That clears up that possibility, then. Now another matter—will you please dictate to the sergeant here, the details of all the clothes your husband was wearing when you last saw him. *Everything*, Mrs. Field, if you please. Begin with the hat, gloves and overcoat. I presume he wore all three—and finishing with the underclothes."

Sergeant Bland opened his notebook. "Brown soft hat, lightish-coloured single-breasted overcoat," began Claudia Field, "brown suède gloves—dark brown. . . ." she continued in this manner until the list of sartorial effects was complete.

Bernays listened carefully and attentively. When the lady had reached the end of the list, the inspector leant over to her again. "Now his personal effects, Mrs. Field. Describe those to Sergeant Bland, will you, please? And do your best to think of every thing as you did the clothes, no matter how small or insignificant it may appear to you to be."

Claudia Field nodded. "Plain gold ring on second finger of left hand—I know that's missing. Gold wrist watch with illuminated dial—that's gone too." She shook her head. "Much of this is conjecture, inspector. You must understand that. Until I check Julian's things when I get home again I can't be absolutely certain of what he had on him."

Bernays nodded his understanding. "Tell us what you think, Mrs. Field—the things you would expect—normally—to find on him."

"A small nail-file—a 'Wilkinson,' cigarette case, lighter, white handkerchief, keys probably, fountain pen, money, I suppose—couldn't possibly tell you how much—railway ticket, pocket-book—I can't think of anything else."

Bland nodded several times as he listed the articles. "Now, Mrs. Field, please," he said, "can you let me have those in greater detail? Each of them. The cigarette case for example, describe it in detail—will you please?"

Claudia Field obliged as best as she was able and Sergeant Bland took down the various details she gave him. Again, the inspector leant over to her.

"Now isn't there something else, yet, Mrs. Field? What about your husband's professional—er—belongings? He must have been carrying something of that kind—surely?"

"Of course! How stupid of me not to think of that before. And yet—"

Claudia Field hesitated. Bernays pounced on the irresolution immediately. "And yet—what, Mrs. Field?"

"Well—it's strange—but I can't remember noticing that my husband was carrying his usual case when he went out yesterday afternoon. That's another matter which I must check when I get back to the house again."

"But surely, Mrs. Field—on a professional visit? The doctor was on his way to a consultation—he would be bound to—"

Claudia Field shook her head. "No—I have known him go out on occasions with a stethoscope pushed into his overcoat pocket. And, of course, if he thought—"

Bernays nodded. "That can be gone into, of course—when we establish contact with the patient—Mrs. Stanhope. After all, you and I here this evening, don't even know the nature of the consultation. Now another question, Mrs. Field. Your husband—er—his practice? Was it just an ordinary practice that he had in King's Winkworth—or did he—er—specialize?"

"In King's Winkworth he was just an ordinary G.P. Although he did have hopes, I think, of becoming a specialist later. When, as he used to say, he had managed to make a bit of money, his idea then, was to branch out as a specialist in chest diseases."

"Thank you, Mrs. Field—what you have told me should tend to help us considerably. As early to-morrow as I can manage it—I'll co operate with the police at King's Winkworth. There's the burglary their end—and this other dreadful business at mine. So expect me some time at your house. 'The Bartons,' isn't it, High Street, King's Winkworth?"

Mrs. Field confirmed the address. Inspector Bernays smiled at her. Poor girl, he thought. To lose your husband in a nasty affair like this. Make a mess of your life—I don't doubt.

"When you see me next time, Mrs. Field," he said "perhaps you'll be able to tell me with certainty what was stolen from your house after you were enticed away. Then we shall begin to know more where we are—and perhaps, too, why your husband was killed."

Claudia Field's handkerchief was in evidence again. "Inspector Bernays," she said, "I haven't heard yet—please would you tell me—how did my husband die?"

"Ah now—but I wish you hadn't asked me that. He was found hanging in the porch of St. Mark's Church at Fullafold—that's a little village—"

"I know that," replied Mrs. Field in a voice scarcely more than a whisper—"that was in the paper. But—that's all I do know. Was he actually hanged? I mean—did that kill him or was there—"

Bernays cut in. "According to Dr. Depard—that's the Divisional Surgeon who made the P.M.—he was dead before the rope was put round his neck. From certain marks on his throat and bruises on his body, generally. Dr. Depard is of opinion that your husband was strangled after a terrific struggle and was dead when he was strung up. There are discolorations round the throat which were undoubtedly caused by a man's fingers. But your husband undoubtedly fought hard for his life."

Claudia Field stood up. She swayed a little. "Thank you, inspector," she said in a hard strained voice. "Thank you for telling me. And thank you for having been so kind—all the way through."

4

After her departure, Bernays rubbed his chin and looked at Sergeant Bland.

"You know, sergeant," he said reflectively, "it was funny she should have asked that question. At least that's how it struck me."

"Which one do you mean, sir?"

"Why—the one about how the man died. You'd have thought that knowing what she did know—from the newspaper I mean—that she'd have accepted the hanging idea and been satisfied. As I said—that's how it appeals to me."

Sergeant Bland sniffed audibly. "I don't know, inspector—she's not quite an ordinary woman—you know—she's the wife of a doctor. Gets a different angle—being that. That's my impression, inspector."

"H'm. May be. May be not."

"Ve-ry peculiar case," went on Bland—"say what you like about it. Nothing like anything that's come my way before. What have we got so far? Plenty of nothing! You've been over the ground. So have I. No prints anywhere. Lantern clear—and the hook. No tracks that show bar the marks of the car tyres on the road at the foot of the slope. Which may have nothing to do with the affair whatever. If you want my opinion—they haven't."

"H'm," grunted Bernays again—"early days yet."

"So they may be—but you know as well as I do—early soon becomes late. Doesn't take long."

"I tell you, sergeant, what does shake me," said Bernays after a somewhat lengthy pause.

"What's that, inspector?"

"Why—the places that pop up in the affair. Almost like a railway time-table. Did you notice that yourself?"

"How do you mean? I don't quite—"

"Why, look at it this way. Field, the dead doctor, starts off from King's Winkworth. We'll call that Point A. He travels to Stoke Pelly. That's the place at the other end of the show as it were. We'll call that Point B. Between the two points is a distance of forty-odd miles. Mrs. Field said so and I know that wouldn't be far out. In between King's Winkworth and Stoke Pelly—and served by the same railway line are Four Bridges, where you and I are now, Greenhurst, which is the station for Fullafold where the body was found, and also Friar's Woodburn, the place where Mrs. Field, the widow, was sent on a fool's errand. Do you know, Bland, I can't help thinking that we're missing something."

Bernays leant forward and gazed deeply into the flames of the station fire. Sergeant Bland grinned at him.

"You do—eh? Well—whatever it is—you won't find it in there, inspector."

Chapter III

1

A week after Mary Whitley's sensational discovery, the almost inevitable happened. At least—that was how Inspector Bernays regarded it. After three interviews with the Chief Constable of the county, that latter-mentioned gentleman decided to invite the immediate assistance of the "Yard."

Sir Austin Kemble, the Commissioner of Police, who had his own hands unusually full at the time, adopted one of his customary formulae, and called a conference consisting of Supt. Hemingway, Chief Det.-Inspector Andrew MacMorran and Anthony Lotherington Bathurst. Inspector Bernays travelled from Four Bridges, and was also present. Sir Austin himself presided and called on Bernays to make the introductory statement. The Four Bridges inspector responded in a most able manner. His language was well chosen, his facts were marshalled in logical sequence and order, and as a whole his statement was both clear and concise.

Anthony Bathurst listened to it with grave and interested concentration. And it must be confessed—with a certain amount of pleasurable excitement. For nearly a year now, crime had eluded him and he had enjoyed the longest rest from activity in the science of deduction since his baptism, many years before, in the famous "Billiard Room Mystery" at Considine Manor in the County of Sussex.

The result was, that, hearing Bernays tell his story brought all the old urge back to him and the fascination of the chase touched him again with its spell-binding fingers. When Bernays reached his conclusion, the Four Bridges inspector pushed back his chair and his face sought Sir Austin Kemble's with a look of intelligent inquiry. The Commissioner nodded to him. He knew what Bernays's look meant.

"Any questions from anybody?"

"Well," said Hemingway—"there are one or two, at least, I'd like to put to Inspector Bernays—and I've no doubt that my colleague here—and also Mr. Bathurst—are much in the same boat. But there's just this point. Inspector Bernays tells me that the inquest is fixed for to-morrow, and in that case—"

Anthony made his first contribution. "I agree with the super, sir. In fact I was about to say what he's just said. I understand that the inspector has to return to Four Bridges this afternoon and I suggest that Andrew MacMorran and I blow along to the inquest to-morrow morning. We shan't be starting from scratch exactly—we can't—it's too late for that—but this procedure I've indicated will give us almost the next best thing. Anyhow—I'm pretty sure we can't do better. I'd like to hear Andrew MacMorran's own views on the matter."

"Suits me, Sir Austin," said MacMorran—"Inspector Bernays has given us the main features of the case and I take Mr. Bathurst's point—the evidence at the inquest will elaborate them for us."

When Bernays had taken his departure, the Commissioner of Police smiled across the table at Anthony.

"Well, Bathurst, what do you think of it?"

"From what I have already read in the Press, added to what Bernays handed to us, I think it's a beauty, Sir Austin! A case after my own heart."

Anthony Bathurst rose to his full height and rubbed his hands.

2

Anthony and Andrew MacMorran travelled to Four Bridges on a sun-drenched morning in November. They travelled by car and passed through King's Winkworth and Greenhurst on the journey.

"Look at 'em, Andrew," said Anthony, "these places we're passing through—we shall see 'em all again, more than once, in the near future—never fear!"

The Coroner's Court, which they entered at twenty minutes past ten—the inquest was timed to start at 10.30—was held in the Council Chamber of the Four Bridges Town Hall. For a medium sized country town, this was quite an imposing building. At least a dozen reporters had already taken up their positions in the seats provided for them. This fact occasioned Anthony no surprise—as he was aware as to the degree of sensation which the murder of Julian Field had created, not only in the immediate district, but throughout the country as a whole.

When the coroner took his seat, the little man (as he proved to be) was almost fluttering with excitement, nervousness and consciousness of self-importance. For this one day he had ceased to be a country solicitor. For one day he had become the central figure who basked in the blinding glare of national publicity, and more than a merely central figure! He had become the controlling figure of a national drama. It brought him happiness and he had chirped to himself more than once on his way to the court that morning, that he would do his best to be entirely worthy of his ephemeral eminence.

As Anthony made his way with MacMorran to their seats, he had time to spare a glance at the members of the jury. These were seated in two rows of six each, on the coroner's right. They were in every way typical, Anthony thought, of the district they represented. They wore their best suits in varying degrees of discomfort, and looked in the direction of the coroner, sheepishly and solemnly. The coroner, himself, by now was fussing at his table. He resembled a bird, Anthony thought, and if any credence can be awarded to Pythagoras he had undoubtedly *been* a bird. His beady little eyes shone through his gold-rimmed glasses and the movement of his head and neck was strangely like that of a bird pecking. His nose was sharp as a beak and his throat was parchment-like and stringy.

Just as Anthony was on the point of whispering in MacMorran's ear, the proceedings opened and a slight hum began to buzz through the court. The first witness called was Claudia Millicent Field, the wife of the dead man, who gave formal identification of the body. Under the judicious handling of Mr. Bessemer, which was the coroner's name, she told in effect the same story, in the main outline, as it affected her late husband, that she had related to Inspector Bernays in the police station at Four Bridges.

Anthony, from his seat near the front, watched her carefully and listened with concentration to every word she uttered. On the whole he was favourably impressed. As favourably impressed as Bernays had been. The questions which the coroner saw fit to put to her were similar in purport to those Bernays had asked her and her answers tallied. Upon occasion she touched her eyes with her handkerchief, but she always retained her self-possession and her voice, although low-pitched, was clear and distinct throughout the whole time she was called upon to give evidence.

Towards the conclusion of her hearing, a member of the jury asked her a question. Not without a certain amount of embarrassment.

"I should like to ask you, Mrs. Field—were you and your husband on good terms with one another?"

"Certainly we were," came the prompt reply. "No two people could have been happier."

The juryman who had evinced the temerity, murmured a conventional "Thank you," and proceeded forthwith to a gallant attempt to efface himself from the future proceedings.

Shortly afterwards, the coroner intimated that nothing more would be required of the witness, so Mrs. Field stood down and made her way from the stand. The next testimony to be taken by Mr. Bessemer was that of Mary Whitley, the finder of the body. Most of the reporters present began to write feverishly, for here, obviously, was savoury fish for their nets. Another good witness, thought Anthony, for Mary told her story without flourish and devoid of frill, just as she had told it to her father in his cottage and to Sergeant Bland when he had called upon her later. The police evidence which followed, was, so Anthony thought, rather guarded. He felt that both Inspector Bernays and Sergeant Bland had made up their minds beforehand to say as little as possible—within certain limits. It was certainly colourless—and to Anthony's way of thinking—rather enigmatic.

But there were sensations yet to come. For which, Anthony and Inspector MacMorran were unprepared.

"Call the Rev. John Moffatt," said the coroner.

3

John Moffatt took his stand. He was a tall, thin, cadaverous man, clean-shaven, with black hair and fierce burning eyes. The eyes of a zealot. His arms and legs were as thin as his body and they moved in a strange, jerking, almost disjointed manner. Anthony had the fancy, as he watched the man take the stand, that if he listened carefully enough, he would hear the creaking of Moffatt's limbs. But the coroner was speaking.

"You are a Clerk in Holy Orders."

"Yes, I am the senior curate attached to the parish church of Fullafold—St. Mark's."

Moffatt's voice was in keeping with the rest of him. It was harsh and fiercely intense.

"Please tell the court what you found."

The senior curate of St. Mark's, Fullafold, proceeded to inform the court that at seven o'clock in the morning of the day that the body of Doctor Field had been discovered, and before the police had examined the church interior, he had entered the church and in the font had found certain articles of clothing neatly folded. They comprised coat and waistcoat of a grey chalk-stripe suit, pants, vest and socks. Evidently missing from what the dead man had worn when he started on his journey, were the trousers, hat, overcoat, scarf, tie, soft collar, shirt and shoes. The articles in the font were, as he had stated, neatly folded and quite clean. He at once informed the police authorities of his find and a sergeant whom he now knew to be Sergeant Bland, came to the church in response to his call, and removed the articles.

The coroner thereupon brought him assistance. "And these articles of clothing, I understand, reverend sir, have since been identified by the widow of the dead man as having been worn by him on the day of his death."

The Rev. John Moffatt bowed in assent. "That is so, Mr. Coroner."

The reporters' fountain pens travelled like wildfire over pads of paper.

"Thank you, again. That will be all, thank you."

The Reverend John Moffatt bowed for the second time and withdrew.

This time Anthony was able to whisper to MacMorran without interruption. "This is a most extraordinary case, Andrew," he said, "I wouldn't have missed it for worlds. That evidence to which we have just listened is really remarkable. Something to set your teeth into there."

The coroner's voice was heard again. "Call Arthur Charles Trott."

Anthony and MacMorran looked up. The man who took the stand in succession to the Rev. John Moffatt was, like his immediate predecessor, tall and thin, but nevertheless of an entirely different physical type. He was scraggy, his hair was "thin," his blue eyes were protuberant, and the size of his Adam's apple had to be seen to be believed. He deposed that he was a ticket collector in the employment of the Southern Railway at Greenhurst Station. A man, whom he had since identified as the deceased, had alighted from the "up" train which reaches Greenhurst at 7.43 p.m. (schedule time) on the evening before the body was discovered. He surrendered the return half of a ticket which had been issued that day from King's Winkworth available for use between that station and Stoke Pelly. "Doctor Field at that time," stated Trott, "explained when he gave up the return half of his ticket, that he had been suddenly called upon to break his journey. He then asked me if I could direct him to Cornelius Steps and how far it was from Greenhurst Station. I said I couldn't, because I'd never heard of the place."

"Did he seem agitated when he said this?" asked Mr. Bessemer.

"No, sir—I wouldn't say that. He seemed quite ordinary-like to me."

"Did he leave the station at once?"

"Yes, sir—as far as I know. At any rate he didn't stay on the platform. The last I saw of him was descending the staircase which leads into Greenhurst High Street. But as far as I know, sir, there's no such place as Cornelius Steps in Greenhurst—or Fullafold."

Again the coroner expressed his thanks to the witness.

"The plot thickens, Andrew," said Anthony to MacMorran, "look at the Press table. None of 'em can shove the stuff down fast enough."

"Call Philip Coomber Stanhope."

Anthony looked up again. A tall, well-built, distinguished-looking man walked to the witness stand. "Stained with the ruddy tan," thought Anthony, "God's air doth give a man."

4

"You are Philip Coomber Stanhope?"

"Yes."

"Gentleman farmer of 'Gifford's,' Stoke Pelly?"

"Yes."

"Will you please tell the court of Dr. Field's visit to your house on the afternoon before his death?"

"I shall be pleased to do so."

"Another good type," said Anthony to himself, "not one bad witness yet."

Stanhope began to speak. "I had been in consultation with the late Doctor Field for some months, now—in relation to my wife's health, which for some time now has been giving me a certain amount of anxiety."

"Was Doctor Field your—er—regular medical attendant?"

"Oh, no. I had got into contact with him purely as a specialist. He had some considerable reputation for his knowledge of chest trouble."

"I see. That explains itself. Now will you please inform the court, Mr. Stanhope, of what happened on the afternoon of the 27th of October."

"Arrangements had been made for Doctor Field to come to my house for another examination of Mrs. Stanhope. He was to arrive by the train timed to arrive at Stoke Pelly at nine minutes to four. I met him at the railway station with my car and drove him to my house. Mrs. Stanhope had a thorough examination at the doctor's hands, in very great detail if I may my so, and somewhere about half-past five I should imagine it was, we sat down to tea. The doctor sat down with us. On the occasion of his previous consultation at my house which took place about a month ago, Doctor Field caught the 7.3 train back to King's Winkworth. He desired, so he said, to do the same on this occasion. I drove him back to the railway station accompanied by my son and I suppose we arrived there about five minutes before the train was due. I couldn't be certain to a minute. I actually walked with Doctor Field to the door of the booking office where we stood for a few seconds. I then accompanied him across the bridge on to the platform where his train came in. His last words to me were that he would let me have the report I wanted with regard to my wife in the course of he next three days. We shook hands just before the train went out and when that happened Doctor Field was standing at the window of the compartment. That was the last I saw of him."

Mr. Bessemer lifted his head and made a pecking movement in the direction of Stanhope. "He was in good spirits?"

"Quite—I should say."

"You got no impression that he had any worry or—er—trouble on his mind?"

"None. He was as normal and as cheerful—shall we say—men, as he had been all the afternoon and evening. If there was any anxiety—it was on my shoulders."

"Thank you, Mr. Stanhope." Mr. Bessemer stroked his upper lip and made certain notes. It appeared to Anthony that he was searching for something. "Ah, Mr. Stanhope," continued the coroner, "there is another question I'd like to put to you before you conclude your evidence—and that is this. Did the late Doctor Field give you any indication—at any time during his visit to you—that he intended to break his return journey at Greenhurst—or anywhere else?"

Stanhope shook his head emphatically. "None at all."

"Thank you—er—Mr. Stanhope—thank you again."

As the coroner spoke, Stanhope raised his chin and Anthony, watching him intently, wondered what was coming next.

"There is something else, Mr. Coroner," said Stanhope, "that I'd like to tell the court—it may be trivial—it may not. That is not for me to judge. But it may help the police authorities."

"By all means, Mr. Stanhope," interrupted the coroner, "give us all the information that lies in your power. That—er—ahem—is why you are here."

"Quite so," replied Stanhope, a faint tinge of colour coming to his neck, "and that is also why I mentioned the matter. I need not have done."

The coroner made a strange noise as though he were on the point of saying something. Stanhope, however, didn't wait.

"When Doctor Field left me," he said, "he had two things with him which weren't in his possession when he arrived. The first was a very fine dark red rose which he admired so much when he walked round my garden just before tea, that I cut it and presented it to him, and the other was a specimen of Mrs. Stanhope's sputum. The doctor placed the rose in the button-hole of his overcoat. These two matters may, I suggest, be of some interest to the police." Stanhope squared his shoulders.

"Those—er—facts—will be duly noted," replied Mr. Bessemer drily, but with a hint of firmness in his voice which he deliberately attempted to put there, "and you may stand down, Mr. Stanhope."

Stanhope stepped briskly away.

Nothing more of importance transpired until the advent of Dr. Depard, the Divisional Surgeon. By special arrangement with Bessemer, his evidence was taken last, as owing to pressure of duty, he had been compelled to keep two other official engagements in the earlier part of the day. Depard was laconic—even to the point of being terse. Death, he said, had been caused by strangling. By somebody's bare hands, he thought. From certain tests he had made of the body's temperature he would put the time of decease at about six hours before he himself was called to the body. The body was nude when he came to it. At about eight o'clock, say—but this must be regarded as *extremely* approximate. There had been some sort of a struggle. Bruised chin showed that—and there were other signs. Superficial. But the man was most certainly dead before he was roped up in the church porch. The contents of the stomach showed that deceased had partaken of a meal a few hours before death.

"Any questions of Doctor Depard? None? Thank you, doctor."

The divisional surgeon bowed and made his exit.

Anthony looked towards the coroner, Mr. Bessemer removed his glasses, wiped them ostentatiously and put them on again.

5

The coroner coughed twice behind his hand and began his final address to the jury: "You have viewed the body of the late Doctor Julian Race Field. You have heard the medical evidence of the Divisional Surgeon, Doctor Depard. He states that in his opinion death took place about four hours before Mary Whitley discovered the body. But our good friend the doctor, as is very natural, covers himself there with the margin of an hour or so. At the same time, you, the jury, will be entitled to draw your own conclusions. The dead man was strangled, says Doctor Depard, by human hands—and that, after a struggle. There was a bruised chin to support this statement." The coroner paused to refer to his notes. "It is significant, too, that the evidence of Arthur Charles Trott, the ticket collector at Greenhurst Station, of Philip Coomber Stanhope, whose house the dead man had visited and with whose family he had tea, and of Doctor Depard—all may be said to tally. They link up together, as it were. Each, in part, is confirmatory of the others. That, to my mind, is the strongest and—er—most illuminating feature which emerges from their various—er—testimonies. The point that then suggests itself to us, and the suggestion is both persistent and disturbing—is what was the reason which made the deceased leave the train at Greenhurst Station? Was it to meet somebody? Was it—I'm compelled to mention this possibility—was it something in the nature of an assignation? And by the word assignation I am bound to admit I am using it in its usually accepted sense. Deliberately so. The members of the jury must ponder over these things. As far as can be ascertained, the deceased was a good living man, his character and personal integrity have not been assailed in any way; he was a man, too, of high professional skill and standing, very likely on the threshold of a distinguished career and nobody has brought forward the slightest suggestion that he was worried in any way. There has been no hint from my direction at all of trouble, of anxiety, of apprehension—he was not in debt—he had been successful at his profession—and he was married—and recently at that—to a very charming lady. A lady whom we have seen in the witness box to-day. To that lady, on your behalf—and speaking for myself too—I extend the most sincere sympathy and the very deepest condolence in what to her must be an agonizing sorrow." Mr. Bessemer paused again.

"In conclusion, and before I request you to consider your verdict, I must draw your attention to the extraordinary evidence given to the court by the Rev. John Moffatt. With regard to certain articles—er—wearing apparel—which had been worn by the deceased and which had since been found in the font of St. Mark's Church, Fullafold. You are aware from what Doctor Depard told you that the body was nude when he was called upon to examine it. From that you would have expected—er—reasonably expected that if *some* articles of the deceased's clothing had been placed—hidden, may I say—in the font of the church—all of them would be there! But they were not—as you have heard from the Rev. Moffatt. Why were the clothes divided—separated—in this most remarkable way? What could be the reason for it? Why were the—er—" Again Mr. Bessemer made reference to his notes, "trousers of the suit, the hat, the overcoat, the scarf, the tie, the shirt and collar—er—soft collar and the shoes not with the other articles of clothing? Certainly a most remarkable feature. You will do well, members of the jury, to consider all the evidence that has been placed before you. And of course there can be no thought of suicide. That contingency can be ruled out with certainty." The coroner pushed his notes to one side and put his elbows on the table.

"The various points to which I have drawn your attention may be legitimately considered by you in arriving at your conclusion. I desire you, therefore, to consider your verdict."

A buzz of excitement rippled through the court. Within the space of a few moments the foreman of the coroner's jury rose and stated that the members of the jury did not desire to retire. There was no necessity. Their unanimous verdict was "Murder—by some person or persons unknown."

The Council Chamber began to empty—fast. Anthony and MacMorran sat in their places for a few moments watching the others go out. In a moment of comparative quietude the latter turned to Anthony with a question.

"Well—what do you think of it?"

"What do I think of it, Andrew? As a case—do you mean? Why—it's a gem! Of purest ray serene! I wouldn't have missed it for all the tea in China. I suggest we have a spot of lunch—it's late now—and then we'll blow back to Bernays and Bland at Four Bridges Police Station. What do you say?"

"That's O.K. by me," replied Andrew MacMorran.

Chapter IV

1

Anthony and Inspector MacMorran went to the "Nepean Arms." "I spotted this place on the way down," said Anthony, "not too bad from the look of it."

They found a luncheon-room and a waitress. "You're only just in time," she said—"we don't serve lunches after half-past two. And it's just on that now."

"Lady," said Anthony, "upbraid us not. We are servants of the public. Ours not to reason why. What have you for lunch?"

"Most of it's off," she said petulantly—"you'll have to have rabbit-pie."

"Even so," said Anthony, "poor puss."

As the waitress placed the meal in front of them, Anthony turned to MacMorran.

"I have two thirsts to be assuaged, Andrew. One for beer—the other for information. The local brewer will attend to the first—you shall administer to the second. How does that appeal to you?"

"It'll pass. Go ahead. What can I do for you?"

"I want to know what you thought of the witnesses. My need is urgent. Tell me, Andrew."

"Well—I wouldn't cross swords with any of them on to-day's showing. As far as I could tell from watching them and listening, they all seemed to be telling the truth. As the old boy said—their respective stories linked up. That doesn't always happen, you know." MacMorran shook his head with an air of profound wisdom. Then he tossed the ball back to Anthony. "What did you think of them yourself?"

"Oh—I wouldn't quarrel with you at all. My impressions were much the same as yours. At first blush, if I did desire to pick a hole or two, I *might* fall back on the widow."

"Good lord—why? She rang very true to me."

Anthony shrugged his shoulders. "Can't tell you why. Admit that at once. Just a hunch perhaps. She rang true—you say. Perhaps, I thought, *too* true. Can't tell yet. Early days. But I'd bet on one thing, Andrew, with regard to her. She's of the type to find speedy consolation. She's an attractive wench." .

"She may be that—and still pass," replied MacMorran drily—"speaking for myself, I'd put her in the clear without the slightest demur—or hesitation."

"I don't altogether agree," responded Anthony, "and I'll tell you why. Field, the murdered man, may have been the possessor of a roving eye. Mrs. Field may have been aware of the fact. Hence—a roving eye on her side. Two roving eyes—and trouble comes aboard. That's one possible angle on the problem. What did you think of Stanhope of Stoke Pelly?"

"Good chap. Liked the way he counted out the change for the coroner. Didn't turn a hair either."

Anthony grinned. "Pretty sound that, wasn't it? How did the reverend gentleman strike you?"

"Oh—typical. Far from the world and fervent. How did he appeal to you?"

"Well—that's rather a nasty one to answer. How shall I put it? I think—in this way. That when he found Field's everyday raiment in the font, he was much more concerned with the defilement the font had suffered than with the actual finding of the clothes. I say, Andrew, this isn't a bad pie, when all's said and done. The pastry's excellent."

MacMorran mumbled his agreement. "Our trouble, Andrew," went on Anthony, "is the usual one. The one that's as old as the hills. We're expected once again to lay our noses on a cold scent. All the same—it's a beautiful case. With five, I think, of the tightest knots in it that I've ever been called upon to unravel."

"Five?"

"I said 'five,' Andrew."

"What are the five?"

Anthony ticked them off on his fingers after putting his plate to one side. "A—the mysterious 'phone message which sent Claudia Field careering off to Friar's Woodburn. B—the appearance of Julian

Field at Greenhurst en route for the hook in the porch of Fullafold Parish Church. C—the strange separating operation that took place in respect of the dead man's clothes. D—the almost sadistic treatment of the body after death—stripped to the buff and strung up in a church porch. E—the conversation which Julian Field had with Trott, the ticket collector at Greenhurst Station when he surrendered his railway ticket."

MacMorran knitted his brows. "I get the flavour of the first four—but I'm hanged if I get the fifth. Or 'E' as you described it."

"Why, Andrew? You remember what Trott said, don't you? Wot Trott said wot Field said?"

MacMorran thought it over. "Yes. I can remember. Field said that he'd been forced to break his journey, and then inquired of Trott as to the whereabouts of a place called Cornelius Steps. Trott said in effect—'there ain't no such animal.'"

Anthony grinned. "Full marks, Andrew." He leant across the table to the inspector. "Now I'll tell you something else. Friar's Woodburn! Where Claudia Field wasted some anxious hours. Ever been there, Andrew?"

"Never. Look out—here's the apple-pie coming."

Anthony drew back. The waitress deposited the two plates. "So you've never been to Friar's Woodburn? Well I have, Andrew. And this is where it begins to get interesting. You listen. To the best of my memory'—there's a little place near Friar's Woodburn by the name of Cornelius Stones. There are a number of stepping stones there across a stream—I fancy it's called the Pidge. Perhaps its only a tributary. Does the coincidence appeal to you at all, Andrew?"

"It's significant, I agree. We shall have to put it on a plate for Bernays. With or without parsley sauce. Your point is, of course, that Julian Field alighted at Greenhurst because he wanted Cornelius Stones, whereas where he really should have got out was Friar's Woodburn? And in view of—" MacMorran stopped abruptly.

"In view of what, Andrew?"

"Why—what the coroner hinted at. The assignation idea. Would this Cornelius Stones place be a sound investment for something of that sort?"

"Excellent, Andrew. Just what the doctor would have ordered! All the lovers in the district have used the Stones at some time or other. The nooks beyond the river are a paradise for the amorous. You've arrived where I arrived, Andrew."

The waitress planked the bill on the table with a frown and looked significantly at the clock on the wall.

"Thank you," said Anthony, "thank you for everything. The pie, the beer, the sweet, the service, and the smiling face."

2

"You've arrived—you two gentlemen—at what I've heard described as the psychological moment," said Inspector Bernays. He smiled as he spoke.

"That's interesting," replied MacMorran, "we always do our best to oblige in that way. What's the special significance this afternoon?"

"Come in the next room," replied the local inspector, "and I'll show you. Sergeant Bland's in there now. Later on, he'll be getting back to Greenhurst."

Anthony and MacMorran followed Bernays into the inner room. Bernays jerked his head towards one end of the table. "Look over there."

Anthony looked and saw a heap of clothes. MacMorran moved over towards them. Bland stood by them—a broad grin on his face.

"More for the rummage sale," declared the sergeant—"but it's plain daft—all of it."

Anthony began to understand what had happened—but Bernays was on the point of explanation.

"Here," he said, "we have—(a) pair of trousers (grey chalk-stripe), (b) brown soft hat, (c) light overcoat, (d) silk square or scarf—colours red, black and silver, (e) tie in similar colours, (f) light fawn-coloured shirt, (g) collar to match, (h) pair of brown shoes—size about 9, I should think—and (i) pair of dark brown gloves. That's the clothing part. At the side, if you look carefully, a heap of miscellaneous articles. We'll number 'em this time. (1) Gold signet ring, (2) gold wrist watch—nice article that, I must say—(3) cigarette case, (4) white handkerchief, (5) nail-file. (6) fountain pen, (7) cigarette lighter,

(8) wallet, (9) stethoscope, and (10) a heap of money amounting to threepence in all and comprising six half-pennies, (11) note-case—empty, and (12) one red rose that has seen better days. There you are gentlemen, bar the money that's obviously missing from the note-case—I suggest he must have carried *some*—his keys, and the return half of his railway ticket, there you have the remaining possessions that the late Dr. Field carried on him when he entered Stanhope's place at Stoke Pelly and when he left it. Plus the buttonhole."

Anthony rubbed his hands. "With, I think, one exception," he remarked. "That is to say, with regard to when he left."

"What's that, Mr. Bathurst?" inquired Bernays quietly.

"The specimen of Mrs. Stanhope's sputum. My remarks, of course, are based on the evidence given at the inquest."

"Quite right, Mr. Bathurst. I'll let you have that one." Bernays smiled again.

"Decent bloke," thought Anthony—"better than some I've knocked up against."

"Most extraordinary case of my career," went on Inspector Bernays—"Sergeant Bland here keeps on saying it's plain daft—and 'pon my soul—I'm inclined to agree with him. Whoever's croaked this doctor fellow took all his big money—he must have had some—and left him with six halfpennies, a gold ring and a jolly valuable gold wristlet watch. Then he hangs him up, after stripping him and playing silly buggers with his clothes." Bernays scratched the back of his head. "Doesn't make anything like sense to me. Must be the work of somebody from the looney-bin over at Abel's Common. Somebody who's escaped."

Anthony looked at him shrewdly. "Two things you haven't yet told us, inspector. In which, I confess, that I have a great deal of interest."

"What are they, Mr. Bathurst?"

"Firstly—how long have these clothes and articles been in your possession—"

Another smile from Bernays. "When you and the chief came in just now—" Bernays looked up at the clock—"I'd had 'em exactly five minutes. Don't you recall my remark concerning the 'psychological moment'? That was what I intended to convey. Sorry if it missed fire."

Anthony gave grin for grin. "That's O.K., inspector, I get it. Now for my other question—which you know you're waiting for me to ask. Where were these things found and who found 'em?"

Bernays gave him a queer glance. "Wait for it," he said, "and hold on to somewhere for support. They were found early this morning by the Rev. Theodore Ingram Henson, Vicar of Friar's Woodburn."

"Where exactly did he find 'em?"

"I should have thought you'd have guessed that," replied Bernays—"he found 'em in the font of Friar's Woodburn Parish Church. Dedicated, so he says, to St. Mary Magdalene."

MacMorran came over to stand by Anthony. "Perhaps I did guess it," said Anthony Bathurst.

"Yes," continued Bernays, "they were all neatly folded, so the good vicar says, just as the Fullafold lot were. It's still plain daft, isn't it?"

"I'm not so sure," said Anthony.

MacMorran shook his head. "Maybe it's been made to look like that deliberately."

"I think you've got something there," added Anthony, "because that's the pattern as I'm beginning to see it." He turned suddenly to Bernays. "Oh I say, inspector—Field's wallet that you mentioned—been through it yet?"

"No, Mr. Bathurst—not yet. That is to say properly. There are a few papers and such like in it. They're on the side there. We'll run through 'em now if the chief's agreeable. What do you say, chief?"

"Yes—by all means," replied MacMorran.

The three men sat down at the table and began to examine the contents of Field's wallet. Bernays described the articles as he looked at them in turn.

"Hotel bill receipted. Last July. St. Mawes, Cornwall."

As Bernays handled the documents one by one, he passed them to MacMorran who relayed them to Anthony.

"Book of stamps. Remains of a five-shilling's issue. Stamps in it now—worth—let me see—three shillings and fivepence. Pocket time-table—local publication—trains and bus services evidently. Letter from a lady—evidently a patient—making an appointment at Field's surgery for a consultation—what's the date? Fortnight old now. Lydia Carson, 'The Ferns,' Beechcroft Crescent, King's Winkworth. Wonder why he kept it? Tailor's bill—unpaid this account—from Messrs. Cotter and McCormick, tailoring experts, Cornhill, London. Nothing much else here. I'm afraid. Hallo—what's this?"

Bernays' running fire of comment died away suddenly. His companions watched him as he read the document to which he had last made reference. When he handed it to MacMorran, he spoke quietly. "H'm. Distinctly interesting. Looks as though we've got something there, gentlemen."

Anthony waited in patience while MacMorran read. Without further comment, the latter handed the letter to him. It was neither dated nor addressed. The handwriting was unusual. That was the adjective which Anthony first applied to it. Not strange or peculiar. Not ill-formed or illiterate. Just unusual. Anthony read the letter carefully. It was worded as follows:

"My dear Julian. Yours to hand. Thursday will suit me. Will meet you as before, same time, but different place. I'll come out as soon after tea as I can make it. The other side of Cornelius Stones, but I won't risk anything. When you say that we must find a way out, I agree entirely. Anybody will direct you to C.S. if you ask. All my love, darling. Till Thursday, then. Mary." Anthony returned the letter to Inspector Bernays. Bernays waited for the inevitable comments. But his impatience got the better of him.

"Well?" he enquired with an almost sharp insistence, "what about it?"

MacMorran smiled one of his most enigmatic smiles. Anthony spoke. "Won't Bessemer be pleased?" he remarked drily—"he's holed in one."

"Assignation?" declared Bernays.

"No doubt about that," supplemented MacMorran.

Anthony extended his hand to Bernays. "Let me have another dekko, inspector," he said to Bernays—"something's just occurred to me."

Bernays produced the letter again. Anthony scrutinized it for the second time. The others watched him.

"What's the point?" asked Bernays—"anything about it strike you particularly?"

"Don't know," replied Anthony—"just wondering—that's all. It reminds me of something I've seen somewhere and I haven't succeeded yet in remembering what it is. Shall have to wait for it to come to me."

"I'll tell you how it struck me the first time I read it," said Bernays.

"How was that?"

"Well—it didn't strike me as being typical of a girl's writing."

"How do you mean exactly?" queried Anthony.

"Well—put it like this—more suggestive of a man's fist than a woman's."

Anthony shook his head. "I don't think there's a lot in that, inspector. Many women nowadays write in a very similar style to men. In fact, I have three of my own acquaintance whose handwriting is typically masculine. If I didn't know to the contrary I'd swear that their handwriting was a man's in each instance. No—it's not that which was troubling me. Something else and I can't give it a name yet awhile. As I said—I'll wait for it."

Bernays shrugged his shoulders. "Maybe I was wrong. It wouldn't be the first time." As he spoke, he swung round to MacMorran. "When I was in town yesterday, you said something about visiting the church at Fullafold. When would you care to go up there? It stands at the top of a rather steep slope, you know."

"We were wondering," answered MacMorran, "if you could run us up there this afternoon? The sooner the better—by all means."

"That's O.K." responded Bernays. "I'll get a car. We'll take Sergeant Bland along with us. Are you fit?"

"Ready when you are, inspector."

"Good. I'll get cracking at once, then."

"Ain't life a scream," murmured Sergeant Bland.

3

The car stopped at the foot of the slope on the Greenhurst side. "Here we are gentlemen," said Inspector Bernays—"X marks the spot."

Anthony looked round. "This, I presume," he said to Bernays, "is where Mary Whitley alighted from the bus on her way home?"

"That's right, Mr. Bathurst. At this very spot. The bus runs along the road we've just come from Greenhurst. Mary Whitley got out here and went up the slope just as we shall."

"Where does the bus run to?"

"Little place called Minnow."

"Where does it start?"

"Four Bridges. Travels exactly the same route as we've just covered—as far as this. Then it goes on to Minnow through Stoat's Green. There is no service that actually touches Fullafold. Mary Whitley had been to the cinema in Greenhurst—she picked the bus up there. Are you ready?"

"Just a minute, inspector. Won't keep you waiting long. Just a word with Sergeant Bland here—if you don't mind?" Anthony turned to Bland. "You were on duty at Greenhurst station when Mary Whitley's father telephoned for you? That right?"

"S'right, sir," said Bland. "I do duty at Greenhurst on certain evenings in the week. That's where the girl's father ran me to earth. I wasn't half pleased to hear from him—I can tell you."

"Thank you, sergeant. I just wanted to get the true picture in my mind of what happened—that was all."

"That's right, sir. When Whitley reported what his girl had run into up at the church, I got hold of a constable—Nye his name is—and we cycled over here pronto. Got off the bikes just here as we're standing now."

"Thank you again, sergeant. I get you. Lead on, inspector."

The four men ascended the slope that led to the church. "Get a rare crop o' thistles here in the summer," remarked Bernays.

"S'right," contributed Bland, "they send the force out here to graze when the thistles get too numerous. Some o' the locals say it's their favourite food. A policeman's life in these parts ain't a doddle."

"That lane down there," said Bernays pointing back, "that lane we've just come from is known as Strangler's Lane. A young girl got it down there donkeys' years ago."

"It's livin' up to its reputation," remarked MacMorran, "I reckon the locals, as you call them, will be givin' it a miss on dark nights."

"Now stop here for a minute, will you please?" The words came from Bernays. The four men halted. "This is just about where Mary

Whitley fainted. Just by the edge of the grass here. According to her reckoning she was about two-thirds of the way up the slope—she's been over the ground with me so that I've got the bearings pretty well—when she heard somebody cough and then a voice—'murmuring and mumbling' so Mary Whitley describes it. She was so frightened—scared stiff she says—that she stopped. Just about here. Footsteps came towards her and she reckoned she was for it. Then—she passed out."

"What time was that?" asked MacMorran.

"In answer to that, chief, I'll give you exactly what Mary Whitley has given to me. The 'flick' she saw packed up about twenty minutes past ten. She reckoned she waited ten minutes for a bus in Greenhurst High Street so that, approximately, she'd get away from Greenhurst about half-past ten. I put inquiries through to the cinema people and to the omnibus company—and their times confirm what Mary says. That means she'd alight at the foot of the slope there about 10.45. Quarter to eleven. Five minutes or so walking up the slope—say ten to eleven. Or, if its easier to reckon by—say eleven o'clock."

"Thank you, inspector." MacMorran acknowledged the information.

"When Mary came back to consciousness, she says she heard a clock striking twelve, probably, I should say, the clock on the Town Hall at Four Bridges. When she pulled herself together, she went towards the churchyard. You know all about the noise she heard—you were in the coroner's court this morning when she gave evidence. So—like Mary Whitley—we'll make our way towards the gate of the churchyard on the Greenhurst side. By your leave, gentlemen."

Bernays moved forward. The others followed him. Bernays opened the gate and the four men passed between the tombstones.

Chapter V

1

Inspector Bernays waited for the others at the porch. Anthony came slowly and brought up the rear. He desired to see and to understand the general lie of the land.

"Here we are, gentlemen," said Bernays, "this is where Mary Whitley stood when the dead body of Field swung against her face. You can guess the kid was scared all right. I shouldn't have cared much for the experience myself. Especially in the dark."

"On the foggy side, too, wasn't it?" queried MacMorran.

"I wouldn't say foggy, exactly. Bit of a ground mist—there had been. When Mary got here, however, it had begun to lift a bit." Bernays moved farther in. "The lantern had been removed. It had been placed at the back of the porch—with a hook. Probably brought as a spare. The lantern usually hangs, as you can see if you look closely, on a stout hook which is screwed into the beam. The beam is solid oak. On this hook was another—such as a butcher uses—strong metal. From this second, curved hook hung a shortish length of rope with a noose which held the dead body of Field. We've replaced the lantern as you see—the curved hook, the spare hook, and the rope you can inspect when we get back to the station."

"Any prints?" demanded MacMorran—"on the lantern—or on the hooks?"

"Not a smell of one," returned Bernays with emphasis.

Anthony went up a little and stood directly underneath the lantern. It was of the old-fashioned type—square almost—and suggested to him those he had seen in pictures as carried by the watch in years gone by.

"What's the height of the oak beam. Inspector?" he asked of Bernays.

"As nearly as possible—eight feet from the ground."

"H'm. What was the height of the dead man?"

"Five feet seven and a half. The description we shoved out put him as medium. I'd call him on the short side."

"Weight?"

"Just over eleven stone, Mr. Bathurst."

Anthony turned to Sergeant Bland. "You were the first man on the scene, sergeant. Will you be good enough to tell me just what the dead man looked like? Tell me just how he struck you when you first saw him."

Anthony closed his eyes. Bland, a trifle surprised, perhaps, began to speak. "Well, sir, I wouldn't call him a sight for sore eyes. Not on your life. When I shone my torch on 'im and saw his clock—gave me a bit of a turn it did. I'd be a liar if I said it didn't. I thought he was a foreigner at first glimpse. S'fact I did. Pale—sallow face. Dark hair—dark eyes and a 'beaver.' Beg pardon, sir, a beard. Small-pointed sort of beard. That's what gave me the impression, I suppose, that the bloke wasn't a Britisher. Fair creepy, it was—to see that naked stiff swingin' there on the hook. Matter of fact, I thought old Whitley was going to put his supper in the churchyard somewhere. His eyes almost fell out. And he looked proper uneasy round the gills—I can tell you."

Anthony opened his eyes. "Thank you, Sergeant Bland. I can almost see the body there now. Thanks to your most able description."

"You thank your lucky stars, sir, you can't! Reckon I'll dream about it more than once before I hand in my dinner-pail."

"Now," said Bernays, "I'll take you in to look at the font. Where the Rev. Moffatt found the clothes. You'd like to see it, of course."

MacMorran pushed his hands into his overcoat pockets. "Take us in there, inspector."

Bernays pushed open the door of the parish church. As he passed through into the church, Anthony glanced at the report of the previous Sunday's offertory. He desired to see the signature. The report was signed "Godfrey M. Atherton, M.A. (Oxon)." Anthony noted the name. He presumed it was the vicar's.

"Here's the font," Bernays was saying as Anthony joined the group—"half a dozen paces from the main door. No more. If the clothes were all ready, it would be but the work of a moment for the murderer to drop them in."

Anthony scratched his cheek as Bernays spoke. "Where were the other clothes, then, I wonder? What was the reason why they didn't go into the font with the first consignment?"

"Search me," replied Bland.

"Search me, too," smiled Inspector Bernays. MacMorran looked down into the font. Then he shook his head—as though the problem was too much for him.

Anthony came at Bernays again. "The church porch and the churchyard generally, inspector? They have been subjected, I take it, to a thorough search?"

"They have—Mr. Bathurst. You can take it from me that there was nothing left behind anywhere which looked anything like a clue. Especially when we knew what the reverend gentleman had picked up. Will you endorse that, sergeant?"

Bland was in like a flash. "We've been over all the ground, all over the church itself and the precincts thereof"—Bland grinned—"with the old small tooth-comb. Not a sausage."

"I'm satisfied," said Anthony.

Bernays looked at MacMorran. "Anything else you want to see here, chief?"

MacMorran shook his head. "I don't think so, inspector—thank you. We may as well be getting along again."

"Before we go, inspector," interposed Anthony—"I'd just like to have a glance at the other side of the churchyard. Isn't Fullafold the village that nestles at the foot on that side?"

"Quite right, Mr. Bathurst. If you come along now—I'll show it to you."

The four men crossed the churchyard and went out through the second gate. "There's Fullafold," said Bernays—"it lies at the foot there. Right on the downs."

Anthony looked at the cluster of small houses which was Fullafold. Sergeant Bland came and stood at his side.

"You see that swirl of smoke from a chimney-pot just down there, sir?"

Anthony looked and nodded. "Well," went on Bland, "that's just about where the Whitley's cottage is. It's in that row somewhere. Pretty little village—that. One of the 'show' places of the district."

Anthony stood there for a moment or so and looked round. His eye took in the line of country. MacMorran joined the two men.

"Had enough? Shall we get cracking?"

"Yes, Andrew. Stag at eve—me! I'm ready to return to Four Bridges. This is a very pretty little business."

"I told you that, sir," said Sergeant Bland. "Fullafold's one of the prettiest—"

"I wasn't referring to the village, sergeant," said Anthony. "I was referring to the problem itself. The case of the swinging death."

2

When they reached Four Bridges and entered the police station again, Bernays said laconically—"Come with me. I'll show you those other murder impedimenta. I mentioned them when we were up there in the church porch. All ready for the Black Museum? Come along through the yard, will you?"

They followed the local inspector as he had requested them. Bernays produced a bunch of keys and unlocked a door. To Anthony's eye, it looked like the door of a cupboard set in a wall.

"There you are," said Bernays—"one coil of rope—with noose. One screw hook. One curved butcher's hook."

MacMorran handled the three articles.

"The rope may lead us somewhere," continued Bernays—"the hooks—well—there must be thousands of them knocking about the length and breadth of England."

Anthony looked at the rope with its sinister noose and made a mental assessment of its length. What he saw satisfied him.

Bernays threw the articles back into the cupboard and re-locked the door. "Now where do you two gentlemen think of staying?" he asked.

MacMorran looked enquiringly at Anthony. "Somewhere," said Anthony with a smile, "between King's Winkworth and say—Stoke Pelly. They're the two places which seem to me to be the poles, as it were, of the affair generally. And, in between those two given points we have, don't forget, Greenhurst, Four Bridges, Fullafold, and Friar's Woodburn. Each one of which, you will admit—is not entirely devoid of interest."

"You mean," persisted Bernays, "that you haven't yet made up your minds?"

"Leave it at that, inspector," replied Anthony—"and you won't be far out. But as soon as we have fixed up—we'll let you know where we are."

"O.K. Put a ring through to the station here."

"That shall be done, inspector."

MacMorran and Anthony shook hands with Bernays and Bland. "The car's in the corner of the yard," said the inspector, "I had to have it shifted back a few yards. I'll be seeing you." He waved his hand.

3

Anthony, with Andrew MacMorran at his side, halted the car by the clock tower in the main street of Four Bridges.

"Well, Andrew," he said—"which shall it be? Which of the different places makes the appeal and tickles the MacMorran nostril? Apart from considerations of convenience?"

MacMorran rubbed his nose with his forefinger. "Well, to my way of thinking, the choice lies between Four Bridges and Greenhurst. They're the more central—for one thing."

"I agree, Andrew."

"Suppose then, we decide on Greenhurst? Suit you?"

"Andrew—you're a man after my own heart. Greenhurst is my choice. As we came through on the way down, I spotted a rather attractive little pub. What do you say? Shall we make for there now?"

"That's the idea," replied MacMorran—"a spot of dinner and we'll talk things over."

The pub to which Anthony drove the car, bore the sign of "The Horse and Groom." Preliminary negotiations proved admirably satisfactory and Anthony, with Andrew MacMorran, sat down to dinner at almost exactly seven-thirty.

"Mutton cutlets, Andrew. The landlady apologized for same and intimated her intention to 'do better' to-morrow."

"Sounds all right."

"Looks all right, too. I've seen 'em."

MacMorran took his seat at the dinner-table and extracted a letter from his pocket-book. "I borrowed this from Inspector Bernays," he said—"I fancy it may repay a little further study."

Anthony saw it was the letter found in the wallet that had been carried by Julian Field. MacMorran spread it out in front of him. Anthony watched him.

"Seems to me," said MacMorran, after a somewhat lengthy pause, "that this must be regarded, very definitely, as Clue Number One. If we can't get somewhere from this, it's time we retired and kept bees."

Anthony grinned at him. "Mary's a grand name, Andrew."

"Eh? What's that?"

"I said Mary was a grand name."

"It is. I confess to a liking for it myself. So we're in agreement on that."

"S'right, Andrew, as Sergeant Bland might say—you and I and thousands of others. Had the name been Cassandra now or Desdemona—" Anthony broke off and shrugged his shoulders.

"Yes," said MacMorran. "I get your point. But things may not be so bad as you're inclined to think. Look at it for yourself. Friar's Woodburn isn't London, or Birmingham. Neither Manchester nor Liverpool."

"Or even Glasgow—eh, Andrew?"

"You've said it."

"Very true, Andrew. All that you've just said. But I'm not taking Friar's Woodburn from you. Oh—no!"

"Why not? What's the matter with Friar's Woodburn?"

"Nothing at all. And there's nothing the matter with Greenhurst either. Or even with Maidenbridge and Great Bosway—the two main places between Friar's Woodburn and Stoke Pelly."

The inspector was silent. Anthony pressed home his point and held out his hand for the letter. MacMorran passed it over to him. Anthony read through it again carefully.

"It may be assumed, and assumed with some degree of confidence, that the lady who wrote this certainly resides somewhere in the locality. Take this sentence as confirmatory. 'I'll come out as soon after tea as I can make it.' I think that indicates almost certainly that she hadn't a great distance to travel to the place of assignation. Namely—the Cornelius Stones."

MacMorran nodded. Before he could reply in words, the waitress arrived with the dinner. After the brief interval thus necessitated, Anthony took up the thread again.

"And remember, Andrew, she and Field, according to this, had met before. Same time—but different place. She then nominates the

Cornelius Stones. Later on in the communication which was obviously written in haste, she has a kind of afterthought, that she hasn't given Field any directions as to how to find this new place of rendezvous. So she slips in the phrase—'anyone will direct you to C.S. if you ask.' Are you with me so far?"

"Absolutely," replied MacMorran between mouthfuls.

"Good. Well—now—let's go on from there. And we can proceed infinitely well. Let's turn the floodlights on to Julian Field. What does Field do—in relation to the terms of Mary's letter? Field, who resides in King's Winkworth, and who may or may not be familiar with the country between King's Winkworth and Stoke Pelly, to which place he has been twice on a professional visit, *gets out at Greenhurst*! Whereas, had he been properly directed by the lady anxious to receive his attentions, he would have got out at Friar's Woodburn. That to me, Andrew, is as plain as a pikestaff."

Again MacMorran nodded. "Yes. I think you're right. That's very sound, all of it. That is to say—if the train stopped there."

"Thank you, Andrew. You were always the gentleman. But I haven't finished yet—I haven't anything like finished. For the reason that we can proceed still farther." Anthony leant over the dining-room table towards the Yard inspector. "Now—why exactly—did Julian Field leave the train at Greenhurst?"

"Because he thought it was the nearest station for this Cornelius Stones, I suppose."

"But he didn't know where the Cornelius Stones were, Andrew. If he had been familiar with them, he wouldn't have given them the wrong name. Don't forget what he asked Trott, the Greenhurst ticket collector. He inquired the way to Cornelius Steps."

"What's your point then?"

"Why this, Andrew. To my mind, it's almost a certainty that Field alighted at Greenhurst because Greenhurst was the station where he had got out when he kept the previous tryst with the amorous Mary. And—don't forget this—he chose a train which *didn't* stop at Friar's Woodburn. I've checked that. There you are, my lad, pick the bones out of that."

MacMorran was silent for some seconds. "Once again, I think you're right," he said eventually.

"Once again, then, thank you, Andrew. Shall we go on from there to the next base?"

"O.K. I'm listening. I'm one of the worr-ld's greatest listeners."

"So you ought to be," grinned Anthony, "look at the practice you get listening to me. Anyhow—here we go. The next point of deduction from that, and which sticks out a mile, is that the love-lorn Mary resides in the neighbourhood of Greenhurst. And, also, the probability is, that she used a car to get her to her assignation with Julian Field. What's the sweet, Andrew—can you see?"

The inspector craned his head in the direction of the waitress. "Some sort of fruit-pie with custard. But she's coming over. You'll soon know."

Anthony did. "Mulberries, Andrew—and very nice, too. Now where were we? Oh—I know. That Mary resides near this 'ere village of Greenhurst. Where we dine off succulent mutton cutlets and luscious mulberries. Anyhow—let's go on once again. Something else emerges from all that preamble, Andrew, which strikes me very forcibly."

"Come again," said MacMorran.

"I'm now going to bring a third person into the cast. Can you guess who?"

"Trott—the ticket collector?"

"No—somebody playing a much bigger part. Claudia Field, relict of Julian. Think of this point, Andrew—because it's fat with all kinds of possibilities. To what place did Claudia's 'phony' message tell her to go? You heard what Bernays told us."

Anthony replaced his dessertspoon and fork and rubbed his hands as he put the question to MacMorran. MacMorran thought.

"To the railway station at Friar's Woodburn."

Anthony's grey eyes gleamed with excitement. How well MacMorran knew that sign!

"Well, then, Andrew—doesn't that look extremely like the fact that Friar's Woodburn was the place where Julian Field was *expected* to be?"

Anthony slopped abruptly and his eyes took on a far away look. He seemed to be mentally criticizing his own statement. "Either expected—or meant to be," he added. And then, almost under his breath MacMorran heard him say, "I wonder whether—now that's something I *hadn't* considered."

4

"I'm beginning to get you," said MacMorran—"I can see where you're going."

"Where, Andrew?"

"Well—you're endeavouring to clear up something that's troubled me right from the very outset. And that's the question of motive. Frankly, look as I might, I couldn't see one anywhere. Now—you're showing me one of the oldest of all. Perhaps the one that's got the longest whiskers of any. The eternal triangle."

Anthony drank coffee. "I didn't say so."

"Not in so many words. But you hinted at it pretty strongly. Good Lord—what other angle could I get out of what you've just said?"

Anthony stirred his coffee—almost absentmindedly. "Tell me what you're thinking, Andrew. I mean—give me the picture as you see it now. Following on my remarks brought about by this letter." He tapped the letter to Field which still lay on the table between them.

MacMorran seemed a trifle mystified, but he nevertheless fell in with Anthony's suggestion. "I should have thought," began the Yard inspector, "that the picture had become pretty plain. The broad lines of it, as I see it, or rather as you've shown it to me, are these. Field is running an affair with a girl in the Greenhurst district. We'll call her Mary 'X.' On the occasion of his previous visit to Mrs. Stanhope at Stoke Pelly, he has killed two birds with one stone—if you like it better—combined pleasure with business. The opportunity was there—he took it. Mary 'X,' in all probability, is a married woman. Her husband tumbles to her little game—and he's the guy that put Field out of mess. Quite frankly—I thought that was your own idea."

"No, Andrew. Strangely enough—seeing the way you've put it—it wasn't. I see now, though, that it might have been. Perhaps, indeed, I ought to have said 'should have been.'" He drummed with his fingers on the table-cloth. "Tell me, Andrew," he said suddenly, "what makes you think that our love-sick Mary is a married woman?"

MacMorran wagged his head in an attempt to suggest infinite wisdom. "Psychology. A fragment of my own."

"Embroider it, then—so that I may understand."

"Well, I'm getting a wee bit old in the tooth now—and I'll tell you this. I've noticed that when a medicine man runs off the matrimonial lines, you can lay ten to one that the siren who beckons to him is married. Doctors seem to fall much more for the married kind than the other sort. At least—that's my profound belief."

MacMorran sat back in his chair, looking very satisfied with himself. Anthony pulled at his top lip—an old habit of his when assailed by doubt.

"Not bad, Andrew. Haven't enough data to argue it out with you. Going back to where we were—I'll make a confession. I wasn't thinking of 'Mr. X'—the spouse of Mary."

"You weren't? You surprise me then. He was the first proposition to enter my head."

"So you've said. No—my thoughts were wandering round in the direction of Claudia. At the other angle of the triangle. The fair-haired, blue-eyed Claudia. I was wondering whether we might find an admirer of hers lurking in the background somewhere. It's that faked telephone message which is worrying me. I don't like it at all."

"Why—so particularly? I don't know that I get that." Anthony took a cigarette. MacMorran shook his head at the offered case. "No, thanks. I'm going to have a pipe."

"Right-o. We'll adjourn to the lounge, then. I didn't think it looked too bad as we came through just now."

MacMorran followed Anthony into the smoking-lounge and they found that they had the apartment to themselves. A comfortable seat for each near the fire completed a satisfactory situation.

"Coming back to Claudia's 'phone call," continued Anthony, "first of all let's look at it from the angle you've put up. That Field was murdered by a Mary connection for the love of Mary. If that's the goods—why send Claudia to Friar's Woodburn?"

MacMorran made no answer. He drew comfortably at his pipe. Anthony waited for him. Eventually the inspector found words. "Go on—make your point more clear to me."

"Well—why revenge yourself alone on Claudia? Why send Claudia—the innocent party—the wronged wife—on a wild-goose chase to Friar's Woodburn? The murderer—your murderer, Andrew—had no grouse against *Claudia*. The triangle was the wrong way round for that. Do you get me now?"

MacMorran smiled. "The point is taken, kind sir. As an alternative, then, what is *your* explanation? How do you account for Mrs. Field's telephone call?"

"I can't account for it—and that's a fact. I suspect it! It smells. Its offence is rank and cries to High Heaven. You must have that 'phone call checked, Andrew. Because if it's a wrong 'un and the fair Claudia is double-crossing us—it throws the whole case out of gear completely."

"Bernays is working on that. I've already discussed it with him."

"Good. Another thing, Andrew. If the murder be the work of a jealous husband—and mind you I don't deny the strong possibility of that—especially on your showing this evening—why divide the clothes? Why separate the garments, Andrew? There must be some point in that. Otherwise, why all the time and trouble?" Again the inspector had no immediate answer. Anthony pounced on the fact of his reluctance.

"You can't answer that one, Andrew. I can't answer it, either. And until more data come our way, I don't think I shall attempt to."

The Yard inspector nodded. "I don't disagree with that. Now let's discuss the general plan of campaign. Where do we attack first?"

"Well—there's Mrs. Field, there's the Stanhopes, there are the two ecclesiastical contacts, St. Mark's, Fullafold, and St. Mary Magdalene, Friar's Woodburn—to say nothing of certain comparatively minor ports of inquiry. I'm inclined myself to start with King's Winkworth—Field's house and the blue eyed Claudia."

Anthony tossed a cigarette stub into the fire. "In the morning, Andrew, I'll run up to King's Winkworth while you and Bernays go through some of the routine stuff. That suit you?"

"Suits me," replied MacMorran.

Chapter VI

1

On the following morning, Anthony drove MacMorran to the police station at Four Bridges.

"I can leave you here, Andrew," he said, "and then run up to King's Winkworth on my own. It will only take me about half an hour's travelling time and, in addition, I shall be able to come in and have a word or two with Bernays."

The last-named met them upon arrival and nodded with apparent satisfaction. "You're early," he declared, "didn't expect you much before midday. Where have you fixed up?"

"At the 'Horse and Groom,' Greenhurst," replied MacMorran—"and up to the moment, we're very satisfied with the choice. Good dinner last night, decent bed and a thundering good breakfast this morning."

Bernays seemed pleased to hear the Yard inspector's news. "Good work. I'm glad you're early, all the same. As a matter of fact I've a fragment of news for you. This will interest you particularly, Mr. Bathurst."

"Oh—what's come in, inspector?"

"Come inside for a couple of minutes and we'll talk it over." They went into the inspector's room. "I've had the idea, Mr. Bathurst," said Bernays, "that you were more than ordinarily interested in the telephone call which Mrs. Field states she received late in the evening of the murder. Am I right?"

"You are, inspector."

"I thought so. Well—as I told the chief yesterday—I've had a check on it. I got the full dope about an hour ago. The telephone people have been in communication with me. It was a 'pukka' call all right and was received by Mrs. Field just as she stated. Now—where do you think it came from?"

Bernays looked first at Anthony and then at MacMorran. "I'll have a stab at that one," responded MacMorran—"my guess is Friar's Woodburn."

Bernays turned to Anthony. "What do you say, Mr. Bathurst—same as the chief?"

"Well, inspector—I won't deny that you've placed me in somewhat of a quandary. According to what you've told me—the call was genuine. As you know, I've always been inclined up till now to regard it with suspicion. So that to a certain extent I'm forced to re shape my ideas. Give me a minute to think."

"O.K. Take your time."

"My opinion," said Anthony, "is from Fullafold itself."

Bernays seemed a trifle startled at Anthony's answer. "You're right. Fullafold it was. From a call-box on the Four Bridges road. There are only two anywhere near the village—all told."

Anthony nodded as though he had been considering something. "Yes," he said, half to himself, "my opinion can still stand—in a way. There's the possibility still there." He looked at the two professionals. "You see what happened, don't you?"

"How do you mean?" This from Bernays.

"Why—you appreciate the sequence of events? As I visualize it, the telephone call was put through to Claudia Field as soon as the body of her husband had been disposed of. It was swinging in the church porch at Fullafold. That part of the murderer's campaign had been accomplished. But why not Greenhurst?"

"What do you mean?" intervened MacMorran, "what do you mean—why not Greenhurst?"

"Why this, Andrew. If Mary Whitley's story is to be believed—and I see no reason whatever to doubt it—she heard the murderer coming down the slope from the church on the Greenhurst side. The side of the slope she herself was ascending."

"That's a fact," contributed Inspector Bernays.

"I must think that out," said Anthony—"it requires certain explanation." He relapsed into silence.

"Look here," said MacMorran suddenly—"I'm getting fogged over this. To use your own phrase of last evening—or something like it—why send the bad news—and false information at that—to Claudia Field—and bung her off to Friar's Woodburn?"

"Andrew," replied Anthony quietly—"I've been acting like a prize idiot! I deserve to be kicked in the pants till further orders. I haven't been merely shortsighted—I've been as blind as Bartimeus. Eyes have I—and yet I saw not. My spell away from crime and criminals must have denuded me of any brains that I may have ever had. I've been looking for intrigue and the double cross—and all the time, the solution that I sought was there in front of me—money for old rope. The phone call to Claudia was just the time-honoured expedient to get her out of the house! Nothing more—and nothing less."

"Of course it was," said Bernays—"I could have told you that."

"I'm sorry, inspector—of course you could."

"The murderer," went on Bernays, "wanted something valuable from Field's house. When Field was dead—he went up and got it, having made certain in the meantime that the coast would be clear when he arrived there. That's elementary."

"I should be the last person in the world to contradict you, inspector—nobody's more aware of that humiliating fact than I am," Anthony spoke quietly—"but I think you're wrong."

"Oh?" Bernays seemed disconcerted. "How do you arrive at that conclusion?"

"What I think is this," replied Anthony—"I think that the murderer was compelled to go to Field's house after he had killed Field. I agree with you that he went to get something 'valuable,' but I think that its value was something entirely different from that which you are imagining. Still—tell me. What did you really mean by 'valuable'?"

Bernays was undoubtedly impatient by now. "What does anybody ever mean by 'valuable'? Something of high monetary worth—of course."

Anthony nodded. "Yes—I thought your mind ran that way. And that's where I differ from you. In my opinion, the murderer went to Field's house to lay his hands on something which, had it come to be discovered, *would have pointed unerringly to him as the murderer*. That's the reason why I said just now that he was *compelled* to go. Have I made myself clear, inspector?"

2

Bernays scratched his chin. "Oh—it's clear all right," he remarked, "but that isn't to say I agree with you."

"Time will tell," replied Anthony, "but I'm confident I'm on the right track in that respect. Anyhow, I can now ask you what it was my intention to ask you when I came this morning. Re Mrs. Claudia Field. You've been over Field's house, I take it, inspector?"

"As carefully as I know how, Mr. Bathurst. Why—what made you ask?"

Anthony grinned at Bernays's question. "Oh—I was just interested—that's all. Did you get anything?"

Bernays shook his head. "Can't say that I did."

"I see. Everything quite normal—eh?"

"Yes—pretty well. You could say that was so and you wouldn't be telling a lie."

"What does Mrs. Field report as stolen from the house while she was at Friar's Woodburn? I would be interested to hear that."

Anthony thought that Bernays hesitated a trifle before he answered. "Well—that's the strange part about it. She can't definitely say that she's lost anything."

"The explanation of that is, of course, a simple one. The article or articles that were stolen belonged to her husband. And it's quite on the cards that Claudia Field was, and is, entirely unaware of their existence."

"I take your point, Mr. Bathurst. Maybe you're right." Anthony could see that Bernays wasn't giving anything away. "How did the burglars get in?"

MacMorran, who had been in close conversation with Sergeant Bland, came up to join Anthony and Bernays. He listened attentively to Bernays's reply to Anthony's question.

"Well, in rather an unusual way, perhaps. At the back of the Field's house is a room with a balcony. This room was originally used as a bedroom. According to Mrs. Field—this was in Dr. Wolff's time. Wolff was Field's predecessor. Since however the Fields bought the practice—or rather since Field did—they've used the room as a kind of library and study. Chiefly for the reason of the pleasant outlook. By the side of this balcony there's a drain-pipe. The man who entered while Mrs. Field was at Friar's Woodburn, climbed up this drainpipe and from there was able to make the balcony. The rest would be comparatively easy."

Anthony thanked Bernays for the information. "You know, inspector," he said, "what you've just told me confirms the opinion that I expressed just now. You described your 'valuable' article as something of high monetary worth—your own words, if you remember—and yet Mrs. Field can't put a name to it."

"In that direction, Mr. Bathurst, permit me to recall your own words. That the valuable article belong to her husband." Anthony shrugged his shoulders. "O.K., inspector—skip it. I'll leave you to the tender mercies of the chief." He winked at MacMorran and walked back to the car.

3

Anthony came by car to King's Winkworth. He selected a public parking-place with more care than usual and contented himself, to begin with, with a stroll round the little town. Ascending the incline that leads from the railway station, he soon came to the main street which held the market and a rather imposing war memorial. To Anthony's eye, the place seemed quite a prosperous little market town and he soon found himself entering Bridge Street which escorted him to the Royal Bridge and to the river. The river itself was skirted by a pleasant stretch of green sward. The whole was attractive— made even more so by the brown and dark green of early November. Anthony stood and watched the river. Away upstream he could see an eyot nestling in the water, and on it the white bodies of the swans in active preparation for the winter which was not far behind this burst of November sun.

A charming little place—King's Winkworth—for a man to spend his days. Or a woman, either—come to that. He retraced his steps to the town and crossed the main road that runs between King's Winkworth and Four Bridges. He came to a smithy—thatched and white-washed—and to the post office which is not a hundred yards or so from the Norman parish church. Anthony walked up the hill and looked down again at the water of the Mower, glinting and shining in the November sunshine. In early summer, guessed Anthony, the waters of the Mower must be well fished and earnest fishers doubtless gather at the many King's Winkworth inns.

Anthony looked at his watch. The time was half-past eleven. He would direct his steps now to the house where Julian Field had lived—"The Bartons" in the High Street. His journey was soon over. It was a pleasant house of dark green paint and white shutters and stood cheek by jowl with a solicitor's offices and an inn. The inn had the sign of "The White Bear" and hard by "The Bartons" was the inn's courtway.

As he rang the bell, Anthony saw Field's brass-plate. He noted his qualifications for the practice of medicine and allegiance to the oath of Hippocrates. A pleasant house, thought Anthony, as he stood there, not large or pretentious—but attractive and almost dainty. Maybe—it was the paint and the doll's house-like shutters. His luck was in—for as the door opened to him—he saw that he was facing Claudia Field.

Anthony raised his hat. "Good morning, Mrs. Field. I know you're Mrs. Field, because I saw you yesterday at the inquest on your late husband. My name is Anthony Bathurst."

He added words of additional explanation. Claudia Field nodded. "I shall be pleased to see you," she said, "but could you possibly make it after lunch? I happen to be engaged just at the moment—and if you could—"

"By all means, Mrs. Field—name the time that will suit you." Claudia thought. "Well," she said, "could you possibly make it—say—a quarter-past two?"

"That will suit me admirably, Mrs. Field. Very many thanks."

Anthony withdrew in good order. He walked up the street past the "White Bear." He was wondering, as he walked, what the precise nature of Mrs. Field's pressing engagement was. If, indeed, there were one. Anthony walked a little distance and then stopped. After a moment's thought, he crossed over and walked back on the opposite side. A baker's and confectioner's, with the sign "morning coffee" displayed in the window, caught his eye. The chairs and marble-topped tables were in the shop itself and not in the parlour at the rear. The baker's was almost exactly opposite the cobbled yard of the "White Bear."

Anthony was pleased at what he saw, for an idea had been born within his brain. He entered the baker's shop, ordered a coffee and buns and took a seat near the window, from which he was able to command the front door of the dark-green house with the white shutters. The activity might yield him nothing, of course, but nothing venture—nothing win. The girl who had taken his order, brought the coffee and the plate of buns and Anthony sat comfortably to take his time. With the exception of himself, the shop in which he sat was devoid of custom.

"Pretty little place, this," he remarked to the shop-girl. "Yes—and gettin' famous now." The girl seemed anxious to talk.

"Oh—how's that?"

"Haven't you heard of the murder?"

Anthony simulated thought. "Oh—yes. Of a doctor—who lived here. I've got it right, haven't I?"

"That's right. Dr. Field. That's his place just opposite." The girl jerked her head towards the other side of the road.

"Which one do you mean?" Anthony stood up, coffee-cup in hand and gazed questioningly at the houses.

"The house next to the 'White Bear.' The one with the white shutters. 'The Bartons' is the name. See it?"

"Well, now—that's very interesting," said Anthony—"I remember reading about the affair. It's by way of being a mystery, isn't it? I mean—there's nobody been arrested for the crime."

"It's a proper mystery—if you ask me," replied the girl—"Mrs. Field's in there now. I saw her go in about an hour ago. Her cousin was with her."

The young lady means to talk, thought Anthony—and who am I to stand in her way? "Is that so?" he said casually.

"Yes—Mr. Courtenay. That's his name. Mr. Ernest Courtenay. Nice-looking fellow, too. Like Ray Milland in features. He's Mrs. Field's cousin," she repeated.

"Yes. I think you said her cousin went in with her. At least I understood you to say that." Anthony poised his coffee-cup. "This coffee's excellent. Can I have another cup?"

"Certainly—as many as you like."

The girl came from behind the counter and took the cup from him. During her absence, Anthony watched the door of the Field house. Nobody came out. The second cup of coffee arrived.

"Only married last year—they was," continued the shop-girl. "Doctor Field and his wife. About Whitsuntide it was. She was a Miss Allison. The Courtenays are her cousins. She was spending a holiday with them when she met the doctor. It was a proper surprise to all of us here in King's Winkworth when the engagement was announced."

The tone of voice employed to express the last statement was indubitably provocative. Anthony played up, therefore, in the approved fashion.

"Oh—why was that? Why were you all so surprised?"

The girl screwed her face up as though she were about to impart information of the most secret and highly confidential character. "Why—because everybody in King's Winkworth thought that she and Mr. Ernest Courtenay would pair up together. 'E was 'ead over 'eels in love with her—or at least that was 'ow it looked. Stuck out a mile it did. Always together—they was." The girl shrugged her shoulders. "But there you are—you don't never know when it comes to 'Oly Matrimony. Up pops Dr. Field and lo and be'old there's a wedding and Mr. Ernest is left standing in the cold. Doctor Field must 'ave bin a fast worker. I'll say 'e was."

Anthony was still watching the door with the dark-green paint. The news—or gossip, would be the better word—fell rather pleasantly on his ears. The pattern which was beginning to show, was a pattern which entirely suited him. It was in keeping with the early ideas which he had permitted himself to form. He had always felt that if there were an amorous triangle, it might well be on the reverse side to that which Andrew MacMorran suspected.

"Well," he replied to the girl, feeling it was high time he said something, "the doctor's dead now. Maybe—Ernest Courtenay will yet come into his own. Evidently he and Mrs. Field are still great friends—you say he's with her now."

"Yes. I saw him goin' in. About 'alf an hour ago. Do 'er a bit of good—it would—there is that about it."

"Oh—how come?"

The girl looked at him almost as though he had shocked her. "Of course," she said. "I keep forgettin' you don't come from these parts. The Courtenays are very wealthy people. They've lived here for many years. Old Mr. Courtenay is the owner of the big factory down there by the river—you know—boot and shoe polish. You must 'ave heard of 'Courtenay's Cleeno.'"

"Of course I have. And they're those Courtenays—eh?"

"That's it. Fair rolling in it. Everything the old man touches turns to money."

Anthony put his coffee-cup on the table. "Well—now—as I said before—that's all very interesting. How much do I owe you? I mustn't stop here all the morning—otherwise I shall be—"

The girl came towards him and began to fill in his bill. Suddenly she stopped—her pencil on the pad almost slipped in her excitement.

"There 'e is—look! Comin' out of the house now. That's Mr. Ernest Courtenay."

4

Anthony walked to the window and looked across the road. He saw a young man coming away from the house with the white shutters. He was tall, lithe and slender. He was well-dressed and he moved with an easy grace that was, perhaps, especially unusual in these days of careless walking. Anthony, as he saw Courtenay walk away, was scarcely aware of the interested girl who was standing almost at his elbow. Her voice, when she spoke, almost startled him.

"Don't you think he's like Ray Milland?" she cried—"his features? He always reminds me of him."

"Yes," he replied diplomatically, "perhaps you're right." He smiled. "I seem to have come in here just at the right moment. To hear all the news and see all the sights."

"It does seem like it, doesn't it?" she smiled at him.

"Well," said Anthony, "what's the damage? You were going to tell me."

"Tenpence, if you please."

Anthony gave her the money—"and there's sixpence for yourself. So that was Ernest Courtenay—eh? I suppose his people live near here?"

"That's right, sir. In the big red house almost on the corner of the main road to Four Bridges. Lovely place they've got there, too. The garden runs right down to the river. If you 'appen to be going in the direction of Four Bridges, you can't miss it."

"Perhaps if I'm out that way later, I'll have a look at it." He returned her smile. "You've got me right down interested. By the way—which is the best place for lunch?"

"Either the 'White Bear' or the 'Dragon.' The 'Dragon's' in Bridge Street. P'raps the 'Bear's' the best, though. Most people seem to think so. They're a bit more generous with their 'elpings."

"Good. I'll try it a little later. Many thanks!"

Anthony made his way from the shop. It seemed to him as he walked towards the Four Bridges road, that his early estimate of Claudia Field had not been a bad one.

Chapter VII

1

A few minutes later he stood and looked at the red-bricked house which was the Courtenays. Everything about it denoted opulence.

"Very nice, too," said Anthony—"and all out of 'Courtenay's Cleeno.'"

He walked round it. It had most of what it takes. Trim lawns, tennis courts, kitchen garden and fruit orchard. "And Claudia chose the doctor, when she might have had the son of the house. Now—I wonder why? For once the importance was not Ernest's."

Anthony walked along the Four Bridges road and saw the distance which the grounds of the Courtenay house ran down it. The story which the girl in the baker's shop had told him, might have points about it. He turned in his tracks and journeyed again towards the "White Bear"—and, he hoped, a satisfying lunch.

His hopes were not misplaced and precisely at a quarter-past two he stood again before the dark green door of the house with the white shutters. As he put his finger on the bell, another hope ran through him—that he wasn't being watched from the shop opposite. He grinned at the thought. As before, Mrs. Field came to the door. Anthony remembered that Bernays earlier on had mentioned that the Fields did not keep a maid. Mrs. Field had told him they were unsatisfactory, dishonest and that she got far better results from a daily woman.

"Please come in, Mr. Bathurst," said the girl who had been so recently widowed. "I expected you to be punctual, so I got rid of the luncheon things as soon as I possibly could." She piloted him into a room which did duty, obviously, as a lounge. "Please sit down."

Anthony took advantage of the invitation. "Before we start to talk, Mrs. Field," he opened, "you might care to look at that." He handed her the card he carried, accredited and signed by the Commissioner of Police, Sir Austin Kemble.

Mrs. Field read it and quietly handed it back to him. "Yes," she said, "Inspector Bernays, from Four Bridges, told me the other day that the 'Yard' would be called in on my husband's case. So that, more or less, I've been expecting somebody to call."

"Naturally," replied Anthony. Claudia Field continued: "I hope I didn't inconvenience you when I asked you to rail again. Left alone as I am—there is so much to do. And for one pair of hands—" She broke off—but Anthony waited for her to go on.

"I was doing a job of sorting out," she continued—a little lamely, perhaps—"and it would have been a terrible mess for you to come into."

"Quite so," said Anthony—with a thought for the attractive Ernest Courtenay.

Claudia Field faced him calmly and folded her hands in her lap. "Now tell me please, Mr. Bathurst, what is it I can do for you?"

Anthony smiled at her. She was an attractive girl—there were no two opinions on that score. "Well, Mrs. Field, I should like to ask you just a few questions. After expressing to you my very deep sympathy."

She inclined her head. "Thank you, Mr. Bathurst. I appreciate your kindness. But I've answered so many questions which, chiefly, have been put to me by Inspector Bernays, that I really don't think there are many more that can be asked me. If you see what I mean."

"Very possibly—still—we'll see. Please forgive me if you find any of them—er—painful."

She shook her head. "I'm positive that you can't ask me any that I haven't been asked. Still—go on."

"Thank you. Dr. Field and you—you were on good terms with one another?"

"Excellent—as I have already said." Claudia answered without the slightest hesitation.

"You are certain that your husband had no other attachments?"

"If you're alluding to love affairs—absolutely certain. He was as much in love with me the day he was murdered as he was when we were first married."

Anthony made a mental note of the singular pronouns. He wondered what she would think when she heard of the letter found in Field's wallet.

"Well—that's as definite as it very well can be," he said—"he had no worries?"

"None that I was aware of—again as I've already stated." Anthony waited. Claudia went on, as he had hoped that she would. "His practice was flourishing, he was acquiring a certain reputation as a specialist for T.B., he always seemed to have plenty of money—and we were ideally happy. Why then, should my husband have any worries?"

There was no mistaking her emphasis and certainty. She went on immediately. "That isn't a question of my opinion. It's a point of fact. It can be proved. Take the professional engagement that took him to his death. Right away at Stoke Pelly. Over forty miles from here. Why did Mr. Stanhope consult my husband with regard to his wife's health—if Julian's reputation as a specialist wasn't becoming known—and growing too—all over the county? That's really why he bought this practice. From Doctor Louis Wolff. Dr. Wolff was a chest specialist—one of the best in the South—and that was the line which Julian always hankered after. He's told me that scores of times—he hoped and anticipated that many of Doctor Wolff's connections and professional contacts would become his. And they did. More and more of them were coming to him. Why, then, should my husband have had any anxieties or worries?"

All the time that Claudia Field had been talking, Anthony had watched her intently. He was forced to admit to himself, assessing her as he was, that every thing which she had so far said appeared to be sincere, candid and truthful.

"The burglary you had, Mrs. Field, whilst you were at Friar's Woodburn—have you been able to discover yet what was stolen? The last time I discussed it with Inspector Bernays—he didn't seem too sure as to what had been taken."

"Well, frankly, Mr. Bathurst—I'm still not at all sure myself. I really couldn't go into the witness-box, if I were called upon to do so, and swear that *anything* had been stolen."

"I see. Tell me then, please, what actually happened." Again there was no hint of hesitation in her reply. "Julian's surgery had been—well—turned over, is, I think, the best way to describe it. I saw it directly I entered the room."

"What was it precisely that you saw?"

"His papers, generally, were disturbed and disarranged. One of the drawers of his desk wasn't properly shut. In a manner in which Julian would never have left it. He was a most tidy man in his habits—and extremely methodical."

"But you can trace nothing which you think has been stolen? That sounds Irish—but you know what I mean." Anthony smiled.

"I can't, Mr. Bathurst—and that's a fact."

Anthony resolved to strike a very definite note. "Mrs. Field," he said, with grave determination in his voice, "I'm determined to do everything in my power to bring the murderer of your husband to justice. That is why I am here with you to-day." He paused—he desired to see how she would react to that statement. Claudia Field was not found wanting. "I cannot thank you enough, Mr. Bathurst, for saying that. You aren't alone in that either, for I range myself at your side."

"I know that, Mrs. Field. I know, too, that I shall need all the assistance that you can possibly give me."

"That, Mr. Bathurst, you shall have." Her blue eyes met his with fearless candour.

"I am going back a little now," said Anthony, "to the afternoon when your husband left this house to keep his professional appointment with Mrs. Stanhope at Stoke Pelly. The last occasion you saw him alive."

Claudia Field looked at him strangely, as though she were in doubt, perhaps, as to what he really meant. There came the suspicion of a pause.

"Yes," she said eventually, "the last occasion I saw him alive."

2

"Take your mind back, Mrs. Field," continued Anthony, giving no sign that he had noticed her hesitancy, "to that afternoon. To the particular period of it, immediately preceding Dr. Field's departure. Do you follow what I mean?"

"I think so. But please go on."

"Visualize, if you can, the exact details of your last conversations with him. Where you stood, where he stood, what he did, how he looked, what he said, what you did, what you said. In other words try to re-live that particular scene all over again. It may help you—if you close your eyes. I often find that trick of great assistance myself, if I'm endeavouring to do something like I've just asked you to do."

For a fleeting moment, perhaps, Anthony thought that the girl looked a trifle scared. But the mood soon passed and he saw her nodding to him. Claudia Field closed her eyes as Anthony had suggested.

"Now try," continued Anthony, "to re-capture as many details as you can of that last physical and mental contact that you had with him. I won't bother you in any way for, say, a couple of minutes."

Anthony sat back in his chair and watched the girl facing him with eyes closed and one of her hands covering them. The only sound the room revealed was the ticking of the clock on the mantelpiece. Anthony gave her ample time. When he eventually broke the silence, he said—"Well—anything you feel you'd like to tell me?"

Claudia showed on her face that she was puzzled. "What sort of thing do you want?" she inquired.

"I'm glad you asked me that. Because I feel that my answer to your question may help you. Did your husband say, or do, anything which you, knowing him as you did, might regard, reasonably, as— shall we say—strange—unusual—or abnormal? Anything, for example, which you didn't expect, or anticipate, or understand immediately he either did it or said it? Look—you know that game when you have to pick out 'intruders' from certain lists which are given you? For example—you're given say 'King Lear,' 'Hamlet,' 'Macbeth,' and 'Midsummer Night's Dream.' Which is the intruder there? Obviously the 'Dream'—because it's the one comedy in the list. Well—was there anything like an intruder anywhere in either your husband's actions, say, or in his conversation?"

"Yes—there was," flashed Claudia Field—"and I've only just thought of it. Something he said which was definitely unusual—and which I remember now—I couldn't understand at the time he said it."

"Oh—excellent, Mrs. Field!" returned Anthony—"what was it?"

Claudia leant forward towards him, her hands resting on the arms of her chair. "Well, just before my husband left the house—he was standing by his desk in the surgery—I went to ask him what time I should expect him back. I think I said to him 'would he be back by the same train as the one he had caught when he went to Stoke Pelly on the previous occasion.' Anyhow—he told me the train—it was the same one—and as I went out of the surgery I heard him say 'This time I hope to persuade a reluctant lady'—and as he said it, he laughed. There—that's the 'unusual' remark of his that I've remembered."

Anthony repeated the words after her. "'This time I hope to persuade a reluctant lady.' You didn't interrogate him—as to what he meant exactly?"

Claudia Field shook her head. "No—I half-intended to—but he hadn't too much time—and that was that."

Anthony's mind at once reached out towards the two possibilities. There were two ladies in Julian Field's orbit for the rest of that day—the day when he had used those words. Mrs. Stanhope—the patient—and the amorous Mary, whose tryst had been liked for the Cornelius Stones near Friar's Woodburn. Claudia Field's eyes were searching his.

"Well—is it any good to you? Can you build anything on it?"

Anthony smiled. "Who knows, Mrs. Field? Who can say yet awhile? But I've put it away on the shelf of my memory. Maybe there will come a day when I shall take it down from that shelf, dust it and use it. I'll tell you, though, what I should like you to do now."

"What is that, Mr. Bathurst?"

"I'd like you to take me into your husband's surgery, where the disturbance took place. I'd like to look round it. Perhaps you can give me certain further information with regard to it."

"Inspector Bernays has been all over it. I don't think he found anything to help him."

Anthony shrugged his shoulders. "I may be in like position, Mrs. Field—or on the other hand—"

3

Anthony followed Claudia Field into the hall and then into the late Julian Field's surgery. It was a neat, compact, square room with the desk hard against the right-hand wall. The waiting-room was on the left as you entered. Anthony noticed it.

"I take it, Mrs. Field," he said, "that your husband had no surgery to keep on the evening of the day he went to Stoke Pelly?"

"Oh—no. That's why he fixed up to visit Stoke Pelly on that particular afternoon."

"Of course." Anthony looked at the desk. "Show me, Mrs. Field, please, where the disarrangement and disturbance were, of which you spoke to me just now?"

Claudia Field walked over to the desk. "This drawer was open—about six inches, I should think. About like this." She pulled open the drawer in demonstration.

Anthony saw that it was the second drawer on the right-hand side. "I see. Thank you. Anything else?"

"Those files on the top of the desk there had obviously been pulled about and turned over."

"Those green ones?"

"Yes. And I *think*—although I can't be altogether sure—that that's where the theft may have taken place. Something may have gone from there. I've had an idea for a day or two now that there aren't so many green files on the top as there used to be. There don't *look* so many. Probably, however, only my husband could tell you."

Anthony looked at the files. He removed the contents of the three files. They were, in each instance, case papers of patients who had placed themselves in the care of the late Doctor Field. He replaced the files on the top of the desk.

"That drawer which was partly open, Mrs. Field—was anything taken from there?"

"No, Mr. Bathurst."

"Certain of your ground?"

"Pretty well—as certain as one can be."

"I see. Now—I must ask you this, Mrs. Field—you'll pardon me, I'm sure. May I see your husband's cheque-book? The current one, say—and the two or three immediately preceding it?"

"With pleasure."

Claudia Field went to another drawer in the desk and extracted a cheque-book which was obviously in current usage. She handed the cheque-book to Anthony. He flicked over the used counterfoils. There were seventeen of them. They seemed all ordinary and in relation to normal financial obligations and commitments such as one would expect a G.P. in Field's position to have. The late doctor had evidently made it a practice to show on each counterfoil the balance on his current account as each cheque was drawn. Anthony noted the final figure. It was over £1,400.

"Did your husband run a deposit account at the bank, Mrs. Field?"

"Oh—yes. He transferred amounts from the current account from time to time."

"May I see the deposit book?"

Claudia, using a key this time, found the book for which Anthony had asked.

"Thank you, Mrs. Field." He looked through the amounts which Field from time to time had placed on deposit. Normally, they seemed to occur at intervals of approximately three months.

"I think," contributed Claudia, "that my husband would have made another transfer in a few days. Had he lived."

"Yes. From the incidence of the dates I think you're probably right."

"There are the other cheque-books you asked about. The last three used-up ones."

Anthony thanked her again and examined the counterfoils as he had those in the current cheque-book. He saw nothing in any one of them to excite the slightest suspicion or comment. Claudia Field had merely told the truth when she had stated that Julian Field had had no financial worries or anxieties. Anthony had ample proof from what he had already seen, that Julian Field had been in possession of a flourishing, rapidly developing and lucrative practice. He handed the cheque-books back to Claudia Field.

"All in order?" she inquired—a trifle archly, he thought. "Yes, Mrs. Field. All in order. Or at any rate, there's nothing apparent to the contrary. Now—another thing. Did your husband keep an engagement diary."

"Yes. Inspector Bernays went through that very thoroughly. It's at the back here. I put it away when the inspector told me he had finished with it. Let me get it for you."

The lady rummaged at the back of the desk and produced the diary for which Anthony had inquired.

"What kind is it?" he asked.

"How do you mean?"

"Why—does it tear off as you go along, or fold back? So that reference may be made to what's happened in the past?"

"Here you are—you can see for yourself." Claudia put the engagement diary in his hands.

"Good," he remarked. "It's of the second kind I mentioned. Folds over. See what I mean?"

Anthony demonstrated to her. "At the back here, we shall find the previous months of the year."

Claudia Field looked and nodded. "Yes. I see."

Anthony looked at the top sheet of the diary. The last entry thereon was an engagement which Field couldn't have kept. There were doubtless others, way ahead in the future, of a similar nature. He looked at the entry in respect of the day of Julian Field's death. "Mrs. Stanhope, Stoke Pelly. 2.22 from K.W." All in order again! This entry had been made in ink—underneath was something else, very faintly scrawled in pencil. Anthony examined it closely. As far as he was able to make out, it read—"Query meet M.E." As he read this, Anthony felt a glow of supreme satisfaction. He felt certain he knew the significance of the last two letters. The letter "M" stood for Mary. The "E"—that remained to be discovered. He turned back the pages of the diary as he searched for another entry. The date of Field's previous visit to Mrs. Stanhope. He remembered the evidence which Philip Stanhope had given at the coroner's inquest. "About a month ago." That would make it somewhere about the middle or the end of September. Yes—here it was, 22nd September. "Mrs. Stanhope, 'Gifford's,' Stoke Pelly. 2.22 K.W." This time there were two additional entries in the rest of the space allotted for that day. The first had been made in ink, similarly to the main entry. It read the one word "refusal." The second entry was in pencil again and had been made right down in the right-hand corner of the day's space. It was curt and to the point and read thus: "Saw M.C.S." Anthony felt that he must rub his hands. What had Bernays made of these entries he wondered. Had he seen them before the letter had been found in Field's wallet from the church font at Friar's Woodburn? Anthony put his finger on the pencilled entry in respect of the twenty-second day of September.

"What do you make of this, Mrs. Field?" he asked.

Claudia bent down and read it. "Is that the day of Julian's previous visit to Stoke Pelly?"

"Yes. This is the day."

Claudia knitted her brows. "I take that to mean—'saw Mrs. Stanhope.' I expect my husband was in a hurry when he made the entry and he did it carelessly. It's obviously carelessly written—and it's probably carelessly phrased as well."

"In that case, Mrs. Field, what do you take the letter 'C' to stand for?"

"Mrs. Stanhope's Christian name—of course."

Anthony considered the answer she had given him. "Do you know that for a fact, Mrs. Field?"

"Oh—no, Mr. Bathurst. I don't know the lady's name—haven't the foggiest. But that's my suggestion—I think it's a perfectly natural one, too."

Anthony decided to let the matter ride. After all—what he knew was nobody's business. "Maybe your hunch is the right one, Mrs. Field. Anyhow—we can easily find out."

He returned to a further examination of the engagement diary. But although he carefully covered the ten months' entries commencing on New Year's Day, he discovered no more references of especial interest.

"Still—all in order?" she inquired as he gave her back the diary.

"I expect I feel much the same about it as Inspector Bernays," he replied non-committally and then deliberately switched her thoughts before she came at him again with another question concerning the engagement diary.

"There's one more thing, Mrs. Field. May I have a glance at your late husband's paying-in book?" He diverted her again. "There's one thing that we must face, Mrs. Field—and that's this. A few days ago there was a man—or woman—whose heart was so full of enmity for your husband—that he or she didn't stop at murder. And who knows the best way by which that guilty person can be traced? We must stop at nothing."

Claudia Field unlocked another drawer and handed him a bank paying-in book.

4

Anthony looked at the date on the first used counterfoil. It was 26th May. Judging by what he saw in the book, Field had the habit of making two payments into the bank per week. Almost invariably on Mondays and Thursdays.

"What's the address of your bankers, Mrs. Field?" Anthony put the question as he turned over the counterfoils. "What I mean is— how far is your bank from here? I see your husband usually paid in twice a week."

"Two minutes' walk—no more. Just round the corner. I usually took it for him."

"I see. No trouble at all, then."

Almost all the counterfoil slips seemed normal. The payments, obviously, were almost without exception made up of cheques from patients and various amounts of cash. There were two payments in, however, which arrested Anthony's attention. Their dates, also, conveyed to him a certain significance. The first was on the 26th June. The amount paid into the bank was shown as £61 11s. 7d. and according to the details on the counterfoil had comprised three separate cheques totalling £11 11s. 7d. and an amount of £50 in currency notes. On the left of the printed narration "Notes" there were pencilled the letters "G.M.A." The second of the payments in which had specially interested Anthony was under the date 2nd October. The amount paid in on this occasion was £73 14s. 9d. £23 14s. 9d. was made up by five miscellaneous cheques and again there was an item of £50 in currency notes. Also the pencilled letters "G.M.A." were again to be seen on the edge of the paying-in counterfoil. Anthony scratched his cheek dubiously and began to think.

An idea occurred to him. Were there any more pencilled initials to be found on any of the remaining counterfoils? He began to check the matter methodically. After some little time his patience and industry were rewarded. He succeeded in tracing two payments in, dated 9th June and 8th September, where the figure for currency notes was £50 in each instance with the attached initials "T.J.H." and an additional two payments dated respectively 23rd June and 16th October, with £25 in currency notes banked to Julian Field's credit on each of these dates and the entries initialled "J.D.M." He looked up at Claudia Field.

"Have you any of the doctor's previous paying-in books handy, Mrs. Field?"

Claudia shook her head. "I'm afraid I haven't, Mr. Bathurst. My husband kept only the current book. If the items agreed with those in his pass book—which he invariably checked—he always said that there was no point in keeping them. Why did you want them?"

Anthony finessed. "Well—this book—the current one—commences on the 26th May, which gives me just about five months of the year only. I thought, perhaps, it would be more satisfactory if I covered, say, a full year. Still—no matter—if the books aren't here—they aren't."

Anthony rose from the seat which he had been occupying and returned to her the current paying-in book. "Thank you, Mrs. Field. Now—one last question before I go. And forgive me once again for bothering you. The urgent nature of the case must still be my justification. You heard Mr. Stanhope's evidence at the inquest?" Claudia nodded. "What was your reaction to your husband's wearing the rose in his overcoat when he left Stoke Pelly? The flower from Stanhope's garden which he had admired so much?"

"My reaction? I don't—"

"Well, you were his wife—you knew him and his habits—you were in daily contact with him—you were aware of his tastes and of his foibles—was the action typical of the man?"

Claudia answered slowly. "Well—he wasn't mad on flowers if that's what you mean. He just liked them ordinarily—as I think most men do."

"Did he make it a practice to wear flowers—as buttonholes?"

Claudia Field made denial. "Very seldom, I should say. Of course, it was made quite clear that his visit—the professional part of it—was over when Mr. Stanhope gave him the rose. There is that about it. And, of course, he might wear a flower for a special sort of occasion. I have known him do that. But otherwise—" Claudia Field stopped.

"Well—we know that he did wear this particular flower because, as you are aware, it was found in the lapel of his overcoat. So that we can harbour no doubts about it. But nevertheless, you wouldn't assert that it was inevitably in keeping?"

"I would not," replied Claudia with unmistakable emphasis.

"Unless he had a special appointment?"

"Exactly. Then—well, he might wear one."

"Thank you again." declared Anthony. "I regard that as most interesting. You, of all people, should know."

He said good-bye to the lady and went back to the place where he had parked his car. In the car, he jotted down on the back of an old envelope three sets of initials, "G.M.A.," "T.J.H." and "J.D.M." As he did so, one of them seemed to strike a familiar note—but he couldn't make up his mind then and there as to which. Anyhow—it could wait. A little exercise in concentration later on would give him the necessary answer to his query. In the meantime, he had much he desired to discuss with Andrew MacMorran and Inspector Bernays.

As Anthony mused this, Claudia went to the telephone and dialled a number.

"Is that you," she said—"he's gone—and—oh boy—am I relieved!"

She listened for the reply.

"You bet I did," she returned.

Chapter VIII

1

Anthony rejoined Inspector MacMorran at the "Horse and Groom," Greenhurst. It was fairly late in the afternoon when he got back and the "Yard" inspector was already there waiting for him. MacMorran grinned at him as he entered the smoking-lounge.

"Well," he opened, "when's the arrest?"

Anthony shook his head. "Deep waters all round us, Andrew. As deep, I think, as you and I have ever encountered. But first of all, how did you get on with Bernays? Tell me, Andrew."

"We've instituted pretty searching inquiries with regard to that length of rope. It may or may not yield results. Personally, I'm not banking too much on it. We spent a certain amount of time as well, on the lantern question. But there you are—"

MacMorran shrugged his shoulders. Anthony pulled the armchair up beside the fire.

"How long till dinner, Andrew?"

MacMorran looked at his watch. "A good hour yet. Why? The worms biting?"

"I'm hungry, Andrew. I'm always hungry. There's always that ravening wolf way back in my pedigree." He stretched his long lithe body in the comfort of the big chair.

MacMorran took the chair on the opposite side of the fire. "You said something about deep waters. What have you got?"

"A heck of a lot, Andrew. Too much—if one can pick up too much on a problem of this nature. And it don't please me! It doesn't all run the same way—for one thing. If it did—I might be rubbing my hands and thinking the case was open and shut. But it's not—by a long way," concluded Anthony quietly.

"Get it off your chest," said MacMorran curtly.

Anthony smiled at him. "Don't rush me, Andrew. Before I give you my basinful—I just want to think one or two matters over."

MacMorran waited. Anthony found his cigarette case and offered it to the inspector. MacMorran took a cigarette. Still no further words were spoken. The two men lit up and eventually Anthony began to talk.

75 | THE SWINGING DEATH

"When I heard Mrs. Field testify at the coroner's inquest, Andrew, I was, on the whole, rather favourably impressed. I was inclined to 'label' her, I know—but I was bound to admit—taking it by and large—that she had been a good witness. All the same, I carefully placed her on one side, as it were, for further observation. Then—just after the inquest—something turned up. The assignation letter found in Julian Field's wallet." Anthony paused—to continue.

"'Right,' said Andrew MacMorran. 'That's you! Unfaithful husband, development of inevitable triangle, plans go awry—murder.' A conclusion with which I have no right or justification to quarrel. Andrew MacMorran suspects the husband's infidelity—certainly the husband gets it in the neck—*I'm* more inclined to put the wife under the microscope. Level pegging, you say? O.K. But mark you, the lady insists all the time that marital relations between her and her husband were entirely unsullied. And—moreover—she doesn't protest too much! She doesn't parade the point, she doesn't belabour it—she simply says so when she is asked. There, Andrew, roughly, you have the mental state of the poll this morning for my visit to the widowed lady. 'You'll soon find consolation, my lady,' say I and lo and behold, the first thing I run into is a handsome male cousin fluttering at her side. Whose companionship is so congenial to her—so I am entitled to argue—that when she answers my ring at the bell—she calmly requests me 'to call again this afternoon.'

"The interval which my lady so kindly granted me, however, was not wasted. For I culled much and sundry from the local pastry-cook's. Whoever he is, he happens to employ an assistant with an appetite for gossip. She talked. I listened. Andrew—I heard a heck of a lot."

As Anthony finished, MacMorran tossed his cigarette stub into the heart of the fire. "This is getting interesting," he remarked.

"Whoever cleaned your shoes this morning, Andrew, may have used 'Courtenay's Cleeno'—invaluable for black or brown shoes. And boots—come to that. Well—the handsome male cousin happens to be none other titan Ernest Courtenay—son of the house of Courtenay and presumably heir to the Courtenay coinage. Doubloons and all that."

MacMorran whistled. "Hallo—hallo," he said, "so that's how it is, is it?"

"You wait, Andrew, my lad! You wait! It's not so easy as all that—believe me. The fair Claudia, so the tongues of King's Winkworth say, spurned Ernest, whose hand, heart and ha'pence were hers for the taking and the late Julian reigned in his stead." Anthony paused. When he continued, he said: "So you see, Andrew—there I was—one up—one down."

"I take it you're still in the pastry-cook's? All ears?" Anthony nodded. "I was. But I moved. When I came out, I took a quick 'dekko' at the Courtenay mansion—nice drop of stuff, believe me—had lunch at a pub called the 'White Bear' and then drifted back for my second look at the puzzling Claudia. She couldn't have co-operated better. She refused me nothing I asked her. It's all right—don't worry—I behaved myself—and generally speaking couldn't be faulted."

"Bernays had been over the ground before—of course?"

"Oh yes. But I don't think that made any difference." Anthony paused again. MacMorran noticed the pause. The latter translated his thoughts into words.

"Did you get anything?"

Anthony leant forward to dispose of cigarette ash. "Yes—and no, Andrew. Up—and down. That's how I was all the way through the interview—and that's how I am now."

"Tell me," said MacMorran simply.

"Well—I had a look at most of the things I wanted to see. I was on the finance side in the main. And you can take it from me that Field had no money worries or troubles. Claudia told the truth all right. He was doing very nicely, thank you. Practice on the up and up—no shadow of doubt about that. I picked up one or two points, though. I'll come back to 'em a little later. Amongst other matters, I took a squint at Field's engagement diary. Bernays had been there before me, by the way. I must have a word with him about it. Now listen to this, Andrew." Anthony left the armchair and began to pace the room. "It was one of those diaries, Andrew, that fold back. So that underneath lies the past as it were. Get me?"

MacMorran nodded.

"First of all, I looked at the space on the diary in respect of the day that Field 'had it.' The Stanhope engagement at Stoke Pelly was down there, all right—time and all details corresponded pretty well with what we already know about it. But listen to this one, me lad! The principal entry had been made in ink. But underneath was rather faintly scrawled in pencil 'Query meet M.E.' Do you get it, Andrew?"

"Of course! Good lord—yes! And it seems to me to shut the case up. M.E. are the initials of the lady whose note we found in Julian Field's wallet. All we have to do now—"

Anthony cut him. "Is to find the lady—eh? That the idea?"

"That's it. Why not?"

"I thought you'd say that. More or less. More or less I said that to myself when I spotted the pencil marks. And yet—"

"And yet what?"

"Well—wait till you've heard the rest of the story. There's a whole heap more yet for your ostrich-like digestion. After I'd spotted all that, it occurred to me to turn back to the day on the diary when Field had made his previous visit to Mrs. Stanhope at Stoke Pelly. I thought I'd have a smell round that."

"I agree. That's exactly what I should have done next myself."

"I remembered that Field's previous visit to his patient had taken place about a month previously, so I knew pretty well where to look. And—I had no trouble. There was the Stanhope engagement entered all Sir Garnet—under date 22nd September. In ink, again, too. Also in ink, Andrew, was another word, close to the principal entry. The word was 'refusal.' You wouldn't have expected that, would you?"

MacMorran was on the point of reply, but Anthony summarily closured him. "Wait for it, Andrew—there's still a drop more in the bottle. Right in the corner of the diary-space dedicated for the day was—in pencil this time—'Saw M.C.S.'" Anthony rubbed his hands. "There you are, Andrew, my bonnie old fighter—that finishes the first instalment. What do you make of it?"

"What we thought—surely! Field was combining business with pleasure when he visited Stoke Pelly."

"Tell me how you get to that."

"Simple enough, isn't it?"

"Not sure. In doubt myself. Just want to know how you translate it."

"Well—firstly there was the pencilled reference to 'M.E.' which I thought we agreed meant Mary Evans or Edwards or Eisenhower, or what you will, and now there's this second pointer of yours in relation to the previous Stanhope visit—'Saw M.C.S.'"

"Which being interpreted—?"

"Saw Mary at Cornelius Stones, of course."

Anthony nodded approvingly. "Thought you'd come with that one. Considered it myself. Then I put the 'Saw M.C.S.' entry in front of the bereaved lady. Asked her what she made of it."

"Well—what was her solution? Something entirely different?"

"You've said it, Andrew. Mrs. F. looked at it quite dispassionately and read it as 'Saw Mrs. Stanhope.'" Anthony chuckled. "Weren't anticipating that, were you? I know I wasn't."

"But that doesn't tally," expostulated MacMorran. "M, isn't Mrs.—and what about the 'C'?"

"I agree. But the lady explained that away by saying that Field had been in a hurry when he had made the entry and had written carelessly. Actually, as a fact, I'll subscribe myself to the carelessness part. It looked very much like an entry you scrawl hurriedly in a diary as a sort of afterthought."

"Shucks," retorted MacMorran gracelessly—"those initials mean what we think they mean all right. They couldn't be better. I wish I were as sure of a thousand quid."

"I'll have a word with Bernays," went on Anthony—"but we mustn't forget one point with regard to that angle. And that's this. Bernays probably saw that engagement diary before he had Mary's little letter. All the difference—you know! I had the advantage."

"I'll tell you what," said MacMorran. "I've an idea. I rather think I've got something."

"Andrew," said Anthony with mock solemnity, "you're ultra-modest. You've got *everything*."

2

"No—I'm serious," continued MacMorran, "you listen. It's my turn to do the talking."

"O.K. I'll listen. But I shall want you to listen to me again later on. My bottle's not empty yet. To say nothing of the fact that you've ducked one or two nasty ones. But what's your big idea?"

"This. Stanhope lives at Stoke Pelly?"

"Right."

"Field was in practice at King's Winkworth?"

"Go on."

"Distance between the two places—forty-two miles?"

"Keep it up."

"Why send for a doctor to consult about your wife's health—all that distance away?"

"Specialist. Man with big reputation. Lung trouble. Suspected T.B. That's all right."

"So it may be—but why Field?"

"Why Field? Why anybody? It had to be somebody—didn't it?"

MacMorran stuck doggedly to his guns. "You still haven't answered my question," he persisted—"I repeat why Field? You're not going to put into me that Field—a man with a three-year-old practice in a comparatively obscure country town like King's Winkworth—had such a terrific reputation as a specialist that when a case of T.B. is suspected, everybody shouts with one accord—'We want Julian Field.'"

"His reputation as a lung specialist had been growing for some considerable time, Andrew. You've got to remember that. And it was all in the county—you know. King's Winkworth and Stoke Pelly." Anthony's voice changed. "Nevertheless, Andrew—your point is well and truly made. I take it! Go on from where you left off."

"Good. We're getting somewhere. The rest of my point is this. I should say that Stanhope got in touch with Field for another reason. He was *recommended by somebody*! Somebody—at least this is my idea—who knows Stanhope and his wife and who was aware that the lady wasn't too good from the health point of view and who sang Field's praises. The man you want for the missus is Julian Field—the King's Winkworth chap. Marvellous bloke. *The* coming man! Nothing in Harley Street fit to wipe his boots. They'd almost ordered my wife's cousin's coffin when she went to Field. Now she's a champion 'all-in' wrestler. You know the stuff."

"Well, you may be right, Andrew. Quite likely. I won't argue with you. But does it matter to us who whispered 'Field' into Stanhope's ear? Where will that get us?"

"It *might*," replied MacMorran, portentously, "get us a rare long way. It might even take us all the way we want to go."

"How do you work that one out, Andrew? I'm curious."

"Well," replied MacMorran with triumphant slowness, "there might be somebody living either at Stoke Pelly, or near Stoke Pelly, at Friar's Woodburn for instance, who knew the Stanhopes and who also knew Doctor Field—and who—" Anthony laid his hand impetuously on MacMorran's arm. "Good for you, Andrew! You've opened my eyes. You mean Mary E?"

"I had," replied the inspector modestly, "been thinking more on the lines of Mary E.'s husband."

Anthony stood upright in the middle of the floor and stared into space.

3

"Dinner," said Anthony, "has come as a most pleasant interruption. When it was announced, I had something of a shock. I had no idea that the time had passed so quickly. Because, Andrew—there are still some more things I'd like to talk over with you before we meet Bernays again."

MacMorran lowered his glass. "Let's have 'em now, then. They say there's no time like the present."

Anthony sat back after disposing of his soup. "Right. Do you remember my saying you'd ducked just now? I'll take you back."

"You often do that. Get along."

"When I was telling you about Field's engagement diary, I mentioned that in the space allotted to the 22nd September I came across two 'postscripts'—as we may very well call 'em. You were quick to deal with one of them—'Saw M.C.S.,' but you were strikingly reticent with regard to the other. Now you aren't going to get away with that, Andrew! No evasions! What's your reaction to the other chap?"

MacMorran frowned. "Yes—I remember now. Thinking and concentrating on the one diverted my mind from the other. It was the word 'refusal'—was it not?"

Anthony nodded his confirmation. "It was, Andrew. And I'm not permitting it to apply to you. What do you make of it?"

"Well—it seems to me that it's something to do with the woman who had the assignation with Field—our lady friend, Mary. I can bring something, too, in support of that. What was that phrase in her letter? Wasn't it something about 'finding a way out'?"

"Quite correct, Andrew. That was the expression used."

"Well, then, she and Field, or perhaps Field on his own, had to come to a decision about something. Possibly about winding their affair up. Very likely things were beginning to get a trifle too hot for them—maybe Mary's husband was imagining something that wasn't a vain thing. Field was determined to tell Mary when he kept that appointment with her, that he had decided to refuse to carry on. He was going to pack it all up. So he jotted the word 'refusal' down in his engagement diary."

"As a possibility. I'll give it full marks, but only as a possibility. Because now I'll tell you something else."

"Been keeping something back—eh? Play the game, you cads."

Anthony grinned. MacMorran was evidently enjoying the dinner with which the "Horse and Groom" had provided him. "When I was interviewing Mrs. Field, I asked her to carry her mind back to that afternoon when her husband left her, en route for the final Stanhope consultation at Stoke Pelly. Asked her to visualize again everything that had taken place between them. Whether anything abnormal or out of pattern had stuck out anywhere. You can guess the idea. Well—after a time—she cottoned on to what I really wanted." Anthony paused. "Eventually—she came out with this. She told me that just as Julian Field was leaving the surgery on that last afternoon, he volunteered the following remark. 'This time, I hope to persuade a reluctant lady.' Does that fit in all right with your theory?"

MacMorran exhibited signs of excitement. "Of course it does! Why it almost seals it up! The previous time he saw his lady-love, she wouldn't agree to his proposals. This second time he hoped to persuade her to his own way of thinking. What's wrong with that?"

Anthony smiled. "I could answer your question, Andrew, if I knew better what these proposals of Field were."

4

"You can bet your life they were what I've said they were. Field wanted to call it a day. The lady didn't. The situation's as old as the hills. Older!"

Anthony put his dinner plate on one side. "O.K. We'll go on from there, then. You shall have the final drop from that bottle I mentioned. Finance! I looked at Field's most recent cheque books, his deposit account, and at a recent paying-in book. As I told you when we were in the smoking-lounge before dinner, Field was doing quite nicely. Very cosy practice. There were, on the face of things, no anxieties. He was doing a great deal better than I anticipated. In fact, I've been wondering on the way home if he weren't doing just a little too well!"

Anthony scratched his cheek and waited for his last remark to sink home. MacMorran looked up.

"And what do you mean exactly by that cryptic remark?"

"Wait before I reply. I'll hand you out some more data. When I went through Field's paying-in book, I ran across certain regular payments to his account. Occurring, roughly, at quarterly intervals."

"Not much in that." MacMorran shook his head. "He may own property. Rents—ground rents—financial interests of that kind. Probably does, I should say."

Anthony came again. "These payments-in, to which I refer, Andrew, were invariably in *cash*."

"Cash?"

"Cash! Nary a cheque reared its ugly head amongst any of 'em."

MacMorran was silent. Anthony watched the expression on his face. The inspector spoke. "May be all right. Some people don't take to bankers, you know. Perhaps Field didn't risk too many bouncers."

"The amounts were more or less static. Even fifties and twenty-fives."

"Looks like rents. So much per quarter."

Anthony struck again. "There were initials in pencil on the paying-in slip counterfoils where these items showed."

MacMorran's eyes were raised again. Anthony still came. "These pencilled initials could have easily been erased. In a few seconds. If the time ever came to make that desirable—or necessary."

"Yes, I suppose they could. What were the initials? Did you make a note of 'em?"

"Andrew—you're askin' for trouble! They were these. 'G.M.A.,' 'T.J.H.' and 'J.D.M.'"

"Not M.C.S.?" joked the inspector.

"No, not that one. Just those three. And do you know, Andrew—it seemed to me that—"

Anthony stopped abruptly and again that far-seeing look of his took possession of his grey eyes.

Chapter IX

1

MacMorran waited for it. He knew that sign of old. Anthony turned to him as the waitress came with the coffee.

"Do you know, Andrew, that's a very remarkable thing. Something came to me a moment ago which had previously been eluding me. When I saw that first set of initials on Field's paying-in slip counterfoil, I knew that I'd seen it very recently. Within the last day or so. But I couldn't connect. I didn't really try—I knew it would come back in time. Well, Andrew, the point is—that it has come back. When I repeated them to you a few seconds ago. I remember now where I saw the 'G.M.A.'"

"Where was that? You don't mean in connection with the murder of Julian Field, do you?"

"You must be the judge of that when you hear. Actually I shall expect your eyes to do a spot of popping."

"Where was it?"

"Question for question, Andrew. Where was Field's body found?"

"In the porch at Fullafold Church. What's that got to do with it?"

"Did you notice anything else in the church porch?"

"You don't mean the lantern?"

"No. Not that."

"You tell me."

"Well—did you notice the monthly offertory report—giving the amounts of the collections for the October services? For the four Sundays? You know—matins and evensong."

"On the wall at the side, wasn't it?"

"Yes. On the right-hand side of the porch as you enter by the main door."

"I know what you mean and where you mean—but I wouldn't say that I really looked at it."

"Well, Andrew, that report on the offertory was signed by the Vicar of St. Mark's. The name was 'Godfrey M. Atherton.'"

MacMorran drank coffee and then rubbed the tip of his nose with his finger. "For crying out loud," he started and then stopped. "I don't get it," he continued after a short interval, "and what's more—I don't see where we're getting to."

"Well, don't for a minute think that I do! Because I don't. But I'll hand this much out to you, Andrew. This case isn't going to break open as I fancy you once thought it would. I said it before—and I'll say it again. We're in deep waters. Very deep waters indeed. But let's have a smoke in the lounge before bedtime. That's a noble fire in that grate which makes me feel a better man."

2

"I know what you're thinking," said MacMorran, as they crossed to the lounge, "your mind's turning to the 'black.' But as I see it, the gallery's wrong. We're mixing here with a priest—a doctor—good class both of 'em."

"Class—as you call it—hasn't yet made people immune from blackmail. At any rate—I've never heard that it has." Anthony stooped to twist his armchair nearer to the fire. "After all, Andrew, why stick the body in the church porch? And why divide the clothes—some at Fullafold—some at Friar's Woodburn. But in the font each time. Great Scott, Andrew—I believe I'm really on to something!"

Anthony leant forward from the armchair, elated with excitement. But his voice was controlled and he spoke quietly.

"What were the initials—the other sets—which I told you about in addition to the 'G.M.A.' set? Can you bring any back?"

"Think so," replied MacMorran with sturdy confidence—"er—'J.D.M.' and er—'T.J.H.'"

"Good man," said Anthony even more quietly, "and the man who found the first clothes consignment in the font at St. Mark's, Fullafold, was the Rev. John Moffatt, who may well be endowed with a second Christian name."

"By George," cried MacMorran as the point came home to him—"that's absolutely—"

Anthony's raised hand checked his further statement. Still in the quietest possible voice, he said: "Also, Andrew, the Vicar of the Church of St. Mary Magdalene at Friar's Woodburn is the Rev. Theodore Henson—no, he had a second Christian name—what was it now—" Anthony thought. "I know—'Ingram.'"

"Well, that's an 'I,' not 'J,'" countered MacMorran.

"Very true—but don't forget that in some respects the letters 'I' and 'J' are almost interchangeable. Take indexing for example."

MacMorran filled his capacious pipe. "Another thing—I must call your attention to it—those three combinations you've been juggling with, 'G.M.A.,'—and—are, I should say, amongst the most common. I doubt whether we've got anything after all—really."

"But what about the churches—the fonts? They've each entered the picture—haven't they?"

MacMorran shook his head doubtingly. "I still favour my original theory—Mister Field was kicking over the matrimonial traces—and paid the penalty. I'm coming back to it again. Husbands are invariably jealous. I've known quite a number like that in my time. You stick to your theory. I'll stick to mine." MacMorran had his pipe well going by now.

"I'm afraid," said Anthony pensively, "that we haven't travelled very far. We've had a lengthy discussion and I've chucked a rare lot of stuff into your lap. Most of it, I admit, bewildering and also cross-grained. Cross-patterned, perhaps, is the better way of putting it. Frankly, I can't get a satisfactory starting point."

"Why's that? You aren't usually in that position."

"I *think*," said Anthony weighing his words, "that there's something 'phony' somewhere. I don't know 'what'—and equally—I don't know 'where.' We must see Bernays again in the morning."

"I agree. When I left him to-day, he was going to work on the assignation letter angle. He has hopes of tracing the lady we know as Mary. It was my suggestion, naturally, but he made no bones about it. If he's successful—the case may fold up quicker than you expect."

Anthony demurred. "Don't you kid yourself! We've a long way to get yet, Andrew—before this case folds up."

3

Anthony and MacMorran conferred with Inspector Bernays at Four Bridges. Bernays seemed despondent.

"After I left you yesterday, chief, I spent the rest of my time over at Friar's Woodburn. I worked on the two ends you suggested. The 'Mary' end and the 'Cornelius Stones' end. Well—there's no point in making a long story out of nothing—I toiled all day—you can fill in the rest for yourself. Field certainly didn't show up at the Friar's Woodburn railway station—not that I thought he ever had—and, to make a clean breast of it, I couldn't get a line on him anywhere. I tried three likely 'pubs' and to finish up I put in a good couple of hours in the neighbourhood of 'Cornelius Stones.' There are a few cottages pretty close to the stream there—and I tried my hand at all of them. No sign of Field. No sign of Mary. The answer may be, of course, that they didn't get there until it was dark. Don't suppose they wanted to—come to that."

"In my opinion," said MacMorran, "that's the place where he was murdered."

"Where?" asked Bernays—"do you mean somewhere in Friar's Woodburn, or actually at the 'Cornelius Stones'?"

"At the 'Stones.' In all probability the woman had been followed from her home to the rendezvous and her husband came down on Field like a wolf on the fold."

Bernays nodded. "It's possible, I suppose. But why muck about with the clothes? That's the part of it I don't get."

"No—nor I, inspector," said Anthony. "If we knew the true significance of those clothes, we should know a heck of a lot. Still—put Mary and the stepping-stones on one side for a moment. There's something else we'd like to discuss with you."

"Carry on," said Bernays good humouredly.

"Yesterday," said Anthony, "I popped up to King's Winkworth. Saw Claudia Millicent Field, widow of Julian. Candidly, I wanted to give Field's place the once over. Candidly—also—I wasn't too sure of the fair Claudia. I still am not."

Bernays shook his head. "She's O.K., Mr. Bathurst. With me she came clean all the way. If that girl's a wrong 'un—well—stick me in charge of the Girl Guides."

"Skip it, inspector—for the time being. Let it ride. I'm with all the way to the extent that she seems frank and open over every thing. Nothing too much trouble for her. Nothing shoved in your way. Mistress Claudia—collaborator and complete co-operator. Yes—sir! But all the same—at the moment—I'm reserving judgment."

He smiled at Bernays. "You'll allow me that, won't you?"

"Oh—quite. But you'll come to my way of thinking in that direction before you've finished."

"Maybe. Maybe not. Anyhow, I went up to King's Winkworth for a nose round generally. Claudia, as I said, played appropriate ball all the time. Now, inspector—this is where I want your advice. Amongst other things I looked at was Julian Field's engagement diary." Anthony stopped.

Bernays came in as Anthony had hoped he would. "Yes. I know the thing. I looked at it myself. One of the chief things that I went to look at."

"I guessed so. Anything strike you about it?"

"Oh—yes. One or two. Wait a moment." Bernays put his hand to his breast pocket and took out a notebook. "I jotted down one or two things in here," he explained. "I'll turn them up."

Anthony waited for him. MacMorran, keenly interested, prepared to listen to the verbal exchanges which he knew were on their way. Bernays began to speak.

"The Stanhope consultation at Stoke Pelly was on the diary all right—for the afternoon when the murder took place. And also underneath—there was a faint pencil entry—'Query meet me.' Do you agree?"

Anthony looked at Bernays inquiringly. "Say that again, inspector, do you mind?"

"Say what again?"

"What you said about the extra entry in the diary." Bernays repeated the phrase. "Query—meet me."

Anthony rubbed his upper lip. "Hear that, Andrew?" he said.

MacMorran laughed. "I heard."

Bernays shook his head. "What's the joke? What's funny about any of that?"

"Nothing funny, inspector. Just another illustration of the superiority of two heads over one. The point is, you see, that your reading of the phrase is so vitally different from mine." Bernays looked bewildered. "Well—I may be a ruddy old fool—but for the life of me I can't see how else you could read it!"

"You don't? I'll tell you then. What you read for the first personal pronoun—accusative case—I read as two initials—'M.E.' You see, inspector," Anthony scratched his cheek, "I had the idea that the 'M' might stand for 'Mary.'"

Bernays coughed. "Well—it's a point certainly—which, I'll willingly admit, never occurred to me. All the same, Mr. Bathurst, I'd like to see the diary again before I give a firm opinion on it."

"I'm not going to be didactic, inspector," said Anthony, "you may be right. But just a moment—let's look round the point together. Would you agree with me that the letters 'M.E.' were rather larger than those of the rest of the entry."

"Yes, I would. I agree with you entirely."

"Well—then—don't you think that tends to swing it over to my reading?" Anthony was surprised at the logic behind Bernays' reply.

"No. I don't. Because I think I can explain the reason for that."

"Go on, inspector. I'm most interested."

"I think," said the local inspector, speaking slowly, "that Field did that for *emphasis*. That what he meant was 'Query meet *me*.' That's how I should have emphasized it when I first read it to you."

Anthony thought over what Bernays had said. The point was good, he thought, and it was certainly novel to him personally. Bernays might well be right. All the same—there was the other—.

"That's very neat, inspector," replied Anthony. "I congratulate you, but don't overlook something else. Can you recall the terms of the diary entry for the day of Field's previous visit to Mrs. Stanhope?"

"I can," replied Bernays with a smile. "There was what I'll call the authentic entry in relation to the actual professional visit, there was the word 'refusal,' and also there was a scrawled phrase—let me see—'Saw M.C.S.' Is that right?"

"Absolutely right, inspector. One hundred per cent! What did you make of that little collection? That's what I'd be extremely interested to hear."

"Well," Bernays was speaking more slowly now, "I took all that—the word 'refusal' and the other phrase with the initials to refer to a consultation that Field had had that same day some time with another patient. But—and you mustn't forget this, Mr. Bathurst."

Anthony nodded. "I know what you're going to say. That when you examined that diary, you hadn't seen the 'Mary' letter. I've already realized that fact, inspector. When I saw the diary I was fortified by information which wasn't in your possession when you inspected it. But tell me—now that you know as much as I do—do you still think as you did? Is your interpretation still the same?"

Bernays thought for a moment or two before he replied. "Yes—I think it is," he said eventually. "I'm of the opinion that Field made the notes in reference to another one of his patients. Somebody, perhaps, whom he'd refused to see, say at a certain time."

MacMorran questioned him.

"You don't think that the 'M' might conceivably stand for 'Mary' and 'C.S.' for the 'Cornelius Stones'?"

"They might," said Bernays still smiling, "but I don't think they do."

"Good for you, inspector. There's nothing like knowing your own mind."

"You're tellin' me," replied the Four Bridges inspector.

4

It was at that moment that MacMorran came in again. "What about Field and finance, inspector?" he inquired. "Are you completely satisfied from that angle?"

Anthony was silent. He was well aware of the reason which had prompted Andrew MacMorran to ask the question. He watched Bernays carefully as he answered.

"I think so, chief. It all seemed pretty healthy to me from what I could see. I should assert with no hesitation whatever that Field was by no means short of brass and that everything was hunky-dory for him in that direction. Another thing—we should all remember this, I think—Field was a professional man—medical. He worked *by* himself *for* himself. No aggrieved business partners. Nobody near him who might be sore at Field playing him a fast one."

Bernays shook his head firmly as he concluded. "No—I don't think that we shall find this murder going back to the money motive."

MacMorran looked across at Anthony. Anthony returned the look almost blankly. MacMorran took the hint and made no attempt to follow up his previous question. Bernays on the other hand, kept the particular matter alive.

"Does Mr. Bathurst think otherwise? Are he and I again in disagreement?"

"Not for a moment, inspector. From the financial point of view, I agree with you that Field was sitting pretty. In fact—it did occur to me that he was sitting almost too pretty."

"Oh—I don't know. There isn't much competition in places like King's Winkworth and the dice was loaded in his favour. His wife is a relation of the Courtenay family. Plenty of money there, too—to say nothing of the influence a family like that can wield."

"I suppose you're right. Now—the clothes, inspector. I understand they've been subjected to the usual tests. Yes?"

"Quite true, Mr. Bathurst."

"Anything come of it?"

"Very little. There was a slight stain on the under part of the right-hand sleeve of the overcoat—the expert reports that it's beer. In addition to that—" Bernays began to speak slowly again—"there was a small patch of muddied grass between the heel and the sole of the left-foot shoe. You know the sort of thing I mean. The foot fails to get a proper hold—slithers a bit—and gets a piece of wettish grass caked on the shoe where the maximum of pressure has been applied. That piece of muddy grass has been through the microscope as you might say and it contains several thistle seeds." Bernays paused—and then went on again. "Which seems to indicate to my way of thinking, that Field was killed somewhere near the church at Fullafold where his body was found. And that, gentlemen, is something I *hadn't* been bargaining for."

Anthony whistled.

"It has always been my impression," continued the local inspector, "that Field had been killed somewhere else and his body taken to the church at Fullafold. But this latest piece of information suggests otherwise. Because it's almost a certainty, so it seems to me, that Field must have walked up the slope that leads to the church."

Anthony waited for MacMorran to cut in. He was wondering how he would react to what Bernays had just told them. MacMorran spoke.

"I have been under the same impression as you, inspector. That Field had been killed elsewhere. Probably, I thought, in the neighbourhood of the 'Cornelius Stones.' Now I don't know what to think. There are too many gaps. For instance, what happened to Field after he got out at Greenhurst Station? Did he eventually go to Friar's Woodburn? Did he find the 'Cornelius Stones'? Did he meet—"

Anthony uttered a sharp exclamation. "Good heavens—what a blind idiot I've been! Of course—of course!"

Bernays looked at him with no little amazement. "Why—what's the—"

Before Bernays could complete his question—there came a tap at the door. "Who's there?" cried Bernays.

"Sergeant Bland," came the answer.

"O.K., sergeant—come in."

Bland came in, grinned good humouredly in the direction of Anthony and MacMorran and spoke to Bernays.

"Something's turned up out of my prowl round Greenhurst yesterday, inspector. At least—that's what I'm hoping. There's a chap outside who reckons he's got some information."

"What do you think of him?"

"I think he's genuine."

"Bring him in then, sergeant—we shall be pleased to see him."

Chapter X

1

The man who entered in the company of Sergeant Bland was short and fair. He was hatless, his hair had begun to leave him and he wore a belted mackintosh tight round his body and buttoned high to the chin. As he came into the inspector's room, he unfastened the belt and then plunged his hands into the pockets of the mackintosh.

"Good morning," said Bernays pleasantly, "just take that seat, will you? Then we can have a talk."

The man nodded. He sat down in the chair which Bland placed for him.

"Mr. Albert Drake," announced Bland, "of Number 17, Waterloo Street. Brought some information concerning the late Doctor Field."

"Good," returned Bernays—"pleased to hear it." He smiled at Drake. "Local man—eh?"

"That's right, inspector. Lived 'ere for a good many years. Know you well by sight. But you don't know me. That's as well says you. So do I, say I."

"I expect you do. Well—what's your story?"

The man in the chair shot his legs straight out in front of him. Then he fished in his pocket and produced a copy of the *Sunday Record*. Pointing to a rather alarming picture and then stabbing with his finger he said:

"That's a photo, I suppose, of the feller what was 'ung in the porch of Fullafold Church?"

"That's so, Mr. Drake."

"Is it a good likeness?"

"Well," said Bernays, "I never knew Dr. Field when he was alive—I admit that—but—er—from what I saw of him dead I should say it's an excellent likeness."

"Right," said Drake—"that's all I wanted to 'ear you say. I'm not one for gettin' myself mixed up with the police, as I told you just now and I didn't want to open my trap this time unless I felt sort of certain that I was doin' the right thing. But the point is this. I see that chap the evenin' he got what was comin' to 'im."

"You're sure of that Mr. Drake?"

Drake nodded confidently. "As sure as there's a 'ole in my—sock."

"Where did you see him?"

"In the private bar of 'The Ram' over at Fullafold. You couldn't mistake 'im! Beard—and all that. 'E was sittin' at a little table near the fireplace with a bird. They was drinkin' together. Glass o' beer each. At any rate, that's what it looked like. Once or twice a week I walk over to 'The Ram' just to 'ave a couple before bedtime and this was one of the nights."

Bernays motioned to Bland. The latter began to make the necessary notes.

"What time would this have been, Mr. Drake?"

"About nine o'clock. I should say. Nearer nine than ten. You see—I noticed the bloke there when I first went in."

"How would you say he was dressed, Mr. Drake?"

Drake pursed his lips. "Well—'e was sittin' down—I couldn't see too much of his clothes—you must understand that—but I'll 'ave a go. Light-coloured overcoat, brown 'at, one o' them soft 'ats—brown shoes—" Drake shook his head—"that's about the bundle of what I could see."

"Good. That's all right. Now—this lady companion of Doctor Field's? Can you describe her?"

"Reckon I can do better with 'er than with 'im. She was a nice drop o' stuff. Real bit o' classy homework. She was fair—blue eyes—medium height—well-dressed. No 'at—long blue coat—collar turned up—it was a lousy night—scarf round her throat—oh—dark blue shoes. Not a local girl definitely." Drake swallowed hard after disposing of the last word. Anthony extended his hand.

"May I glance at your paper, Mr. Drake?"

"Certainly, sir." Drake handed over the copy of the *Sunday Record*.

Anthony looked at the picture of Julian Field and then proceeded to read the newspaper report. MacMorran took a hand.

"What strikes me as strange," he remarked, "is that the people at this public-house—'The Ram,' you said, didn't you?—haven't come forward. A Fullafold house, too—the actual village nearest perhaps to the place where the body was found."

Drake leant forward almost contemptuously and tossed away the suggestion as of nothing worth.

"You wouldn't say that if you knew the 'ouse! It's kept by an old girl named Tattersall 'oo's as near-sighted as a bat and, for another thing, 'alf a dozen's a lot to get in there some nights. That's the reason I use it. You never run into a school. Comes a bit more economical."

Bernays looked at MacMorran. "Does that satisfy you, chief?"

"It certainly deals with the point I raised—to an extent." Anthony handed back the paper. "Thank you." He turned to the others. "I should like to ask Mr. Drake a question, if I may."

"Go ahead," answered MacMorran.

"Mr. Drake," opened Anthony, "was this man whom you've identified as Dr. Field, in the bar of 'The Ram' when you left?"

"No, sir. He packed up and went out before I did."

"About what time?"

"About a quarter to ten, sir, I should think."

"Did his lady companion leave at the same time?"

Drake grinned knowingly. "I reckon she did—although actually she left their table a few minutes in front of him. You can guess why. Went to powder her nose."

"I see. Thank you. Now I want you to think hard, Mr. Drake. You can remember seeing the man you think was Dr. Field sitting at this table by the fireplace in the bar of 'The Ram,' can't you?"

"That's right, sir."

"You had a good look at him?"

"That's right, sir. I couldn't very well 'elp seein' him from where I was sittin'."

"That's good. Remember the overcoat? The light overcoat that he wore?"

"Of course I do. I described it first—now didn't I?"

"You did. I want you to think of it now as you saw it then. You get the idea. Try to picture it now in your mind's eye just as you saw it in the bar of 'The Ram.'"

"Well—what about it?"

"What can you tell me about the overcoat. For instance can you tell us any more than you've already told us?"

The face of Albert Drake which had temporarily clouded over, now cleared. "I get you, guv'nor! You mean the flower! Yes, that's right, 'e was wearin' a red flower as a button 'ole. I couldn't tell you rightly what it was because that side of his coat was farthest away from me, but I can remember seein' it all right. If it 'ad been a bit later in the year I might 'ave thought it was a November poppy. But there you are—I can't say what it was."

"Thank you, Mr. Drake," said Anthony, "that's all I wanted lo know." He turned and smiled at Bernays. "Your witness, inspector."

"Good. Now Mr. Drake—just a question or two more before we finish up. 'The Ram' at Fullafold lies well back from the road—does it not?"

"Quite a way back—yes. It's a very old 'ouse you know. Some of the old wood they've got in it's a fair treat to look at. I 'appen to be a carpenter, so I know what I'm talking about when I say that."

"I see. You wouldn't get many cars at 'The Ram,' I suppose, in the ordinary course of events?"

"Not a lot—no. Occasional of course. One or two pr'aps Saturday night and Sunday. But if you're leadin' up to another question, I can tell you what you want to know before you ask me. There was a car there on the night we're talkin' about. I remember seein' it as I went in. But I couldn't tell you a blind thing about it. I just spotted a car—and that was that."

"H'm. Pity, Still—you weren't to know. When you left 'The Ram' to go home—was this car you've spoken of there then?"

Drake shook his head. "No. It 'ud gone. I'm certain of that. The approach to 'The Ram' was pretty well clear everywhere. No cars—no push-bikes."

"Thank you, Mr. Drake."

Bernays looked inquiringly at MacMorran. The "Yard" inspector shook his head.

"I think that's all then, Mr. Drake. And many thanks for coming along. The police can do with all the help they can get. If we should want you again, we'll let you know."

"O.K. inspector. You know where to find me." Drake pulled the belt round his mackintosh and fastened it. "Good morning, gentlemen all."

2

Bernays stood in the middle of the room and scratched his head. "Takes us along a bit, doesn't it?"

"Tell me what you think," said MacMorran.

"Well—we know now where Field went after he left Greenhurst Station. He met the lady and they adjourned to 'The Ram.' And it's beginning to fit in. All of it. The beer-stain on the sleeve of the overcoat—that tallies with what this chap Drake has just told us. And 'The Ram' is less than a quarter or a mile from St. Mark's Church."

Bernays noticed that Anthony was slowly shaking his head.

"Why?" said Bernays, "why the look of doubt and sorrow?"

"Lots of 'whys,' I'm afraid, inspector. Lot's of 'em are jumping up at me."

"Such as?"

"Why meet the lady at 'The Ram,' Fullafold, when the assignation we're interested in was at the Cornelius Stones at Friar's Woodburn? There's the first 'why' for you."

"Well—it could be answered. He may have met her on the way to the place where they had intended to meet. You know—spotted the car. He knew where she was coming from and made arrangements to intercept her. That's one possible answer."

"Time was a bit hazy for that to happen—you read Mary's note—you'll grasp my point."

"Well," proceeded Bernays, unabashed, "the girl in 'The Ram' may not have been the 'pukka Mary.'"

"In that case, then," flashed back Anthony, "where are we? Floundering! And making a damned good job of it."

Bernays shrugged his shoulders and turned away. Just in time to see Sergeant Bland straighten his face. Anthony came again.

"Another thing, inspector. Another one of my little colony of 'whys.' Why was Julian Field in 'The Ram' at Fullafold at that time in the evening? How was it possible?"

"What do you mean? He's been traced to Greenhurst Station at about 7.45. Trott's evidence gave us that. What was more likely than that he walked over from there to 'The Ram' at Fullafold? That makes sense to me. I wish it all made as much sense as that part does. The time fits all right. Drake says he was there about nine o'clock. What's your trouble?"

"Merely this, inspector. If we are to believe the evidence of Dr. Depard, the Divisional Surgeon, Julian Field had been dead six hours when he was called to examine his body. And that doesn't make sense to me."

Bernays was shaken, but he nevertheless fought back. "Now—wait a minute! I was there when Depard gave his opinion. He said '*very* approximately.' He thought that Field died somewhere in the region of eight o'clock. He may have been a couple of hours out. Quite possible. I'll go farther than that—more than likely! You can't get away with—"

Anthony yielded the ground. "Yes. I'll admit all you say with regard to Depard. All the same—"

"All the same what?"

Anthony shook his head. "It's all wrong, Inspector Bernays. I said that before, I know—but I'll say it again. Certain of the clues we have tally, as you have just pointed out, but there are so many more which are completely contradictory. We must sift the true clues from the false. Take Stanhope's end for example—we've had it confirmed that Julian Field left the train at Greenhurst. But I've not yet had Stanhope's story corroborated that he saw Field on to the train at Stoke Pelly. Was that confirmed at Stoke Pelly Station? You put nobody up, inspector, at the inquest. More than once I've wondered why."

"We had Trott's evidence," replied Bernays. "I considered that was enough."

"It might be," said Anthony, "and yet again it might not. Circumstances alter cases."

"There's one thing I'd like to say," remarked MacMorran. "I didn't say it before because I expected one of you would push it into me. What did you think of Drake's description of the woman who was with Field in 'The Ram'?"

"What about it?" retorted Bernays. MacMorran gave his opinion. "Well—I don't know what you chaps thought—but it struck me how well it fitted Field's wife. Not only physically—but clothes as well."

There ensued a rather ominous silence. "Claudia Field!" exclaimed Bernays eventually, "but surely—"

"I was wondering," contributed Anthony quietly, "how long it would be before one of you mentioned that."

3

"It's always been a possibility, you know," Anthony continued, "that instead of somebody trailing Field, Field himself was trailing—well—if you like—Claudia."

"You harp on that," declared Bernays, "but I tell you you're wrong."

"Shouldn't be surprised," rejoined Anthony cheerfully, "because I'm very much in the dark and I don't mind admitting it. In fact, I can't tell you the extent of my appreciation that the murderer made the mistake he did."

Bernays heard the remark and stared blankly. "Mistake?" he repeated.

"That's what I said, inspector."

"Well—I've no doubt that he has made one—they all do—but I'm hanged if I know the one to which you're referring."

"You don't? Well then, I'll make you a present of it on a plate. Cornelius Stones and Cornelius Steps. Either will do."

Bernays shook his head. "I don't regard that mistake as over-important. Even if he did make it—and I can't see yet that he did. Sorry to disagree with you."

"You don't? To me, inspector, it almost sells the pass. In fact it was only recently when I realized its full significance that the light began to filter into my addled brain." Anthony dropped an eyelid in the direction of Andrew MacMorran.

The mood of Bernays changed suddenly. "Let's look at what we know. Or at what we can reasonably claim to know. Concerning where Field went. Where we *know* he went. I'll take it in stages. If you disagree with any statement that I make, stop me. Agree, chief?"

"Yes. Good idea."

"That's all right then."

Bernays began the itinerary. "One—Field leaves his surgery and goes by train to Stoke Pelly. Confirmed by Stanhope. Two—Field leaves Stoke Pelly just after seven o'clock. Again confirmed by Stanhope. Three—Field leaves the train at Greenhurst. Confirmed by Trott. Four—Field finds his way to the bar of 'The Ram' at Fullafold where he meets a lady. Confirmed by Drake. Field's body found at midnight in the church porch at Fullafold. Doesn't need confirmation. Therefore, he was murdered somewhere between 'The Ram' and the church—and from the time angle between about 9.45 say and half-past ten or eleven o'clock. It's on the cards, as I see it, that Mary Whitley only just missed the actual killing. I don't think she was more than a few minutes late." Bernays sat back in a chair. "Now do you agree on those lines? If you don't, shoot!"

"Not altogether," said MacMorran—"and I don't think Mr. Bathurst will, either. In the first place, inspector, you've used the word 'confirmed' a good deal. I'll show you what I mean. We have only Stanhope's word that Field ever arrived at Stoke Pelly."

"You're wrong there, chief," cut in Bernays—"the outward half of his railway ticket was surrendered at Stoke Pelly Station. The railway company has confirmed that. The corresponding return half was given up to Trott at Greenhurst."

"It looks all right, I admit. But there's no hundred per cent certainty that *Field* surrendered them. Oh—I know I'm splitting hairs—I'm doing so deliberately for the sake of my argument."

"But Trott identified him," exploded Bernays.

"I know. I think you're right and on perfectly sound ground. All I'm tilting against is your contention of confirmation."

Bernays showed signs of impatience.

"Again," went on MacMorran, "Drake doesn't *confirm* that Field was in the pub at Fullafold. He merely comes forward with a plain statement and says he was." MacMorran turned to Anthony. "How do you feel with regard to what I've just said to the inspector."

"I go all the way with you, chief—indeed I'd go even farther. I think you could have elaborated your argument considerably."

Bernays came back. "Hold on a minute. In my opinion you're inclined to forget one or two points. How about *other*—if you don't care for the word—'confirmations'—'supporting evidence.' Go back to what Dr. Depard said at the inquest. You were there and heard it. The divisional surgeon told the coroner that Field had partaken of a meal—a few hours I think he said—before his death. Which again pairs up with what Stanhope had said in his evidence. That the doctor, after his consultation with Mrs. Stanhope, had stayed and had tea at Stoke Pelly. I can't see any sense in deliberately *trying* to find discrepancies. Especially where independent testimonies are in accordance with one another—and thereby rule out discrepancies."

"I'm not," replied MacMorran almost mildly, "far from it. I'm simply sounding a warning note against taking too many things for granted."

"I'll send Sergeant Bland down to 'The Ram' later on," said Bernays, changing the drift of conversation—"a word or two with the landlady, Mrs. Tattersall, won't do any harm. She may have something for him. She may not have been as blind as Drake said."

"Sound notion," declared Anthony. He rose from his seat. "Well, I really think we've made some progress at last. Same as you, Inspector Bernays. Drake's yarn may well prove to be the turning point. Who knows—somebody else may turn up with something?"

"Here's hoping," added MacMorran.

Chapter XI

1

The telephone had rung in the "Horse and Groom." The girl who had taken the call, came bustling in for MacMorran. When she located him—she beckoned—"'phone for you. In my office."

"What's this all about?" said MacMorran to Anthony as he went ahead to take the call.

It was Bernays at the other end. "Is that you, chief?"

"That's right."

"This is Inspector Bernays speaking from Four Bridges Police Station. Some more news for you. Just come in. A young chap from Fullafold on his way to work this morning found a revolver in the ditch at the foot of the slope that leads up to the church. Just where the path comes to the road."

"Which side?"

"The Greenhurst side. He was walking into Greenhurst to his work. As most of the Fullafold folk do. It hasn't been there very long and had probably been hidden under leaves. He says the sun happened to glint on the barrel just as he walked by—so he spotted it."

"What type is it?"

".38 automatic. And there's no doubt it's been recently fired."

"Anything in the magazine?"

"One bullet. Actually—so Chadwick says—that's the name of the young fellow who found it—the striking pin was cocked when he picked it up. He put it right for safety. Lucky he found it, in a way, and not a youngster. Seeing it was still loaded. What do you make of it?"

"Don't know. It's probably something to do with the Field case seeing where it's been found—but well—it doesn't seem to have been used on Field, does it? In that case—why throw it away?"

"I should say the bullet aimed for Field—missed. Then there was a struggle-down went the rod—but Field came off worst. Possibly, in the dark, the murderer couldn't find it. It might have been kicked around anywhere."

"O.K. I'll be over to see you later."

MacMorran returned to Anthony and gave him the gist of the message he had just taken from Bernays. Anthony scratched his cheek as he listened.

"Where exactly did you say this gun was found?" MacMorran told Anthony in the words that Bernays had used. "In the ditch at the foot of the slope which leads to the church. Where the slope-path meets the road."

"That's on the Greenhurst side?"

"That's the idea."

"Been recently fired—and one cartridge still on duty?"

"That's it."

"Any powder marks on Field's clothes anywhere? The shot might have been fired at close quarters."

"Not that I've heard of. The point's a good one. I'll see Bernays about it when I go over there. I told him I'd be over later."

"What does Bernays himself think about it?"

"Oh—what you might expect. A struggle, a shot fired at Field, the assailant dropped the gun and then when Field had been disposed of—couldn't find it. How does all that appeal to you?"

"Not much. I don't think the struggle could have taken place so close to the ditch for one thing. The ditch is too close to the road. Unless, of course, the struggle flared up very suddenly."

"You think, then, that the gun was hidden in the ditch? By the killer—after he'd done the job?"

Anthony shook his head. "I don't know that I even think that, Andrew. At the moment I'm more inclined to the theory that the gun was planted there."

"Planted there? You mean—deliberately?"

"That's what I meant."

"Why? What was the purpose behind that?"

"It was meant to be discovered. That's my opinion. I'll tell you why I think that. If the murderer hid it, or intended to hide it is a better way of putting it, why choose just that section of ditch right by the junction of slope and road? Surely, if the idea had been concealment, the killer would have walked along the side of the ditch and chosen a place right away from everywhere?"

"H'm. I hadn't thought of that one. Maybe you're right. I'll run over to Four Bridges later on and have a word or two with Bernays. Will you come?"

"I may as well, I suppose. I had intended to motor down to Stoke Pelly—but perhaps I'll leave that for this afternoon. I'd like you to come there. After that—there's Friar's Woodburn."

"Right-o. Stoke Pelly after lunch. How long—in the car?"

"Oh—under the hour. We won't do Stoke Pelly and Friar's Woodburn in the same day—too much of a rush. We may have to take our time at Friar's Woodburn. Fit?"

"Give me two minutes," replied MacMorran.

2

Bernays showed them the revolver. As he had stated—it was a .38 automatic.

"Plenty of that sort knocking round," said MacMorran.

"Poked under the leaves—it had been," remarked Bernays—"might have stayed there for months—but for young Chadwick's sharp eyes."

"Hardly likely," said Anthony.

"Why?"

"Too near the road, I should say. There was always the chance that somebody coming down the slope-path would spot it."

"You don't get thousands doing that."

"How many do you get—per day—on an average?"

Bernays considered the question. "Chiefly Fullafold people, of course. Going to work in Greenhurst. Couple of dozen every morning say—bar Sundays."

"There you are, then. Twenty-four fair chances every day. To say nothing of all their return journeys."

Bernays shook his head emphatically. "You wouldn't see anything in the ditch as you ascend the slope. The ditch gets behind you from the very first step upwards—or good enough."

"Even then, inspector, my twenty-four still stand. And as a minimum." Anthony handled the revolver. "As the chief has just said, inspector, there's no limit to the number of this sort of gun. But it might be interesting to find out whether Field had a licence." He handed the gun back to Bernays. The latter seemed surprised at the remark.

"You don't seriously think that this gun belonged to Field, do you?"

"I'm inclined to think so."

"Why? Why on earth should a man in Field's position carry a gun?"

"Come to that, inspector, why does anyone carry one?"

"But, man, Field wasn't exactly *anybody*! He was a professional man out on a professional visit. A professional visit which we *know* he fulfilled. He went to see Mrs. Stanhope—and he saw Mrs. Stanhope. A man doesn't need a gun to go with his stethoscope."

Anthony was unperturbed by the warmth with which Bernays had invested his argument.

"What about the letter, inspector? Where did Field go after he'd seen his patient? Yesterday you prepared his itinerary for us. He may have needed the gun—defensively. It would appear, too, from what happened to him that the need was there."

Bernays was silent. "Well—it can easily be settled. If he had a licence—"

"Agreed. But he *may* have been a law-breaker and not had a licence. That sort of thing is not unknown. Which means that the doubt may not be so easily settled."

For the second time since they had met him, Anthony thought that Bernays seemed despondent. "All well," returned the local inspector—"we don't know, so that we may as well save our breath. We'll just wait and see."

3

Anthony and MacMorran took the winding road at the foot of the downs which leads to Stoke Pelly and after that to Spears and

Crawness. The countryside was beautiful in its young autumnal dress, but Anthony had no intention of loitering on the road and whenever he could with safety, he pushed up the needle of the speedometer.

Shortly before three o'clock, they saw the yellow A.A. sign announcing the propinquity of Stoke Pelly.

"Railway station first of all," growled MacMorran, "and let's hope we find the man we want on duty."

Anthony watched for the pointer and swung the big car to the left.

"I should think, Andrew," remarked Anthony as he drove up the incline which led to the railway station, "that we shall probably find our man. As a rule the staff at little country stations like this doesn't vary much. Anyhow—we'll see."

MacMorran entered the booking-hall and noticed that the ticket-hatch was closed. "No trains on Good Fridays," he grinned. Stooping down, he tapped on the wooden shutter.

There was no reply—so MacMorran was compelled to repeat the performance. Frowning, he was just on the point of a third attempt, when the shutter shot up. "There's my card," he said curtly, "I want a word with the stationmaster."

Meanwhile Anthony had been taking stock of the station, its appointments and its immediate surroundings. There was but one booking-hall, he noticed, and all passengers would be forced to cross the bridge to obtain access to the other platform. He turned to hear the exchange of conversation between MacMorran and a lad. He saw the lad leave the booking office and come out to join the "Yard" inspector in the hall.

"If you come this way, sir," Anthony heard the lad say, "I'll take you along to him."

MacMorran gestured to Anthony and they accompanied the lad down the platform. The stationmaster, a man of rather solemn features was in his office.

"I'm Chief Det.-Inspector MacMorran, Scotland Yard. I'd like a few words with you in private, please. I don't know your name. Perhaps—"

"Plummer," said the stationmaster. His voice was in keeping with the cast of his features. The uniformed youth disappeared.

105 | THE SWINGING DEATH

"Sit down, gentlemen. What can I do for you?" Plummer found chairs, but his small room was uncomfortably full when Anthony and MacMorran took their seats. MacMorran, with an economy of words, explained the reason behind the visit. Plummer nodded.

"I know the affair very well, sir. Mostly through the newspaper accounts, naturally. And, of course, through knowing Mr. Stanhope and his family so well. I've been at this station nigh on twenty years. So you can guess I know Mr. and Mrs. Stanhope all right. Two of the best—and you can take that from me. And there's not a man or woman living in Stoke Pelly who wouldn't say the same. And I can tell you, inspector, that Dr. Field, the man whose body was found in the church porch, caught the 7.3 train from this station on that particular evening."

"You're absolutely certain of that?"

"Positive, sir."

"You saw him yourself?"

"I saw him myself."

"With Mr. Stanhope?"

"With Mr. Stanhope. I can vouch for the fact that what Mr. Stanhope said at the coroner's inquest was gospel true. Everything happened just as he stated. I read the account, you see, being interested like, in the *Four Bridges Echo*. In a way, I wonder your people didn't call me. I tell you—I expected it."

MacMorran looked at Anthony. The latter nodded. "Mr. Plummer," he said, "please remember what you saw. Don't think we doubt your word for a moment. Just give us the picture exactly as you saw it."

"Come along with me." Plummer stepped out of his room on to the platform. He pointed to the other platform. "I was over there on the up side. Getting ready for the 7.3. She'd had the stick for several minutes. I heard Mr. Stanhope's car drive up and stop outside the booking-hall. I saw Mr. Stanhope and the gentleman I now know was Doctor Field walk along this platform where we're now standing, all of us, go up the steps of the bridge there—" Plummer pointed to the bridge which crossed the line—"go over and come down the steps on the up side. They came, I suppose, within about twenty yards of me when this Doctor Field stopped. Just about over there." Again the stationmaster indicated where he meant. "Mr. Stanhope himself waved to me and within a few seconds the 7.3 came in. She wasn't late—or at least, nothing to worry about. I saw Doctor Field get into the train and actually shake hands with Mr. Stanhope through the open window of the compartment."

Plummer stopped, but before either Anthony or MacMorran could speak, he went on again. "I can tell you something else, too—I saw the rose in his overcoat just as Mr. Stanhope said at the inquest."

"Thank you, Mr. Plummer," said Anthony, "that's all very explicit and tells us just what we wanted to know." Anthony turned and addressed MacMorran. "I'm satisfied, Andrew. I don't know whether you have any more questions to ask the stationmaster."

MacMorran shook his head. "I don't think so. Oh—there is just one thing. Which is the quickest way to where Mr. Stanhope lives?"

"I'll come outside and show you," responded Plummer. He piloted them down the platform and back to the booking-hall. "I'll come into the street." Plummer stood on the kerb and pointed. "Turn right—follow the road—that will take you into the village. Carry straight on and you'll come to cross-roads. There's a pub on one corner. 'The Old Oak.' Turn left and you'll come to 'Gifford's.' You can't miss it. It's the only really big house on the road just about here."

"Many thanks." Anthony drove off. He was silent. MacMorran had a go.

"Nothing much wrong there," he ventured.

"Nothing at all, Andrew. It's so good, really, that I'm beginning to wonder if there's much point in our calling on Stanhope. The only thing is he may be able to tell us whether he noticed anything about Field."

MacMorran shook his head. "I don't think so. I haven't much hope of picking up anything in that direction."

"Charming little village," commented Anthony as they passed through Stoke Pelly. "I can well understand people coming to a place of this kind—especially in their later years. It's tranquil. I find an irresistible appeal in tranquillity."

"Good. When I'm pensioned—you shall come and spend a fortnight with me every summer."

"I'd prefer the autumn, Andrew—the autumn's the season that I find most attractive in the country. Here are the crossroads."

"And there's the 'Old Oak.' Turn right."

"Left, Andrew. Left—according to the excellent Plummer. And 'Gifford's' will be the first big house we shall come to. So keep your eyes open."

Half a mile or so up the road, Anthony braked. "Here we are, Andrew—and we're on the right side of the road. Pleasing place, too. Wouldn't scream at this—with £10,000 a year trickling in. Out you get. Or can I take her in a bit?"

MacMorran craned his head, "You can. The gate's open and there's a sort of drive up to the house."

"Good. Much more satisfactory than leaving the car out here."

Anthony drove in and came near to the house. Then he swung the car to the left where he could see ample room for parking. "There you are, Andrew. In a few minutes you can be doing your stuff."

"And you!" replied MacMorran as he opened the car door.

4

"Gifford's" was a house of old-fashioned type with a pillared portico. The garden, which was large, seemed to Anthony to run all round it.

"Don't go to the front door," prompted Anthony, "there's a way in there on the left and if I mistake not, Stanhope himself in the garden."

In this assumption, Anthony was right for Stanhope, having caught sight of them came from the garden to confront them.

"Good afternoon, Mr. Stanhope." MacMorran stepped forward. Stanhope's eyes held a question. MacMorran introduced himself. "And this is Mr. Anthony Bathurst," he added.

Stanhope's demeanour was grave. "I had the idea that Inspector Bernays of Four Bridges was—"

"The Field case has come to the 'Yard,' Mr. Stanhope. That perhaps will give you the explanation you're seeking."

"I see. Well, in that case, gentlemen, come indoors. I shall be happy to give you any information that's in my power."

Stanhope ushered them into a wide, spacious, but low-raftered oak-beamed room that looked on to the garden. There was a wood fire crackling merrily on a great open hearth.

"Sit down, gentlemen," said Stanhope, "and tell me what you'd like to know."

"Just a little on the defensive," thought Anthony.

"First of all," opened MacMorran, "we're trying to get as much information about Dr. Field as we possibly can. You can see the reason for that, naturally."

"Obviously."

"We've been fairly successful. We've been able to trace his movements from the time he left Stoke Pelly Station just after seven o'clock until just before ten. As you know'—people have come forward who have helped us. Trott, for example, the ticket collector on duty at Greenhurst Station. But whereas medical evidence tended towards the time of death as occurring round about eight o'clock—we are of the opinion now that Dr. Field was alive for at least a couple of hours after that."

"I wouldn't know," smiled Stanhope.

Anthony liked the smile. His previous attraction towards Stanhope was confirmed. At the same time, though, there was still that defensive quality about him.

"You see," went on Stanhope, "medicine and I are strangers to one another. I've been lucky enough to have good health all my life— and the result has been, I suppose, that I've never bothered my head very much about medical matters." He smiled again. "I don't know whether you get what I mean—but there it is."

MacMorran nodded. "I think I understand you, Mr. Stanhope. But to come back to Dr. Field. I don't propose for one minute to take you over the same ground again which the coroner covered at the inquest."

"That's pleasant hearing," said Stanhope—"because personally I thought the coroner was a ruddy old fool. Still—that's neither here nor there. I may not be a good judge of coroners. Come to that—I can't be. Old Bessemer's the only one of his kind I've ever seen."

MacMorran laughed. "You've been lucky. My experience, as you may guess, has been very much the reverse. To come back to Field, as I said. Since the coroner questioned you at the inquest, have you by any chance been able to hit on any reason or suggestion as to why Field broke his journey at Greenhurst? Sometimes, when one thinks back, as it were, perhaps even days after an event has taken place, some little point *does* pop up and assume a significance which it didn't hold previously. Now—has anything like that occurred to you since that day of the inquest?"

To Anthony's satisfaction, Stanhope did not reply immediately. He gave MacMorran's question definite consideration before his answer was forthcoming. He shook his head.

"No—I can't say that it has. I really can't say truthfully that I can look back and pick out anything that Field said, or that happened while he was here to give me any clue as to his subsequent behaviour. I should like to be able to, because, naturally, seeing that he was here having tea with us at half-past five, I'm interested in the man's fate and interested also in getting to the bottom of it all. But frankly to-day, as compared with the day of the inquest, well—I'm in *statu quo*. I haven't the slightest idea why the man should have got out of the train at Greenhurst."

MacMorran got up from his chair, walked to the french windows and looked out into the garden. Then he thrust his hands into his pockets and came back again to the middle of the room.

"A plain question, Mr. Stanhope. Did Field strike you as the sort of man who might be on the way to an assignation? I'll be blunt. What I mean is—a man, say, ready for amorous adventure?"

Stanhope smiled his grave smile. "I should say—no. Certainly—no. From the little I knew of him, I should say that the temptations which the gods would scatter in his path, would be of an entirely different nature. No—I think that if I had to find a reason for his going to Greenhurst, it would be that he went to visit a patient. I'm a plain man—not very subtle, I'm afraid—but that, to me, is by far the most likely explanation."

"Unfortunately," replied MacMorran, "we've come across nothing to support that. I can assure you, though, that the possibility hasn't been entirely overlooked."

Stanhope nodded. "Of course. I didn't suppose for a moment that it had been."

Anthony came in for the first time. "Mr. Stanhope," he said, "you made a remark a moment ago which was of considerable interest to me."

"What was that, Mr. Bathurst?"

"You said—in relation to Dr. Field—'from the little I knew of him.' Would you be good enough to enlarge on that?"

"With pleasure. I had actually seen Field only once before. That was in September. I fancy the date was the 22nd. I explained that, I think, at the inquest. You will remember how I told the coroner that I was anxious about Mrs. Stanhope's health. You will agree, I think, Mr. Bathurst, that you can't know all about a man on two showings? That's why I was reluctant to answer your colleague's inquiry as to certain possibilities of character that Field may have possessed. Surely that's reasonable?"

"Oh—eminently. If you'll allow me to put the question—what took you to Field in the first place? I remember your saying something to the coroner in relation to his reputation as a specialist—but I take it there was something, as it were, *before* that?"

"Oh—yes," replied Stanhope—"I'll tell you. The man I really wanted was Dr. Louis Wolff, Field's predecessor in the practice at King's Winkworth. Wolff's name as a chest specialist was a household word in this part of the country. Everybody swore by him. Well—he was killed in an accident during the war—so I've recently found out. I either missed hearing about it at the time or it went out of my mind. When I needed advice in connection with Mrs. Stanhope—I 'phoned Dr. Wolff's old surgery. You can guess what happened—I got Field. Naturally, he told me about Wolff. I didn't fix up with Field then and there." Stanhope smiled. "I'm not that kind of man. I usually like to look round things before I act. To cut a long story short, I made inquiries about Field—found he had a growing reputation in Wolff's own particular field—sorry—that was unintentional—and eventually, after taking everything into consideration, I asked him to come down to have a look at Mrs. Stanhope. I'm glad I did. I don't mean to sound selfish—seeing that it cost the chap his life—but he did relieve me considerably of the anxiety I was feeling about my wife. There you are, sir—that's the story as to how I first contacted Doctor Field."

"Thank you, Mr. Stanhope. You've been most helpful."

"You must stay and have a cup of tea," said Philip Stanhope. "I'll ring and tell them."

"How's Mrs. Stanhope now?" asked MacMorran.

"Oh—almost well. Field's second examination, I think, turned the scale. Of course, we've never had the full report he promised—but he did tell her before he left here that he was almost certain she had no real cause for worry. The first time—in September—he was a wee bit uncertain." The door opened. "Here's the lady herself," said Stanhope, smiling.

5

"Come in, Daphne."

Anthony immediately registered the significance of the Christian name.

Mrs. Stanhope closed the door behind her and advanced towards them.

"There are two gentlemen here," said Stanhope, "who have come all the way from Scotland Yard to see us. I'll include you in the visit."

A charming and attractive woman in the early forties, Daphne Stanhope welcomed MacMorran and Anthony warmly and yet with an entire absence of fuss. She had light brown hair and a pair of sensitive grey eyes.

"And what have we done," she said whimsically, as she seated herself, "to deserve such an honour? Still—I expect I know." She smoothed out a fold in her skirt. "It's about Doctor Field, isn't it?"

"That's so, Mrs. Stanhope," replied MacMorran. "Mr. Bathurst and I are doing our best to solve what is really a most extraordinary problem. And as the dead man spent some hours here with you just before he met with his death—well, you can guess why we came along."

"Can we help you in any way, then, do you think?"

"No. It doesn't seem as though you can. Mr. Stanhope has done his best—but there you are. As he says—he knew very little of Field, really."

"He came here but twice—as you know."

"Yes. Your husband has been making that clear to us."

"You did arrange about some tea, my dear—did you not?"

Mrs. Stanhope smiled the affirmative. The smile embraced the entire company. "My husband's a rare man for his tea," she said.

"I'm a host this afternoon, my dear, besides being a husband."

"It's all being got ready," she said reassuringly—"and it shouldn't be more than a few minutes. So be as patient as you can—and talk to these gentlemen."

Anthony suddenly shot a question at her. "What did you think of Dr. Field, Mrs. Stanhope? I'm a terrific believer in a woman's intuition."

"Also, Mr. Bathurst," she said a little mockingly, "I can see that you're an accomplished flatterer."

Anthony smiled. "Another tribute to your intuition."

"And another example of your flattery." The grey eyes were at their best. Anthony saw that they were almost exactly the same shade of colour as his own. Mrs. Stanhope went on, however, to answer his question. "You asked me my opinion of Dr. Field, Mr. Bathurst. Did you mean as a doctor or as a man? Because, to a woman, there's a great deal of difference between the two."

"Oh—as a man, Mrs. Stanhope. Definitely as a man."

"Well," replied Mrs. Stanhope, staring into the heart of the fire, "I can't say that he appealed to me—or that I even liked him. I think that he was a clever doctor—a very clever doctor—but I'm certain that I should never have liked him as a man." Philip Stanhope laughed lightly at his wife's reply. "You've been spoiled, my dear. You mustn't expect every man you meet to be as nice as I am. Hallo—here's the tea."

Stanhope rose and his wife went to the maid who had brought in the tea-things. "And here are the others," said Philip Stanhope—"now we're all set. What marvellous noses the members of my family have."

Chapter XII

1

STANHOPE made the necessary introductions. "My daughter, Elinor. My eldest, as it happens. And this is Howard, my son."

Anthony looked at Elinor Stanhope and realized that here was Daphne Stanhope, her mother, some twenty-odd years ago.

"Yes," said Mrs. Stanhope—"you're quite right, Mr. Bathurst. We are alike—aren't we? Elinor's my little girl all right."

"You certainly are," remarked Anthony—"and I think you're each to be highly congratulated."

"You know what I said," declared Mrs. Stanhope as she poured tea into cups, "if you're not careful—I shall say it again."

Howard Stanhope was a splendid specimen of young manhood. A giant, ruddy and fair. A very charming family, Anthony thought. Philip Stanhope made a general reference to the Field case, but neither Howard Stanhope nor his sister Elinor seemed particularly interested. Stanhope, having given the cue as it were, presented the opportunity to Anthony to bring the conversation back to the point when the interruption had come. Turning the conversation therefore as neatly as possible, Anthony said, "Would you care, Mrs. Stanhope, to amplify your previous statement with regard to Field? I must confess to being somewhat unusually curious."

"Do you mean as to my reasons for not liking him?"

"Yes. Something of that kind."

"Well—it's because of my judgment of his character. I should say he could be—or could have been rather—entirely unscrupulous. Even cruel! And men of that type, even though they may attain great success, just don't appeal to me." She glanced rather shyly in the direction of her husband. "I like kind men, men of gentle heart. Especially when it's accompanied by real manliness."

As Anthony looked across the table he had the feeling that Elinor's face was wearing a rather strained expression. Howard ate his tea quietly. He was evidently a young man of few words.

"Well, Mr. Bathurst," said Daphne Stanhope, "have I satisfied you? Or are you rating me extremely low as a psychologist?"

Anthony shook his head. "Not at all, Mrs. Stanhope. Actually, I consider that you've done extraordinarily well—on two encounters."

"Ah, but they weren't brief encounters. You must remember that. Why do you look at me so critically?"

The rest of the family laughed. Stanhope himself said, "What do you expect. Daphne, from Scotland Yard?"

Anthony joined in the second laugh which immediately followed. "I must hasten," he said, "to rehabilitate myself. The look was not one of criticism, I assure you. What I was really thinking was that you strongly remind me of a lady whom I knew very well, some years ago. I found myself wondering whether you were any relation of hers. She was a Miss Appleton. Her home, when I knew her, was in Worcestershire."

"No. Sorry to destroy your castle, Mr. Bathurst. There are no people of that name in my family. As far as I know—of course. My maiden name was Bartlett. All my people were connected with the south of England."

"That disposes of my idea, then. All the same, there's an undoubted likeness. Perhaps it goes back to the time when the two of you had a common ancestor who was a King in Babylon."

"More than likely, Mr. Bathurst, that he was a Christian slave." Mrs. Stanhope laughed merrily.

"There is one thing I'd like to say," contributed MacMorran, "as a matter of fact, I intended to ask Mr. Stanhope before about it. I'm coming back, again to the murder of Field."

Anthony saw Howard Stanhope look up sharply.

"What's your point, Inspector MacMorran?" queried Philip Stanhope.

"It's this. Do you know that place at Friar's Woodburn which Field mentioned to the ticket collector at Greenhurst Station? Field inquired, according to this man Trott, for the 'Cornelius Steps.' But from what we've been able to ascertain since, the correct name is the 'Cornelius Stones.' Do you happen to know it?"

"Oh—yes. You must remember that I've lived here a long time. I was born in this house. The Cornelius Stones are well known to everybody at all familiar with this particular stretch of country. I don't think I've ever actually been there—but on the other hand I've passed the Stones in my car—well 'thousands of times'—as the boy said. It's the approved rendezvous for all the courting couples of Friar's Woodburn."

"Shame," said Howard Stanhope. Stanhope smiled.

"Is that a fact," said Anthony—"well, then, I'm left just a little bewildered."

"Why is that, Mr. Bathurst?" said Daphne Stanhope.

"By reason of what Trott said at the inquest, Mrs. Stanhope. Trott told the coroner that Field had asked him where this place was and then he volunteered the information that he'd never heard of it. That's so, isn't it, Andrew?"

"Quite right. Trott said that."

"Well," continued Anthony, "doesn't that surprise you? Bearing in mind what Mr. Stanhope has just told us? Greenhurst is but a handful of miles from Friar's Woodburn and yet we have a railway official at Greenhurst denying all knowledge of a place which is by way of being a household word to the majority of the inhabitants of the district and adjoining area."

Stanhope stirred his tea meditatively. "Don't you think, Mr. Bathurst, that the explanation is probably this? Trott is not a native. He's probably been transferred to Greenhurst from another station. A London station—in all likelihood. The railway does do that—I know. If my memory serves me correctly, Trott said that the Cornelius Stones weren't in Greenhurst or Fullafold. That statement indicates to me that he doesn't know much about Friar's Woodburn. It would be interesting to find out, perhaps, how long Trott has been on the staff at Greenhurst Station. That would show whether I've hit the mark or not."

"I don't suppose," replied Anthony, "that Chief Inspector MacMorran will consider the point important enough for that. Anyhow—it's up to him. Personally, I think, Mr. Stanhope, that your explanation is probably the right one."

"I'm flattered," responded Philip Stanhope, "praise from Sir Hubert is praise indeed. Would you care to walk round the garden—before it's too dark? The evenings are drawing in very quickly now."

"Seven weeks to Christmas," chimed in Elinor—"and the summer only seems a few weeks away. August Bank Holiday seems like the day before yesterday."

"A lot has happened since August Bank Holiday, Miss Stanhope," said Anthony.

"I won't give either of you gentlemen a flower," smiled Stanhope, "in case it's as unlucky as Field's was."

"If it were," replied MacMorran—"you'd find yourself lining up with the Borgias."

Mrs. Stanhope shuddered. "How perfectly horrible you men are," she exclaimed.

2

Anthony and MacMorran drove back to the "Horse and Groom" at Greenhurst. Anthony jerked his head back in the direction of the house they had just left.

"Well, Andrew—satisfied?"

"Nothing else but to be satisfied—is there?"

"I agree. Rather charming people. All the same—I thought the son seemed unusually quiet and the daughter definitely nervy. And I ask myself—why was that?"

"Howard Stanhope's at the silent age and the girl was flustered by the sound of the words 'Scotland Yard.' And I can tell you—there's nothing in that. I've known it happen before. Not once at that—on several occasions."

"Yes. I can well believe it. And, of course, Field left Stoke Pelly by train just after seven o'clock. That's pretty well locked up by now. Also—I'm merely theorizing, Andrew'—if there were any funny business between Field and the Stanhopes—what's the motive? Can't think of one affecting them—can you?"

MacMorran closured the idea emphatically. "Good lord—no. Come off it!"

"And yet," went on Anthony, "I know—as well as I know that my name's Anthony Lotherington Bathurst—that we're missing something. All the same—I'm glad we went to 'Giffords'—it's put the seal on one or two things. There is that about it."

"I'm inclined to think," said MacMorran, semi-whimsically and semi-humorously, "that you're beginning to lose your grip."

Anthony grinned. "How do you get that, Andrew? I'm always ready to learn."

"Well—for one thing in this case, you're suspecting too many people. The Stanhopes don't seem to get by—Claudia Field misses the hundred per cent—there's Courtenay—Mary something or other—"

Anthony cut in, shaking his head. "No. You aren't quite right, Andrew. Because I don't immediately eliminate, that doesn't mean that I necessarily suspect. All the same—it's a rare problem. Only just beginning to take shape in my mind. It's been amorphous for so long. Too long. Never mind—we'll see what Friar's Woodburn can show us to-morrow."

3

Friar's Woodburn was another delightful village. It was old-world from the moment you entered it until the moment you left it. And that's allowing for the possibility that you saw all of it that there was to see before you came away.

"I've been here before, Andrew," said Anthony, "as I told you the other day. Friar's Woodburn is like a hamlet that nestles on the top of a ridge. The main road from London to the coast cuts it off as it were and leaves it self-contained. You'll see what I mean when we come to it."

They came to Friar's Woodburn and to the places typical of a village such as this was—the inn, the general shop which served everything and was a post office as well, the school, the church, the vicarage, the chapel and the rows of cottages with their low tile roofs and sprawling gardens in front.

"See how it's all huddled together, Andrew? The farms lie in the two valleys—to the north and to the south. All round Friar's Woodburn are magnificent trees and if you look at them from a height, the valleys look like lovely lakes of green. But I think the lanes all round attract me most of all. They sort of snake their winding ways into the two valleys."

Anthony stopped the car. "Look—there's the churchyard. Very lovely, isn't it? Look at that great tree in the corner—with the sweeping branches."

"Jolly fine."

"Better than that, Andrew. Grand! Now what's the plan of campaign?"

"First of all," replied MacMorran, "take me to these wretched stones—the 'Cornelius Stones.' I'd like to get some idea of the lie of the land."

"I must try to remember the way. I rather fancy it's straight up and then you bear to the left. It's some years since I was here last. Anyhow—we'll chance it."

Anthony went straight for about half a mile and then swung the car south. "We ought to make it, this way. I remember this road. It's come back to me."

MacMorran grunted approval.

"There's not a lot to see," continued Anthony—"it's a little tributary of the Pidge. I looked it up. What's the name of it now? On the tip of my tongue a moment ago. The Lonner—that's it. Quite charming and there's no wonder the locals regard it as a beauty spot."

"Is it far?"

"We're almost there, Andrew. That is if my memory's worth anything. You'll find the road will begin to drop down in a moment or so—it drops down right to the bank of the Lonner. Here you are—the descent begins just about here."

Anthony drove the car down to the water. The weather dedicated to St. Martin was still holding and the little stream glistened in the pale amber of the sunshine.

"We'll leave the car here, Andrew—and then I'll walk you along to the stepping-stones."

Belts of trees ran away to the horizon and everywhere was thickly wooded. The cottages where Bernays had presumably inquired were about a quarter of a mile away. "Beloved of lovers," said Anthony—"you can easily see that. Apart from its natural beauty."

MacMorran looked down at the stepping-stones across the Lonner water and rubbed his chin reflectively. "Do you know what I'm thinking?" he said.

"No—what?"

"How far's this spot from Friar's Woodburn Station?"

"Couple of miles I should think. Maybe a trifle more. Although—there may be a quicker way—walking—than the road we took. I should think there is. Bound to be. Why?"

"Heck of a way for a man to walk. I'm thinkin' of Field and the assignation angle."

"Andrew—you astound me! What's a walk to a man in love? Or to a man who kids himself he's in love? Good lord—I walked five miles once to cuddle a girl in the snow. Andrew! Have you no romance?"

"You ask my missus. She'll tell you. And I don't believe your snowy reminiscences."

"Believe it or not—it's a solemn fact. My hands were dead until I took her in my arms."

"You were daft, man."

Anthony laughed. "There may be something in that. Well—there are the Cornelius Stones. Do you want to do anything besides look at them?"

MacMorran stood silent—his hands thrust deep into his overcoat pockets. Eventually he turned. "We'll get back to the village, park the car and do what we decided we'd do. What's the time?"

"Ten minutes to twelve. Just about right. What people there are in the place should be round about at this time. When we get to the village—we'll arrange the details."

Anthony and the inspector walked back to the car.

4

"I'll take the railway station and the shops generally," said MacMorran—"you take the inns and the church. Bernays said he called at three pubs—that means there must be two more—smaller ones, I expect—some little distance out. Personally—I think we're on a bad egg. Still—we'll have a cut. What time shall I meet you?"

Anthony looked at his watch. "We'll say 1.15, Andrew. That gives us a little over the hour. Where?"

"At the first of the inns. The one we passed as you drove in. You make that your last port of call—so that you should be in there when I arrive."

"O.K., Andrew. A quarter past one, then. I'll use the car, I think. One of the farther inns may be a good way out. If I'm late—wait for me."

Anthony drove off. He intended to make for the inn nearest to the stepping stones and he took the road, therefore, which he considered would be likely to show him the best results from this particular point of view. Within a matter of twenty minutes he had covered two hostelries, the "Fisherman's Rest" and the "Shakespeare Arms." He drank at each and conversed in the best bar of each with the person who served him. This was a barmaid at the "Fisherman's Rest" and a man who was evidently the proprietor at the "Shakespeare Arms." At the "Fisherman's Rest," Anthony drew a complete and utter blank. By neither oblique reference nor direct statement was he able to find the slightest trace of Julian Field. A sensational murder in the vicinity affords a most workmanlike opening for discussion, but it was soon abundantly clear to Anthony that there would be no necessity for him to produce the newspaper picture of Field with which he had come provided.

He passed on, therefore, to the "Shakespeare Arms." This inn proved as barren and unprofitable as the "Fisherman's Rest" had, and he was soon convinced that Field was also entirely unknown as far as this house of refreshment was concerned. As he passed out of the bar, Anthony half-turned and said, "How far's the next pub?"

"Which way, sir? Into Friar's Woodburn or on towards Maidenbridge, Great Bosway, Beechers and Stoke Pelly?"

"The latter."

"Oh, quite close. Under half a mile. Keep straight on—you can't miss it."

Anthony thought he'd have one more try and a few minutes' driving brought him to the "Marie Elizabeth." It was a pretty little inn—"ought to sell sardines," said Anthony to himself as he went in, "not alcoholic liquors." He ordered a drink, offered the landlord a cigarette and soon had the conversation headed in the right direction.

Contrary to his recent experiences, mine host here was well versed in the details of the Fullafold crime, but in relation to the principal reason underlying Anthony's quest, it was soon patent that he was in the same position as his two predecessors at the "Fisherman's Rest" and the "Shakespeare Arms." He had certainly never seen Julian Field in the flesh or ever heard of him as frequenting this locality.

"That Mr. Stanhope, though," went on the landlord, "the gentleman whose house this doctor fellow had been to—now I know him pretty well. Often pops in here when he's on the road with his car. Rare nice gentleman! All the Stanhopes are! His wife and his family— they've all been in here at odd times. Not often mind you—but I've met 'em."

"His son's a big chap—I've seen him," said Anthony.

"What—Mr. Howard—the elder? Proper giant—ain't he? Mr. Dudley's nothing like so big."

"I didn't know he had two sons."

"No? Dudley's the young one. He hasn't been at home now for a year or two. At college somewhere. Seems only the other day he was quite a nipper."

Anthony looked at his watch and drank up. Time was getting on. He had another call to make before he hung up with MacMorran. He bade the ruddy-cheeked landlord of the "Marie Elizabeth" a cheery "good afternoon," and drove the car back to the church. He hoped to find a copy of the burgess roll somewhere by the main door. As he walked through the lovely churchyard, he remembered that the font of this church of St. Mary Magdalene had been the receptacle for the second instalment of the murdered man's clothes.

There was no copy of the burgess roll, however, visible. Anthony wondered which local authority in the neighbourhood was responsible for the local government of Friar's Woodburn. He pushed open the main door of the church and walked to the font. Yes—just a matter of walking a few paces, taking a quick look round to see that the church was empty and then tossing the clothes into the font. Money for old rope! As Anthony stood looking at the font he heard a light cough behind him. Anthony turned. He saw a tall, bent figure at his back, cadaverous of feature and black cassock-clad. The face of the man was emaciated and on his left cheek was a large mole.

"I have been told," said the man in the black cassock, "that the criminal invariably returns to the scene of his crime."

The voice was hollow and Anthony felt a strange chill engulf him as he heard the words of this cadaverous cleric.

Chapter XIII

1

ANTHONY faced the man and smiled. He felt that this was the best thing he could do in the circumstances.

"Good afternoon, sir. A singularly beautiful church—this of yours—if you'll allow me to say so."

"You, sir," said the priest, "were more interested in the font than in my church."

"He fancies himself as Father Brown," came Anthony's quick thought—"if I'm not careful I shall be late for my appointment with MacMorran—he'll be ringing up the local constabulary."

Aloud he said, "Perhaps I was—when you entered. It's almost the first thing that one sees, isn't it? Have I the pleasure of addressing the vicar?"

"You have, sir," replied that gentleman in sepulchral tones—"I am the Rev. Theodore Henson."

Before the Vicar could elaborate his statement, Anthony had rattled on.

"I wonder if you could help me, sir? Actually I came to the church in the first place to see whether I could run across a burgess roll. But you don't appear to have one here."

The vicar shook his head. "Owing to the terrible European war for which the people of this country, utterly godless, I'm sorely afraid—"

Anthony tried a trick of swift evasion. "My main purpose, sir, was to attempt to trace a lady, who, I think, was resident in this neighbourhood up to fairly recently. Unfortunately all I have to go on is her Christian name which is 'Mary.' It was a surname like Evans or Edwards—anyhow I'm pretty certain it began with an 'E.' Can you assist me?"

Anthony felt that the Rev. Theodore Henson was still regarding him suspiciously.

"Most of the people of my parish," said the latter slowly, "are poor. They live and work on the land and at the farms. Was this lady you mention of good social standing?"

Anthony plunged. "Oh—yes. Certainly not of the agricultural class."

"Then I'm afraid that I am unable to help you. I feel certain from what you have told me that your lady friend was not resident in my parish."

"I'm very much obliged, sir," replied Anthony. "In that case I won't detain you any longer." He placed silver in the offertory box near the main door. As he did so, he felt that the vicar had softly padded behind him.

"Good afternoon to you, sir," said Anthony raising his hat. In the porch he paused. He was looking for a parish notice of sorts. There was one there—an appeal to the parishioners for a fund to purchase new hassocks. As Anthony had hoped—it was signed by the Vicar personally. Anthony scanned the signature, "Theodore I. Henson."

As he walked back to his car, two vastly different thoughts conflicted. They were these. One—that the "I" of the Rev. Henson's signature had been formed remarkably like a "J" and two—that the figure of the vicar in the porch, as Anthony had last seen him, looked horribly like a great bird of uncommonly evil omen!

2

Anthony found MacMorran waiting in the saloon bar of Friar's Woodburn's largest inn.

"You're late," said the professional—"it's turned half-past one."

"Sorry, Andrew. Not my fault. Any luck?"

"Not a sausage! Blanks everywhere. Julian Field never came here."

"You mean never came here—to be seen."

"Hallo? Have you got something, then?"

"Not a glimmer, Andrew! As minus sausage as you are. What about this place itself?"

"Well—as you hadn't arrived, I did the necessary off my own bat. For one thing, I thought it would save time. Nothing doing, though. The answer's always a lemon."

"Do they do a lunch here?"

"Of a kind. I've booked a couple. Thought I'd better—we shall be too late for anywhere else."

"Right-o. We'll have a pint now—and then pop in the luncheon room."

Over the lunch, which was distinctly better than MacMorran's pessimism had painted it, Anthony told MacMorran of his recent experiences, with the accent on his encounter with the Vicar of the church of St. Mary Magdalene. MacMorran found the narrative amusing.

"He's been reading the *Sunday Record*."

"He'd been reading something! I haven't the slightest doubt he thinks I'm the murderer for whom the police are hunting. He's a weird and wonderful cross between Simon Felix, Solomon Eagle and Irving in the Dead Heart."

"Perhaps he's on the phone now to Bernays at Four Bridges. Wouldn't be surprised—unless you've been exaggerating things." MacMorran chuckled.

" I never exaggerate things, Andrew. If anything I'm a master of understatement." Anthony grinned. "You know, Andrew," he said, with a change of mood, "I can't altogether get away from the *two* churches—and the two fonts! Why? Why were those clothes of Field's divided in that manner? Why all the trouble? At the risk of monotony—I tell you again—we're still missing the vital clues. They're there all right—it only needs us to light on them. And recognize 'em—when we do light on 'em."

"More in that than in what you said first. At the same time, I'll admit to you, Mr. Bathurst, that I'm getting a decidedly uneasy feeling that we've almost reached the end of our tether. And it isn't often you've heard me say that."

MacMorran sat back and began to fill his pipe. Anthony lit a cigarette.

"We needn't move for half an hour or so. Go on talking! Go on talking about the case. Just as the maggot bites you. Put your thoughts into words—just as the thoughts come to you. Don't bother one iota about logical order or intelligent sequence—just talk. And I'll listen. Maybe you'll show me something, Andrew, in a different light from that in which I've been seeing it. Desperate conditions, old man, need desperate remedies. We've never had a case die on us yet. Start where you like. All I'll do will be to listen. I won't even interrupt."

"Things must be bad, then," replied MacMorran, "but I'll have a go, as you say."

Anthony exhaled smoke from his nostrils and waited. MacMorran burnt his boats. "The thought that's been uppermost in my mind all the morning, arose out of the story that Drake, that carpenter chap, brought us with regard to the blonde he states he saw with Doctor Field in the 'Ram' at Fullafold."

He paused—waiting for what he had come to regard as the inevitable interruption. None came. Anthony smiled. He knew what MacMorran was thinking.

"I say to myself—why hasn't that girl come forward? Field's dial's in all the newspapers. The headlines have screamed his fate. She hasn't come forward, I say to myself, because she's afraid. Which means she may know something. She may even know why Field was killed and who killed him. I then ask myself—innumerable times—where did

'Mary' come front? We've looked for her round Friar's Woodburn. Why? If the blonde in 'The Ram' was Mary, and Field met her in Fullafold, it seems to me that the odds are heavily in favour of her having come from a place the King's Winkworth side of Fullafold. Considering where they met and where the rendezvous was." MacMorran paused again. "Then I run into another set of conflicting ideas. There are these two str-reams. The 'Mary E.' and the two churches! A vicar finds one lot of clothes—the senior curate of another puts his hands on the second consignment. I can't get any tie-up anywhere. Off I go again on yet another tangent—a nude body is found hanging—the cause of death that the bloke's been strangled—and yet a revolver's found near the spot—with evidence that a shot's been recently fired from it. Again—no tie-up that I can see." Another pause from MacMorran. Then he looked straight at Anthony and said, "How long's this going on for? How about you having a cut now and picking the bones out of what I've said? You don't want too much on your plate, otherwise you'll be inclined to miss something."

"All right, Andrew, if that's how you feel, I'll cut in. First of all, I'll take the case of the blonde at 'The Ram.' You say 'she hasn't come forward.' And from there you go on—quite legitimately—to suspect her possible implication with the crime. My reply to that is this. There may be several eminently sound reasons, apart from her complicity, to keep her away from the police. You know Andrew, there are thousands of people in this land of ours who shy at the police on all occasions. I think it's a heritage they retain from the days of their childhood. When they were threatened with the menacing figure of the policeman for every petty misdemeanour. The blonde in 'The Ram' may have a number of excellent reasons for keeping silent about her presence there. Perhaps, for all we know, she had no business there whatever. Ought to have been miles away. Supposing there's a jealous husband and she had come there to meet her lover—"

Anthony stopped suddenly.

"What's the matter? Solved the mystery?"

"No. I had an idea pop up suddenly. That was all. It can wait. I'll go on. You next mentioned the mysterious 'Mary' in terms of where did she come from. With what you then said, Andrew, I'm in full agreement. It's obvious to me now, no matter which way I look at it, she didn't come from the village of Friar's Woodburn. If I had to hazard a guess mine would be more like Stoke Pelly—because I don't think the blonde in 'The Ram' was Mary. I think you'll be tremendously surprised when you hear the truth as to that lady's identity. With regard to a tie-up, as you call it, of the clothes in the churches and of the gun, with the death of Field as we know it—I agree with you again—I can't see the sign of one anywhere. Now I think that covers most, if not all, of what you said. Does it?"

MacMorran nodded. "Pretty well, I think."

"Right. Now I'll do a 'spot of thinking aloud.' You can cut in on it later as I did on your stuff." Anthony closed his eyes and began to speak. "I find *myself* wondering about most features of this extraordinary case. Certainly, so far, the most baffling that has ever come my way. But when I begin to sort out, as it were, all the things which bewilder me, there are one or two which stand out from the rest. The first is the separation of Field's garments for the filling of the fonts. I give that one an undesirable best! No can do! The second is the bewildering maze which tangles up the assignation. Cornelius Steps, Friar's Woodburn, Greenhurst Station, 'The Ram,' Fullafold, and the final *pied-à-terre* in the church porch. There were thistle seeds, don't forget, in the grass on the dead man's shoes. Also there was a beer stain on the sleeve of the dead man's overcoat. And then, thirdly, I come to something, which, to my shame, I seem previously to have completely missed. And that's this. When Field's possessions, salved from the fonts of Holy Baptism, come to be examined in detail, I believe I am correct in saying that the only defections are (a) an unknown sum of money—presumed by Bernays to be in currency note value—and to have been carried originally in Field's wallet, (b) the specimen of Daphne Stanhope's sputum which Field took from her at Stoke Pelly, and (c) Field's Keys. It is this third object which I don't seem to have yet considered. And the strange thing is that when I do consider it and its significance, I get into a worse tangle than ever. Instead of helping—it's yet another point which hinders. Because I argue to myself in this fashion. Some time after the murder, we have the statement from Claudia Field that she was enticed from the house at King's Winkworth and that during her absence thus effected, her dead husband's surgery was entered and well—we'll say searched. Now—presuming that the murderer stole Field's keys in order to have easy and simple access to his victim's house, premises and surgery—why in the name of all that's logical did he climb up the balcony at the back of the house when he got there? From some points of view, I take that to be the most remarkable feature of the case. I'll stop there for the time being. Now you can pull my offering to pieces."

MacMorran nodded. He looked round and saw that the room had emptied. He got up from his chair and knocked the ash from his pipe on a bar of the grate. He then stood in front of the fire and began to talk.

"My own contribution concerning the clothes and the churches is exactly nil. Whenever I begin thinking of them I invariably end up by shrugging my shoulders. But with regard to the things of Field's which we now know are missing I can put up one or two ideas. The missing money from the wallet comes first. I can deal with that at once. That was stolen. Not a doubt of it. By the murderer. There would be neither trouble nor risk for him in disposing of that. The jewellery and the gold wrist-watch and other articles of that kind were a vastly different proposition. As he well knew. When things of that kind are 'hot'—well—there's always a chance that the chap handling them will get burnt. Anything may have happened to the sputum specimen—chucked away probably. Swabs and matters like that don't take up much room—and for myself, I don't think much importance need be attached to the fact that it's missing. The keys, though, are a horse of another colour. That sounds a bit mixed—but you know what I mean. The main point about them, it seems to me—is—was Field's latch-key or door-key amongst them? The key to the house at King's Winkworth. It may not have been. We can't be sure, can we? What happened then was this. Instead of having the vital key in his possession when he arrived at the surgery, the murderer found that this one key which meant so much to him was missing. Therefore—he was forced to enter Field's house by the way we know he did."

MacMorran began to fill his pipe. "There you are. Free, gratis, and for nothing."

"Not bad, Andrew! But it comes to this. We must look farther into it. Bernays must make sure of that point of the key with Claudia Field."

3

Anthony and MacMorran stopped the car at Four Bridges on their way back to Greenhurst. Bernays was in the police station when they inquired for him.

"Good afternoon, gentlemen. As a matter of fact I thought you'd show up before we put the shutters up for the day. Any luck?"

"Not a whisker." The answer was MacMorran's.

"I was afraid not. I went over that Friar's Woodburn ground pretty thoroughly myself. I should have been surprised if I'd missed anything. It's a rare teaser—this case—and no mistake. Still—I have got a couple of items of news for you. Nothing startling. Just follow-up stuff as it were. That's the worst of these cases. So much time taken up in running round on the check-up parts, and then so precious little to show for all the work you've done. Anyhow, Bland's done a couple of jobs of work and I'll report on his findings. Firstly—he's been over to 'The Ram' at Fullafold and had a word therewith old Mrs. Tattersall, the licensee. You'll be remembering that that Drake fellow mentioned her—said she was as blind as a bat or words to that effect. I sent the sergeant over there this morning to see if he could pick anything up. You shall hear what he has to say, he's in the other room."

Bernays went to the door and called to Sergeant Bland. "Mrs. Tattersall," he said curtly—"just tell the Chief about this morning."

Bland smiled his usual face-breaker. "Well—the old girl's not so blind as our friend Drake made out. Not so hot—I'll admit—but she could tell the difference all right between a couple of bob and half an Oxford. I gradually jockeyed her back to the night of 27th October. She remembered Field in my opinion when I described him to her even though she could never be certain of anybody from the standpoint of identification. Her eyes aren't anything like good enough for that. But when I came to mention Drake's glamour-girl—I had a bit of a surprise. What do you gents think she said?"

"No idea," replied MacMorran. Anthony shook his head.

Bland was evidently pleased. "Well—believe it or not," he said, "according to old Mother Tattersall, the lady who we know as Field's blonde was none other than Mrs. Hetherington from 'The Priory.'"

Bland stopped—to let the information sink in presumably—but then went on again. "According to the old girl again—this blonde goes in 'The Ram' pretty regularly. That's the reason old Mother Tattersall reckons she recognized her."

"Go on," said Bernays. The sarcasm was too obvious to be missed.

"Well," said Bland, entirely unabashed, "you know what I mean. I don't set up to be a linguist. Common or garden copper me."

"Where's 'The Priory'?" said MacMorran, "and who's Mrs. Hetherington when she's at home?"

"You mean when she's out, chief," grinned Bland.

"The Priory," said Bernays, "is the big house on the left of the road between here and Greenhurst. You pass it every time you come here in the car from your H.Q. Belongs to a man who's made a rare lot of money out of road haulage. I should know him by sight—but I can't say the same about his missus."

"On a point of order," interrupted Anthony—"is the name 'Hetherington' or 'Etherington'? You can see the direction behind the question."

"Now—don't say I don't sound the old 'aitches,'" returned Sergeant Bland—"the name is Hetherington with the aspirate."

"Pity. I could have borne it the other way. Especially if the Christian name happened to be Mary."

"Means an inquiry," said Bernays—"no matter which way you look at it. But as far as I know—Mrs. Hetherington's all right and above board. Never heard a whisper to the contrary. Have you, sergeant?"

"Not a squeak, sir. That's why I said the news gave me a bit of a jolt when I heard it. I don't know the lady any better than you say you do—but I've certainly never heard anything to her discredit."

"Well, we'll leave the inquiry to you, Sergeant Bland," said MacMorran—"no doubt Inspector Bernays will see to that all right. What's the other job you've done to-day?"

"The other job," said Bernays, "was in connection with the gun that young Chadwick picked up in the ditch. There was a little division of opinion, if you remember, concerning the licence. Mr. Bathurst here was very confident that the gun belonged to Field. If it did—he hadn't taken out a licence for it. Bland's been on the job and has established the fact that no licence for a gun stands in the name of Julian Field."

"Do you hear that?" said MacMorran turning to Anthony.

"I hear! The news is interesting. To me the case persists in growing curiouser and curiouser."

"That's not the adjective I'd give it," growled Bernays—"I can think of several—much more satisfactory. Twice to-day I've had the Chief Constable on the 'phone. 'Not enough progress.' 'Why no arrest?' I told him one or two things—but they weren't what I wanted to say to him. Not by a long chalk. Curiouser—eh? Call it a proper son-of-a-bitch, and you won't be far out."

Bernays snorted with a mixture of indignation and official disappointment.

Anthony rose. "Tell the inspector, chief, that point with regard to Field's keys, will you?"

4

MacMorran was called to the telephone at the "Horse and Groom" soon after dinner in the evening of the same day. Bernays was the speaker.

"That you, chief? Sorry to call you out of the armchair. I thought perhaps you'd like to hear what Bland's got to say in relation to Mrs. Hetherington. Since you left this afternoon he's been along to 'The Priory,' and was lucky enough to find the lady."

"No business going in for that sort of thing—he ought to know better with all his experience," joked the "Yard" inspector, "what's he got to tell me? Anything or nothing?"

"He's here at my elbow," returned Inspector Bernays—"so he can do the talking himself."

"I'm ready and waiting—tell him," said MacMorran.

"That you, chief?" came the voice of Sergeant Bland.

"O.K."

"Well—the inspector suggested I should take a dekko at 'The Priory' after you left this afternoon so I made all the arrangements this end and as soon as I could, I cycled up there. Got there about half-seven. Just after dinner. I got the fag-end of the whiff. After a bit of chinwag, I was shown into the lounge and there was the lady—with her husband—all waitin' to hear the worst! He's a good many years older than 'er—if I'm any judge and from the way 'e looks at 'er—I reckon she's a very cherished possession. You know—thou shalt not covet thy neighbour's wife—or in other words 'ands off! Well—I broke the ice to the happy pair as gently as I could—wrapped it all up nicely and the lad'll bring it round first thing in the morning—you get the idea—and they both of 'em listened with all ears and never said a word for quite a time.

"I give 'em the murder as the Press has reported it—which, naturally, they knew all about—and a bit of Field's comin's and goin's and I shepherds 'im gradually into the bar of the 'Ram' and sits Field down at the table by the fireplace as comfortable as though I'd bin there myself and all ready to order his wallop. Then I mentions the blonde who come and sat with him and the old feller what's married the glamour girl pricks up his ears and begins to look just a trifle worried. Who's bin sittin' in my chair? Then I come across with what old Mother Tattersall 'as told me—and 'bomb's gone!' When he hears this, the old boy's eyes begin to roll. But not so—the lady! Oh dear no. She just laughs it off. Never turns a hair. 'How thrillin', she says—'but not guilty, sergeant. Not this time. I haven't been in the "Ram" since the evenin's turned dark. Sometimes in the summer—yes. But now—no, sergeant. A thousand times no!'"

"Do you think it's O.K., sergeant? Did it strike you that way?" queried MacMorran.

"Well, chief, 'ang on a bit and you'll hear some more. Directly she came across with the 'not me, sergeant,' she turns to the old boy and says—'27th October, so the sergeant says—I was here with you all the evenin'. Don't you remember?' 'Can't say that I do,' growls the old boy—'you know I never can remember dates. What were we doin'?' 'We listened to the radio, my dear. Don't you remember now? Butterfly'—I'm sure she said 'Butterfly,' chief—'was broadcast from the Garden. You and I listened nearly the whole of the evening.' 'We certainly did,' says the old boy—'but was that the night? That's the vital point, I don't know!' Well—Mrs. H. turns to me, 'Sergeant—you see and you hear, don't you? All that evening I was here with my husband—listening to poor Sheenie's lovely music.' I scarpered soon after that, chief, but since I got back, I've checked up in the *Radio Times*. This Mrs. Butterfly joke certainly *was* on the radio on that particular evening, which seems to let Mrs. H. out, and Bob's your flippin' uncle. Problem—chums—can old Mother Tattersall see—or can she? So long, chief. Proper old blank wall—ain't it?"

MacMorran hung up and walked back to Anthony to pass on the news of the Hetherington alibi. Anthony listened carefully and attentively to the MacMorran version of the Bland visit.

"Taking it by and large," concluded MacMorran, "it would appear to place Mrs. H. in the clear and almost confirm Drake's judgment of Mrs. Tattersall's vision. Do you agree?"

"I think so, Andrew." Anthony sat back in his armchair and put the magazine he had been reading, open and across his knees. "Personally I never thought 'The Ram' blonde was this lady. The wish parented the thought, too, Andrew. So you see I'm not at all despondent over the Bland latest." He picked up the magazine again.

"The clueless crime," muttered MacMorran.

"Clueless?" Anthony echoed the word. "On the contrary, my dear Andrew! Far too many ruddy clues. Our job's to pick out the true from the false. The wheat from the tares. At the moment—I can see three paths in front of me. Each one has a finger-post. On each post I can plainly see the words 'Solution 1 mile.' But do I know which of the three to take? I do not, Andrew. And until I *do* know—I'm not travelling one of 'em. Not until I've made up my mind."

Anthony resumed his reading.

"When the hell's that likely to be?" said MacMorran. "Sometime to-morrow, I fancy," replied Mr. Bathurst.

Chapter XIV

1

MacMorran nodded towards the clock on the mantelpiece. "What about some shut-eye? About time, isn't it?"

Anthony shook his head. "You go, Andrew. I think I'll stay up for a little. I don't feel the least bit tired and I'm rather drawn to a spot of intensive thinking. You know—one of my whole-hoggers. It's

133 | THE SWINGING DEATH

half-past ten now. I'll stick it down here till midnight. You buzz off when you like."

"I think I'll go now. If you aren't tired—I am. Not so young as I was. I'll be seeing you, then."

Anthony waved a hand and MacMorran cleared out. As the door closed behind him, one of the attendants came in from the bar entrance.

"Anybody about?" inquired Anthony.

"No, sir. You seem to be about the last up—from what I can see of things."

"Well, then—do you mind putting out the light? I'll finish my smoke by the firelight. I'll be all right."

The man obliged and Anthony curled up in the armchair in the darkness, broken only by the red glow of the fire. Anthony stared into the heart of it. For one of his habitual exercises in intensive thought, he needed quiet and darkness. More than one problem in the past which for a time had seemed invulnerable had given its solution to him under the conditions in which he now sat. As he had said to MacMorran earlier in the evening, he could see three paths in front of him. Each with its finger-post. And as he had also said to the inspector, he couldn't make up his mind which was the right one to take.

The first finger-post went by way of Philip Stanhope and Stoke Pelly. There was something about the Stanhope atmosphere—for the life of him he didn't know what exactly—that didn't seem "right." And yet the evidence—and it came from the four winds—not one—proved conclusively that Field had left Stoke Pelly railway station—alive. But out of this visit to Daphne Stanhope—one or two matters rather worried Anthony. The rose from the garden was one, the missing keys were a second and the loss of the sputum was a third. Anthony decided after a time to pass Stanhope and have a close look at finger-post number two.

This travelled by way of Claudia Millicent Field. At her side, Anthony visualized the tall figure of Ernest Courtenay, the man whom he had so far seen through the glass of a window only. Assuming that the Bernays-MacMorran version of the eternal triangle were the wrong one, and that an injured husband had not murdered Field for the age-old reason, it seemed to Anthony that there *was* the possibility of Courtenay having played the role of Bywaters to Field's Percy Thompson. Let's suppose, he argued to himself, that Field walked into the bar of the 'Ram' at Fullafold and ran into the blonde unexpectedly and the blonde was Claudia. She and Courtenay, who was near at hand, say, could have killed Field after that—and raced back to the surgery at King's Winkworth. Why? There was documentary evidence there which incriminated Courtenay and therefore had to be destroyed. The telephone call could have been Courtenay—not far off—but why break in and climb the rear balcony if they had the keys? There was a snag there—an undoubted snag! Unless the keys had been lost. Then why again should Claudia marry Julian Field at all—if she were in love with Courtenay? Still—that kind of thing had happened often during our rough island story. Two strings to a bow—the wrong choice—and hasty post-marital repentance, followed by the inevitable swing of the Cupid-manipulated pendulum back to the other love. That was a possibility. Courtenay, too, had been with Claudia for a longish spell when Anthony had spent the day in King's Winkworth. That was a solid fact—not a chance conjecture. Anthony shook his head, uncurled himself in the armchair and leant forward to gaze again into the fire.

The third sign-post! There were no names on this third signpost—yet. Merely three sets of initials, "G.M.A.," "J.D.M." and "T.J.H." Those regular payments to Field. Payment's in cash—none by cheque. Was there just the flimsy chance that Field had "worked the black"? You couldn't escape the fact that "A" "M", and "H" fitted Atherton, the Vicar of St. Mark's, Fullafold, Moffatt, his senior curate, and Henson, the Vicar of St. Mary Magdalene's, Friar's Woodburn. Against that, though, was the discrepancy of Henson's second initial. His name was "Ingram." And Ingram commences with the letter "I"—not the letter "J." Besides, it bordered on the fantastic to think that a doctor of Field's standing would be in a position to put the screw on three priests in holy orders. One—possibly. At a pinch, perhaps, two!

But three in a trot? All of whom resided in the same district? Not so likely!

.Anthony rubbed his top lip with his forefinger—that takes a lot of believing he said to himself. Too much—altogether. And yet—there was the other angle of consideration. Field's body was hung in Fullafold church porch and his clothes divided between the fonts of that church and the parish church of Friar's Woodburn. Why? For the ten thousandth time—why? Anthony began to consider the Friar's Woodburn assortment. He had memorized the various articles when Bernays had shown them to him after the Rev. Henson's find and he thought he would have no difficulty in drawing on that memory now. Hat, overcoat, trousers, scarf, tie, soft shirt with collar to match, gloves, shoes, ring, wrist-watch, nail file, cigarette lighter, cigarette case, handkerchief, wallet, pen, stethoscope, six halfpennies, and a rose which by any other name would have smelt as sweet or looked as dead. Outside the purely sartorial, there were ring, watch, nail file, lighter, cigarette case, wallet, fountain pen, stethoscope, money and the rose.

Anthony sat up suddenly! Bolt upright in the armchair. His blood raced through his veins. He had seen the light! The vital clues were there! But stay one moment, there was something wrong—nail file, cigarette lighter, case, wallet, pen—no—there wasn't! They fitted! Of course they did! Anthony stood up. He knew why Field's clothes had been divided! And why the hell hadn't he known it days before? As he lit a cigarette, on the way upstairs to his bedroom, his hand was unsteady. But, oh boy! "And in the past," he said to himself as he mounted the stairs, "I've called myself a detective!"

2

Dudley Stanhope, who had been playing scrum-half that afternoon for the Cambridge XV against Southshire on the county ground at Spears, had arranged to cut across to Stoke Pelly for dinner at "Giffords." He mentioned this to his skipper as he propelled his eleven stone and a half of muscle and whipcord into the steam of the hot bath.

"Shan't be coming along with the rest of you fellows," said Dudley. "I'm dashing off home. Dinner with the guv'nor. Only a few miles from here—across country. So if you miss me at the 'beer and shove ha'penny' gathering—you'll know why it is."

When he arrived at "Giffords" his mother greeted him in the true Stanhope manner. "Dudley! Just in time! Dinner will be on the table in less than a quarter of an hour."

"Whizzo!"

"Dad and Howard are in the dining-room."

"Good news all round—eh? Any other news?"

"I suppose there is—in a way. Dad'll tell you all about it when you get in there with him. Where's the car?"

"Round at the back. I didn't shove it in the garage. I mustn't be late getting away. You're very quiet. What's the mystery? Anything wrong?"

"Of course not. Don't be silly. Did you win?"

"This afternoon? Oh—yes. 13-3. Good scrap, though."

"Did you score?"

Dudley Stanhope laughed. "Managed to crawl over the line near the corner flag just before no side. The wing-three had done all the work, though. Piece of cake for me."

"Go and tell dad—he'll be delighted. What about Twickenham on that certain Tuesday in December? Cert?"

"Don't you believe it. No Blues awarded yet. Still—livin' in hopes."

"Good. Now go and talk to dad and Howard."

"You seem terribly keen to get me in there. What's cooking?"

Daphne Stanhope laughed. "A very tasty loin of pork, my lad. A fine Black Hampshire has been sacrificed. Which you'll be getting your teeth into within a very few minutes. Now—for the last time—scram!"

Dudley Stanhope flashed another look of inquiry towards his mother, which, however, elicited no more response from her than had attended his previous efforts. Slowly he walked into the dining-room. His father and his elder brother greeted him warmly.

"Victory?" queried Philip.

"Thou sayest it," replied Dudley—"13 points to 3. Good scrap on the whole. They made the 'Varsity go—though."

"I expected they would. These county forwards are big and strong—especially in the loose. Who was hooking for them?"

"The skipper. Hefty lad! Very audible, too. All through the game. Tears off a very juicy strip. I say—" Dudley jerked his head towards the room where his mother was—"what's come over the mater? Sounds all mysterious! What's amiss?"

"We've had a visitor."

"What do you mean—a visitor? What about?"

"Perhaps I should have said we've had visitors. Scotland Yard."

"No! Field?"

"Ah—ha!"

"Nothing in that. Merely routine inquiry. No reason for mother to get all hot and bothered. You agree, don't you?" Philip Stanhope made no immediate reply. Dudley turned to Howard and put the same question.

Howard grinned. "Every time, Dudley, As you say—routine. But you know what mother is, always looking for the crinkled hair in the wood pile."

"Well," said Philip Stanhope, "let's face facts, all of us. Neither minimizing nor emphasizing the position. The local police are stymied. The natural consequence follows. They've asked for the customary help from Scotland Yard. All well and good—and according to Cocker. We mustn't mind the inquiries coming. As Dudley very sensibly points out, they're bound to. And none of us must mind if we're bothered a bit and questioned—because, as I see it, everybody in the least connected with the affair must expect something of that sort to happen. Against all that generalization, there's another point." Philip Stanhope paused.

"What's that," said Dudley.

"One of the two people who came here was Bathurst. Anthony Bathurst."

"Well—what about it?"

"Well—it struck me that he might come again. You're aware of his reputation. And if he does—your mother will worry. Which is the last thing I should desire to happen."

"Thinking of her health again?"

Philip Stanhope made no answer. Dudley came back again. "I take it you satisfied them that we couldn't have had anything to do with the fellow's murder? That was simple enough, surely?"

"Oh—yes—I think so. That followed as a matter of course—didn't it? Bathurst, though, thought he had met mother before."

"Well—what the heck did that matter?"

"Mother told him he was mistaken."

"Well? I should say she was right."

"He fancied she might be an Appleton."

Dudley stared.

"That's it," said Howard Stanhope. "Appleton was the name."

"Well—what about it? What's the point?"

"Mother said that her maiden name had been Bartlett."

"Quite true," said Dudley—"well?"

"It struck me as strange," said his father—"that's why I mentioned it to you."

"I still stick to my original idea—what I said at the beginning—routine inquiry. Mother mustn't mind and she mustn't worry about it. Good lord! I say—that roast pig smells whizzo! I think it must be on the way in."

Dudley Stanhope was correct in his conjecture. His mother and sister brought in the dinner with the maid hovering in the background. Dudley put the tip of his finger lightly on his mother's nose.

"Take that worried look off your pretty face. In other words—count your blessings, mother o' mine."

"How do you know I don't," smiled back Daphne Stanhope.

3

Almost simultaneously with Dudley Stanhope dining in his father's house, "Giffords," at Stoke Pelly, Claudia Field, the widow of the murdered doctor, was dining a deux with her cousin, Ernest Courtenay. Not in the village of King's Winkworth, not in the city of London itself, but in the seaside town of Spears. The same Spears which had welcomed the Cambridge Rugger XV but a few hours previously.

Courtenay had picked Claudia up just outside King's Winkworth and had kept his car at a steady bat nearly all the way to the coast. "We'll have dinner at the 'Ship,'" announced Ernest Courtenay—"can't do better. And we ought to be able to get a spot of dancing afterwards. You usually can there."

Claudia had not demurred at the suggestion and half an hour later sat facing Ernest Courtenay over a table in the "Ship" dining-room.

"Soft lights," quoted Courtenay, "and sweet music. Plus good food and drink—what could be nicer? I confess that I can't think of anything. Can you?"

Claudia shook her head. Her lips were parted and her eyes were smiling. Anyone who knew her and her circumstances would have said that she had had the courage to put her recent sorrow away from her. Courtenay looked both fit and attractive. Besides being tall, lithe and slender, he was fair, frank and fresh, and the possessor of a most determined-looking chin. He handed the menu to his cousin.

"What is it? Made your choice?"

Claudia looked. "Pheasant, I think, Ernest. And ice pudding. Looks the most appetizing on paper."

"I'm with you."

Courtenay ordered. Everything about him was cool, calm and collected, as the cliché has it. He had always been sure of himself—had Ernest Courtenay. He looked across the table at Claudia. "Glad to note the improvement."

"Pour moi," replied Claudia, "glad to hear re noted gladness on your part."

"Yes," went on Ernest Courtenay, "didn't like the physical signs at all—a few days ago. Obvious signs of cracking up. Caused me undue perturbation. Ernest of the ilk Courtenay has but one pretty cousin. And if she accepts physical deterioration—well—one from one—leaves none!"

"Yes," said Claudia. "I was worried. You're quite right. I was hellishly worried. But here's our grub. Wait a sec."

Claudia attended to her cousin's wants and then prepared to enjoy her pheasant. "Goody," she said, "it's a 'gamey' bird. That's just how I like it."

Courtenay nodded and then headed her back again. "And why exactly was my cousin Claudia so worried? The word was worried—wasn't it—not distressed?"

"H'm. Worried."

"Well—tell me why. Don't be so cagey."

"I'm still worried," went on Claudia—"not so much. Nothing like so much. But it hasn't all gone. There's still just a suspicion left."

"My question still stands," said Courtenay. "I won't insult your intelligence by repeating it again."

"You want to know why I'm worried? That can be answered very simply, Ernest. I don't think the police authorities are anything like satisfied."

Courtenay didn't bat an eyelid. His face held the same fixity of purpose that it invariably did. "Well," he said, "I should think that's fairly obvious. You haven't let out anything particularly profound. There's no arrest—and nobody even detained. I shouldn't think the police authorities were satisfied!"

"I wasn't worried at all," went on Claudia, "when I was with that inspector on any of the occasions. I was distressed—as you say—naturally—you can't accept the fact that your husband's been murdered without a jolt—you can take that from me, Ernest—but when Bathurst came to King's Winkworth and put me through the hoop generally—well—I felt vastly different. There wasn't much he missed, believe me. Not even you." Before Courtenay could come in, Claudia went on—"there it's out now. I didn't intend to tell you that—ever."

Courtenay's sangfroid seemed a trifle disturbed. "Me? You say he didn't miss me? You didn't give me a hint of that when you 'phoned me to tell me he'd gone. Why didn't you?" Claudia pushed away her plate.

"That's a simple one to answer. I couldn't at the time. Because—you see—I didn't know."

Courtenay frowned. "Well how do you come to know about it now, then? What's happened in the meantime? As far as I can see—there's been no—"

Claudia interrupted him. "He's bringing the ice pudding. It looks pretty wizard. I congratulate you on your choice of places, Ernest. The 'Ship' has got all that it takes."

"Blast the ruddy ice pudding. Tell me about the great Bathurst and the insignificant me."

"I'm going to." Claudia poised her spoon for attack. "You mustn't be so impatient. I've been married over a year—I've learned to exercise restraint."

Courtenay grinned. This was more like the old Claudia, the Claudia whom he had known before she became the wife of Julian Field.

"Listen—and I'll tell you all about it. You know the pastry-cook's almost opposite the house? Opposite 'Barton's.'"

"I should say so. 'Bulmer's.' Morning coffee show. Coffee and buns—elevenses."

"You've got it. Well—our friend Bathurst was in there. Went in there—after I'd told him I couldn't see him until the afternoon. Remember?"

"What about it? Nothing in that. Where did you expect him to go? To the Museum? He couldn't, my girl—King's Winkworth doesn't possess one."

Claudia went on. "He was in there a long time. I know this—because Sheila—the girl who serves in the shop—has told me so since. At least—I've no doubt from what she says that it was he who was in there."

For once Courtenay's calmness deserted him. "Well—supposing he was? You women amuse me. You're all the same. The slightest little thing and it's talked about and magnified—and—er—exaggerated—until—oh—words fail me!"

Claudia patted the sleeve of his coat. "What you need, my lad, is a little more self-control. Besides Bathurst being in there so long—there's this. He saw you come away from me. Sheila's got the full record. Now listen—if you can! What I'm most concerned about is what the long-tongued Sheila may have tossed into the flames to make 'em burn better! Because I happen to know that the little hussy's got a tongue as long as a week. Now—do you see?"

Courtenay found cigarettes. Claudia stirred coffee as she sat and waited for his reactions. He nodded slowly.

"You mean that when Bathurst did eventually get let in—he'd already had a basinful of you and me." He nodded again. "Yes—I see what you mean. The ground had already been prepared by this girl at Bulmer's. Yes—very likely! Did he question you a lot?"

"Oh—yes. But nearly always with regard to Julian. Professionally—mostly. I can't truthfully say that he showed any disposition to inquire closely into my story. I was a fool, Ernest—I never ought to have agreed to what you suggested. I ought to have turned it down flat. Even now—we don't know that we weren't seen. We can't feel sure about it. Supposing anybody knew us in that pub?"

Courtenay leaned forward over the table and lit Claudia's cigarette for her. "Don't panic. I told you that before. Same advice. Different occasion. Never panic. Nothing's ever been gained yet by losing one's head."

"Ernest," said Claudia very seriously, "tell me. And tell me absolutely truthfully—please. Supposing Anthony Bathurst did find out? I wouldn't put it past him. What would your story be? Have you thought?"

Courtenay leant forward again and fixed her with his clear and steady gaze. Before he spoke, he exhaled smoke from his nostrils. "Claudia Field," he said in a strangely cold, hard, tone—"answer me this and answer me truthfully. Who killed your husband—Julian Field?"

There was an interval of a second or so—before Claudia answered. With the utmost composure and in a voice as even and steady as Courtenay's had been hard and cold, "I haven't the slightest idea," she said.

Courtenay nodded at the words and then relaxed. "Good for you, Claudia Millicent Field. You stick to that story, no matter what's said to you. Don't ever budge half an inch from it. And then you'll find that your clever friend Bathurst will continue to look round at the case in the same way that he's doing now. Looking like Hercules with a big sponge in his mitt and the doors of the Augean stables just opening."

Claudia shook her head. "I wish I felt as confident as you do. But I don't. I admit I don't. I'm at a disadvantage. You haven't met Anthony Bathurst at close quarters. I have! That makes a difference." Claudia knocked her cigarette ash into a tray. "Any dust we chuck about will miss his eyes by yards."

She paused suddenly as though her thoughts had gone off in an entirely different direction. She clutched at his arm.

"Ernest," she said—"I was nearly forgetting—something I've been going to ask you for some time now. It's about Bathurst—so you'll be interested. As I told you—he asked *many* questions—especially when he was in the surgery. Chiefly in relation to Julian and the practice. And he very cleverly made *me* remember what Julian had said to me that afternoon when he went out. I told you that. That bit about persuading a reluctant lady." Courtenay nodded. "But there was something else—something I *haven't* told you. And—do you know,

Ernest—I feel it's terribly *important*. I'll tell you why. Anthony Bathurst was extremely interested in one of Julian's paying-in books. He didn't say so to me—never breathed a word! *That's* why I think it was important. Because he kept it to himself. He didn't know—but I could often see things that he was looking at over his shoulder. He was terribly interested in three sets of initials that he found cropping up more than once in this paying-in book. I looked at the book afterwards to make sure what they were." Claudia paused again. Courtenay was watching her intently all the time and made no interruption.

"I've remembered them," continued Claudia, "they were 'G.M.A.,' 'T.J.H.' and 'J.D.M.' Do any of them mean anything to you, Ernest? Don't answer at once. Think it over before you reply."

Courtenay fell in with her suggestion. He was in no hurry to make denial. After a time he spoke.

"I can make only one suggestion, Claudia. That sky-pilot chap who rolled up at the inquest with the first packet of Julian's clothes—his name was the Rev. John Moffatt. But there was no 'D' for any second name that he might or might not have had. That's the only suggestion I have to offer."

Claudia's brow puckered into a frown. She was endeavouring to remember something. "No," she remarked at length—"it's no good. I can't get anywhere from any of them. I had thought of the Moffatt man—but I think the 'D' puts him out of court. Had he been blessed with a second Christian name it would have come out at the inquest. Bound to have."

Courtenay looked at his wrist-watch. "We ought to be moving. Don't want to cut it too fine at the other end."

"No. Where will you drop me, Ernest?"

"I'll run past your place and pull up round the corner by the flour-mill. It's a pretty dark spot and I don't suppose many people will be taking the air in King's Winkworth by the time we get back."

"That'll suit me nicely. And I think we're wise. It would be extraordinarily foolish of us to set the tongues wagging still more. That's the worst of living in a one-eyed hole like King's Winkworth. Talk about a hotbed of scandal! It's just about the worst place I know."

Ernest Courtenay called the waiter and settled the bill. Despite all his protestations, he wasn't feeling as comfortable as he made out.

4

The drive home from Spears to King's Winkworth was uneventful. Ernest Courtenay, for him, was unusually silent. Almost all the conversation came from Claudia Field. When the car reached King's Winkworth, Courtenay drove past his father's house on the corner of the Four Bridges Road and also past Field's surgery. A few minutes' driving then brought him into the shadow of the old flour-mill. As Courtenay had anticipated, the place was deserted at this time of night. He stopped the car in the shadow of the big granary-hoist and Claudia put her hand on the handle of the door. Courtenay stopped her.

"Don't get out for a minute or two. I want to talk to you."

"My dear Ernest," she replied, "we shan't do any good by keeping on about it. For one thing we shall fray our nerves and simply wear them to pieces."

"Like hell we will," retorted her cousin contemptuously. "No—what I was going to say to you was this. Do you think you'll have a return visit from this Bathurst chap?"

"I can't say definitely, of course—but I'm inclined to think I shall. Why?"

"Well—if he should turn up again—you know what to say and you know how to act. Personally, I think the chances are we're in the clear. If we'd been spotted—we should have heard about it by now."

Claudia was silent. Ernest Courtenay came again. "Well—don't you agree with me?"

"I don't know that I do. They may be keeping it back on purpose. To have something up their sleeve. The police often adopt that course."

This time, Courtenay was silent. Then he shook his head with sudden decision. "No—they'd have been after me long before this. I feel certain they'd never have allowed that to lie. Especially bearing in mind what you told me about that little gas-bag—Sheila. Bathurst would have jumped at it. No—I still say we're in the clear. And if you keep your head and don't panic—that's where we shall stay. Have you got that?"

"If I haven't got it by now, I never shall. Well—anything more to say to me?"

"I don't think so. Not at the moment. Give me a ring any time you feel I ought to know anything. Don't delay, darling. You know what they say about delays."

Claudia nodded and got out of the car. Before she closed the door she leant forward and kissed Courtenay on the lips.

"Good night, Ernest, dear. I'll be a good girl and remember to do all you've told me. Give me a minute or two's start before you cruise back. And I'll see you on Wednesday as we arranged."

She fluttered her hand to him and disappeared into the darkness and gloom of the November night. Courtenay sat at the wheel and waited in the shadow of the flour-mill.

Chapter XV

1

By one of those strange coincidences which Fate or Destiny—have it as you will—so often decides to play, it must have been just about the time of Ernest Courtenay's conversation with Claudia Field in the "Ship" at Spears, that Anthony decided to "have a look" at Courtenay himself. He discussed with Andrew MacMorran not only the question as to whether he should pay a second visit to King's Winkworth, but also the conditions of the line of approach.

"Treat Courtenay as a witness," said the Scotland Yard inspector—"you can play the King's Winkworth card all the time. That's what I should do—and you'll probably succeed in getting a good deal more out of him than I shall. Anyhow—that's the line I should take."

The result was that Courtenay's fears that Anthony would make a second call upon his cousin Claudia were not realized, but it is doubtful whether the alternative procedure—that of visiting him personally—brought him any degree of satisfaction.

Anthony drove to the Courtenay mansion on the corner of the Four Bridges Road in less time than he should have. His conscience was clear, however, because the road all the way had been in a like state. He looked for the second time on this house of red-brick, the garden of which ran down to the river-bank, and thought many things. The white-aproned maid who handled his card with almost fastidious manipulation, lifted the places where her eyebrows had once been and asked Anthony if he had an appointment with Mr. Ernest Courtenay.

"Not exactly," replied Anthony, "but all the same, I think he'll see me. You'll find he'll know the name."

In this statement he was proved correct. Mr. Ernest Courtenay would see him.

Anthony was ushered into what evidently was a morning-room. As he had anticipated, Courtenay's approach lacked nothing in courtesy or personal charm.

"Sit down, Mr. Bathurst," he said, his face smiling. "I can guess why you're here. In a way. It's on account of my cousin's trouble—no doubt?"

Anthony thought—"how much do you know?"

Courtenay thought exactly the same. But the knowledge in each instance was not identical.

"You must forgive me troubling you," said Anthony—"but the truth is we're up against a singularly entangled problem. And it occurred to us that you might be in a position to help us. If only in a comparatively small way."

Courtenay still smiled. He was a good-looking bloke—there were no two opinions about that. As he smiled, he spoke.

"Only too delighted, old chap. If you can tell me—how! Because, candidly, that's what I can't see."

Anthony waited for Courtenay to go on. He wanted Courtenay to talk. But Ernest hadn't come downstairs the day before yesterday and talking was the very last exercise he intended.

"Well," continued Anthony, accepting the situation willy-nilly, "Chief Detective Inspector MacMorran, of Scotland Yard, who's now in charge of the case—as you're aware in all probability—thinks that you're the one person in King's Winkworth who may be in a position to afford us certain assistance. You occupy a unique niche, as it were. Not only did you know the murdered man—you are also a blood relation of his widow. You have all three of you resided in the same little town."

"That's true. As far as it goes. Which surely isn't very far."

Anthony felt positive that Courtenay's tone held relief. Courtenay went on.

"I can deal only with generalities. Julian Field and I weren't bosom companions—or anything like that. He was the King's Winkworth medico—he married my cousin Claudia. They're both statements of fact—but they aren't very much more than that."

Courtenay shut up like the closure of a snapped trap. Anthony knew that he would be compelled to ask a direct question.

"That's a pity. I had hoped—shall we say—for certain different conditions. But you tell me they aren't there. Julian Field. To your knowledge, Mr. Courtenay—had he any enemies? It's a time-honoured question, I know, hoary with age—but there you are—I must ask it."

Courtenay hesitated. Of the hesitation, there wasn't the vestige of a doubt. "I shouldn't be surprised," was his reply.

"That's merely general, isn't it?"

"Oh—quite. It would be impossible for me to go beyond generalities. For instance—I couldn't particularize at all. No names. Not because I wouldn't—because I couldn't. I'm making this statement, you understand, from my own judgment of Julian Field as I knew him."

"As a doctor—or as a man?"

Courtenay seemed a trifle surprised at this last question. "Er—as a man. More as a man than—er—professionally."

"Why?"

"Well—he wasn't everybody's cup of tea. He and I were always very good friends—but he was decidedly aggressive—even pugnacious—and there's no doubt, I should say, that he rubbed a good many people the wrong way."

"Yes—that may be so, Mr. Courtenay—but mightn't it apply to a good many of us? This is murder. Dislike—disagreement—they may lead to a certain unpleasantness, I admit. But murder is activated by hate—or fear. By one of the major emotions, surely?"

Courtenay evaded the main issue. "Yes. I suppose you're right. But there you are—I've answered your questions to the best of my ability. I can't do any more."

There were no smiles on Courtenay's face now. Anthony resolved to play his last card. The "bluff" card which so far he had kept carefully tucked away out of sight.

"I'll take you into my confidence, Mr. Courtenay. I'll tell you something that the police are up against. A strange story has been brought to them. It concerns a lady. A mysterious lady whom so far we haven't been successful in tracing. We have a detailed description of her from the person who brought the story in."

"Oh—and where was this?"

"In the bar of a pub at—"

Before Anthony could complete the sentence Courtenay had changed colour. He paled distinctly. With a big effort, however, he pulled himself together again.

"Fullafold," came Anthony's conclusion.

"Fullafold—eh?" Courtenay had recovered. "That's close enough—to the doings—isn't it?"

"As you say. Close enough—in all conscience."

Anthony watched him closely. Courtenay had most certainly recovered his self-possession.

"Well—if you have the detailed description of her—as you asserted you have—surely it shouldn't be too much trouble to identify her?"

Anthony shook his head. "I'm afraid it's not such a simple task as it may seem. And we certainly haven't run her to earth yet. Although, of course, that may come along at any moment. No—descriptions may be carefully given—and yet fit half a dozen people. Fair hair—medium height—blue eyes—all that sort of thing—you know what I mean. I've no doubt you've noticed that yourself."

Courtenay made no betrayal of feelings. He fended off the awkwardness to the manner born. "Oh—yes. I take your point. I have noticed it." Anthony grasped another nettle.

"Where—in your opinion, Mr. Courtenay, should we look for the murderer of Julian Field? You knew him and he practised here in the town where you reside."

"You flatter me," responded Courtenay drily.

"Not at all. I regard your opinion as distinctly valuable."

"Thanks! Timeo Danaos et dona ferentes."

"Believe me—it's not so bad as all that," Anthony smiled.

"I should look for a jealous husband," said Courtenay—"and I should look for him amongst Field's patients. The wife in the case would be the patient, of course. Don't forget the broken journey at

Greenhurst and the flower of Stanhope's that Field shoved in his buttonhole."

Anthony frowned. "All Mrs. Field says is opposed to that idea. She insists that she and her husband were delightfully in love."

Courtenay shrugged his shoulders. "Loyalty is not extinct. And my cousin Claudia is an exceptional woman. You should be able to draw your own conclusions."

"I see. That's the form your explanation would take. Well—I admit that it's eminently feasible." Anthony rose. "I won't delay you then, Mr. Courtenay, any longer. Many thanks for your kindness. I feel that you've assisted me considerably."

"Only too delighted, old chap. Sorry I haven't been able to tell you more. But as I told you—I'm merely on the fringe of things."

"I suppose so. How was Field socially? Did he mix much? Politics? Church? Freemasonry? Sport? Anything like that?"

Courtenay smiled. "I can answer all those. Quite a change—eh? He was a member of the Conservative Club, of the local lawn tennis club and of the Viscount Valencay Lodge of Freemasons. Next year he'd have been W.M. I don't think religion troubled him overmuch. Don't forget he hasn't been in King's Winkworth so very long. Three years—not much more. He walked into a ready-made practice when Wolff shuffled off—lucky chap."

"What sort of a chap was Wolff?"

"An Austrian—I believe. Made a big reputation."

"Clever?"

"If you ask me—a little too ruddy clever. Glib—and knew all the answers. But there—you don't want me to tell you anything about foreigners. Candidly—I hate the sight of 'em. And what's more I wouldn't let 'em into this country as we do. Few of 'em are any class."

"That's a little too sweeping, Mr. Courtenay—but I think I know what you mean. Well—good-bye—and as I said—many thanks."

Courtenay waited for the sound of car wheels rolling away. When he was satisfied he went to the telephone and dialled a number. When he spoke, he said—after the preliminaries of explanation—"you were right. Things are not so good. They've got something."

He listened for the reply and spoke again. "Now—look—he didn't score a single point against us—and if I'm any judge—what—all right—at Twickenham then on Tuesday week. One o'clock sharp. In the big car park."

2

It had been Anthony's intention to kill two birds with one stone when he had set out from Greenhurst that morning for his talk with Ernest Courtenay at King's Winkworth. He had not, however, mentioned the second bird to Andrew MacMorran. The nest of this second bird was the Vicarage of St. Mark's, Fullafold. Anthony had spotted the site of the vicarage near the foot of the slope on the Fullafold side—when he had gone there with Inspector Bernays. It was an old-fashioned rambling house, mainly built of stone and Anthony rang the bell with a certain amount of misgiving.

In the next few minutes, if he were successful in obtaining access to the vicar, he would have to tread with an excess of care and with all the discretion he possessed. To his pleasure, the vicar himself answered the summons of the bell. To Anthony's eye he looked a man in the middle sixties. He was unusually tall—inches over six feet and in his prime must have been an extremely powerful man, physically. Although he looked like a soldier, turned priest, his face was scholarly and on the whole kindly. But there were fires in his eyes, fires which in the earlier years of his manhood, must have burned fiercely and brightly.

"Yes," he said—the tone was a shade detached perhaps—"what can I do for you?"

"Good afternoon, sir," said Anthony, "have I the privilege of addressing the vicar?"

"Yes. You have. What is it that—"

Anthony presented his card. A shadow crossed the face of the Vicar of St. Mark's.

"May I have—say—a few minutes' conversation with you, sir?"

After a slightly perceptible suggestion of hesitancy, the vicar half-turned and said courteously, "Come in, Mr. Bathurst."

They went to the vicar's study. Anthony was found a comfortable chair. "I presume this visit is concerned with the dreadful business of Dr. Field."

"Yes, sir. With which your church has been so unhappily connected. In two ways. The body in the porch—and the clothes which your curate, the Rev. Moffatt, subsequently discovered in the font."

The vicar smiled. There was sadness in the smile and the veriest soupçon of humour. "In respect of neither of which contingencies can my poor church be blamed," he said, the smile lingering on his face.

"Very true, sir. But in the course of my investigation of the case, I have asked myself the question more than once, if the choice of your church and of your font were deliberately foundationed."

The vicar nodded. "So have I. And I am satisfied that I have found the right answer. The choice was deliberate. But in a different way, I fancy, from the way you meant. My church was chosen because of its loneliness. Right at the summit of the slope of thistles. Few people use my churchyard on the dark nights of late autumn and winter. For no other reason was it so dishonoured amongst churches. At least—that is my solution. And with regard to the desecration of *my* font—well—my reverend brother at Friar's Woodburn was singled out similarly—was he not?"

Again that smile of sadness—almost of sympathy. This time it was Anthony who nodded.

"At times, sir, my thoughts have run parallel with yours. At other times, sir, there have been other manners. The parallels have been missing. Which is why I am worrying you this afternoon."

Anthony paused. The Vicar of St. Mark's bowed his head. "I apportion no blame to you for that. Indeed—I can understand it. I am a great sinner, Mr. Bathurst, like the rest of us, but I do not think that I'm an unreasonable man."

"That's very charming of you, sir. Because it prepares the way for me to ask you a question. If the question doesn't hold water—I ask your pardon in advance for asking it. At the same time, I give you my word of honour that I'm not asking it idly."

The fierce eyes smouldered. "What is the question, Mr. Bathurst? Let me be the judge of it."

"Correct me if I am wrong. You are the Rev. Godfrey M. Atherton?"

The Vicar of St. Mark's looked at Anthony in bewilderment. He half-smiled. "I'm Godfrey Manners Atherton to give the names in full.

As given to me by my godfathers and my godmothers in my baptism. But why—should I be somebody else in disguise? I—a poor priest?"

"No, sir. The really pregnant question comes next. Had you had any previous acquaintance of any kind whatever with Doctor Field—the murdered man whose nude corpse was found swinging in the porch of your church?"

"Good gracious! None whatever, Mr. Bathurst. How extraordinary!"

"Thank you, vicar. Now I'll tell you—if only in justice to yourself, the reason that prompted my question. In Field's private papers—and moreover in a financial relationship—the initials 'G.M.A.' occur more than once. My apologies, sir." There came a silence. The vicar rose from his chair. Anthony was conscious of his towering frame. The vicar walked to the window of his study which showed the garden beyond and looked out. Anthony waited, but had he been taxed he couldn't have said what he thought he was waiting for. The vicar slowly turned and came back into the middle of the room.

"The initials 'G.M.A.' are frequently found, I should say. Take, for instance, the large number of 'Georges' there are."

"That's true, sir. But on the other hand, I don't know that 'M' would run too well among the prolifics."

The Rev. Atherton caressed his chin. "There's another point. I don't suppose for one moment that you haven't thought of it."

"What is that, sir?"

"They may be the initials of a woman. I take it that there's no guarantee that they apply to a man?"

"None at all, sir—they may well refer to a woman."

The vicar turned again—this time towards the window. Anthony knew that the vicar desired the interview to end. There had come an undeniable change in his manner. Difficult to define. Equally difficult to describe. Anthony was at a complete loss to account for it. He became uncertain as to the wisdom of attempting to prolong the interview. Should he mention the two other sets of initials which might fit?

Anthony made his decision. He would not mention them. He would accept the vicar's wish to terminate the interview. He joined the priest, therefore, by the window. Anthony extended his hand.

"My very best thanks, sir. Also my profound apologies—in case I've been a nuisance."

The Rev. Godfrey Manners Atherton shook his head. The gesture was kindly. "Good-bye, Mr. Bathurst. I'm glad we've met. And you haven't been a nuisance."

He conducted Anthony to the main door. "I'm afraid, you know, that there isn't so very much difference, when our accounts are totalled up, between the best and the worst of us. And—er—as I said—'G.M.A.' must be the initials of hundreds of people."

Anthony made no answer. The Vicar of St. Mark's waved to him as he walked towards the car. His huge figure made the gate of the vicarage look absurdly small. Anthony might have been interested to know that nearly fifty years before, he had Put the Weight for Oxford against Cambridge at Queen's Club and that the "Tab" Blue opposed to him had been hopelessly outclassed.

3

Anthony drove back to Greenhurst much more slowly than was his custom. In this remarkable case of twisted threads and serpentine strands, he was constantly being left dissatisfied. Try as he would, he wasn't able to remember a case, way back in the past, when this condition of dissatisfaction had so repeatedly come to him. He was dissatisfied with Claudia Field. The Stanhope ménage had left him wondering. Courtenay certainly didn't satisfy him. The Vicar of St. Mary Magdalene, Friar's Woodburn, had seemed an extraordinary sort of fellow, and now the Rev. G. M. Atherton was another person who had set his brain working overtime.

Moffatt, too, at the inquest had made Anthony think twice on at least three counts. Anthony continued with his mental survey of the case. Take the letter from "Mary." To where had it led? To nowhere and nobody! Drake's information re the blonde in the "Ram" with Field had also almost fizzled out. Mrs. Tattersall's identification of Field's lady companion had merely served to excite a complete denial and an alibi on the lady's part which seemed impregnable.

Anthony's mind travelled back to its latest contact with the Vicar of Fullafold. Even Atherton had left him scratching his mental head.

Why had Atherton's mood changed so suddenly? For changed it had. Anthony reassembled the structure of the interview which had just terminated. Previous acquaintance of any kind whatever with Doctor Julian Field? Good gracious—none whatever—Mr. Bathurst! Plain enough! Categorical! No humming and hawing or beating about the bush there! No hesitation. Not the slightest. No tell-tale sign of any kind on face or hands to indicate that the question had provided embarrassment. Not an earthly. And yet—the vicar had altered. Anthony was as certain of that as he had ever been of anything. The vicar had turned his face away and gone to the window. Had the initials caused a stirring of memory? Anthony looked ahead. The road was deserted. Anthony drew the car into the lee of the hedge and halted. He sat there in deep thought—his gloved hand on the driving-wheel. He sat there for some minutes. Then he reversed and began to drive slowly back to Fullafold.

4

His objective this time was not the stone-built vicarage, but the humble village post office. He had always possessed a partiality for the long shot and he was about to try one now. He entered the little shop and a discordant bell screamed his entrance. An aged beshawled woman came behind the counter.

"I wonder whether you could help me," announced Anthony—"it depends, I suppose, on how long you've been in business here."

The old lady chuckled and produced her commercial medals. "More years, young man, than have passed over your head." A second chuckle followed the first.

"Oh—that's excellent. What I wanted to ask you was this. I was passing through your delightful little village in my car—when an old memory came back to me. Is the vicar a Reverend Atherton?"

"He is, young man, been Vicar of Fullafold for a good thirty-odd years."

Anthony nodded enthusiastically. "I thought I was right. Fullafold's an unusual name. Actually, it's the only one of its name in England that I know. I *think* I was at school with your vicar's son, In fact, I'm almost certain that I was. Is there any remote possibility that he's still residing at the vicarage with his father? If so—I'd like to shake hands with him for the sake of old times."

The veteran postmistress shook her grey head. "You'll never shake hands with young Mr. Atherton again," she said.

"I'm sorry," said Anthony—"is that so? You mean—"

"He was killed on the Somme—1918 I think it was. He was only twenty. Great shock it was, too, to everybody in Fullafold. He was well-loved was young Mr. Richard."

"Well, well," returned Anthony—"and somehow the news never reached me. Or if it did—it passed clean out of my mind. Very many thanks—I'm so sorry to have troubled you."

Anthony resumed the journey back to Greenhurst. His hunch had failed him! The old unsatisfactory position had come back again. "G.M.A." couldn't possibly be applied to a man whose Christian name had been Richard. So far as Anthony could see his two visits to Fullafold that day had produced exactly nothing.

Chapter XVI

1

MacMorran met him in the smoking-room of the "Horse and Groom." The Scotland Yard inspector grinned at him as he entered, but the grin soon disappeared and the look of gloom returned to his face.

"Cheer up, Andrew," said Anthony—"after all—it may never happen. What's the worst news you've got?"

"The worst news I've got is no news at all. Not the whiff of an old oil-rag. Day after day's going by, too! Bernays's backside gets kicked more and more severely every twenty-four hours by his Chief Constable and I don't feel like putting mine anywhere in the neighbourhood of our old man's boot."

"Use mine, Andrew. Use mine. Not such a magnificent specimen as yours—I'd be the first to concede. Indeed a poor thing. But mine own."

MacMorran actually produced a laugh. "How about you, my lad? How did you get on in King's Winkworth? Anything to hang an official hat on?"

Anthony pursed his lips. "Well—I saw Courtenay. I suppose I had an hour with him. Quite an hour, I should say." Anthony paused. As always, MacMorran was quick to seize the implication.

"You weren't satisfied?"

"No. I wasn't. But, my dear Andrew, what is one among so many? Nothing has really satisfied me all the way through the case. Courtenay is simply no exception to this persisting, paralysing rule. Courtenay *knows* something! That I'll swear. What its importance is—" Anthony shrugged his shoulders—"well—that's what I can't feel sure about."

MacMorran scratched his cheek. "Like that, is it?"

"That's the way it goes, Andrew. Courtenay and Claudia Field. Claudia Field and Courtenay. If what I think is the case—why the hell did she marry Julian Field—or—come to that—why the hell any of it. It's all hay wire." Anthony tangented. "Bernays got anything on Mary yet?"

"Nothing. Not a sausage!"

"Then I'll tell you something. He *won't*. Those tracks are covered up all right. So cleverly—that they don't exist. Yes—you may well look puzzled. Work that one out."

"Good lord," replied MacMorran—"you're as pessimistic as I am. I did have hopes of you."

"I had hopes of myself, Andrew. Ah—well—to-morrow is also a day."

"And it's the darkest hour before the dawn," supplemented MacMorran—"I know a lot more. You read 'em in books." Anthony slid into an armchair and picked up a newspaper. It was the *Spears Herald*. "How long before dinner, Andrew?"

"A good hour, I should think."

"I should call it a bad one. The darkest hour before the 'dinn.' Taking liberties with your words of wisdom."

Anthony opened the local paper. He read for a few minutes and then tossed the newspaper over to the inspector.

"That's rather interesting, Andrew. I should imagine our friend Philip Stanhope must be a proud man. I certainly should be—apart from the horrible fact that our hero's wearing the wrong shade of blue."

MacMorran looked at the photograph which Anthony had pointed out to him. He read the caption below the picture which was of a good-looking youngster in a football jersey. "Rugger Blue for local sportsman." Under this heading was the following account: "All local sportsmen generally, and followers of Rugger in particular, were delighted to hear at the week-end that Dudley Stanhope, son of Mr. Philip Stanhope, the well-known gentleman farmer, of 'Gifford's,' Stoke Pelly, had been invited by the skipper of the Cambridge University Rugger Fifteen to play at scrum half against Oxford at Twickenham on Tuesday week. We add our congratulations to the many which Dudley and his father have doubtless received. Never was an honour more deserved. At the risk of offending our readers whose allegiance lies with Isis, we wish Dudley Stanhope a grand game, a fine individual display—and dare we say it—victory over the Dark Blues. Dudley learnt his 'Rugger' at Ampleforth—another feather in the cap of the famous 'Rugger' school."

"I can never understand," said MacMorran with something between a grunt and a growl, "why they call the perishing game 'Football.' 'Handball' or 'Catchball'—yes—but certainly not football. Now—when you see the 'Spurs'—"

Anthony grinned at the inspector. "Each man to his taste, Andrew. If only William Webb Ellis had known what he was doing that day when he stalled it all, he'd have dropped that ball like a red-hot spud. Never mind—come back to what I said. Philip Stanhope's a proud man—I'm pretty certain of that." But MacMorran still browsed in the field of reminiscence. "I saw a Rugger International once. Years ago now. At the Rectory Field, Blackheath. England and Ireland. It gave me the 'willies.' I saw the ball—if you can call the ruddy thing a ball—about three times during the whole game—if you could call it a game. The rest of the time, the ball was either 'out'—'in touch'—don't they call it—or in a scrum affair. Scrum! Then another scrum—and another—and another—till the cows come home. All you saw was a row of heaving backsides. Now take the 'Spurs'—when the 'Lilywhites' get moving, my boy—or the old Rangers when I was in Glasgow—now that *is* football! On the floor all the time—there's the ball—passed and flicked—not shoved into a ruddy scrum every few seconds where nobody can see it."

"I'm not going to argue with you, Andrew. For one thing—I'm tired. I want my dinner and after that, I'm going to turn my attention to an intensive study of Mr. Ernest Courtenay and another gentleman."

"Who's this other chap?"

"I don't think you've met him, Andrew. He's the Vicar of St. Mark's, Fullafold—and once upon a time must have been a remarkably fine physical specimen."

"What's he got to do with the death of Julian Field—apart from the church business?"

"That's just what I don't know, Andrew. See you later. I'll go and wash my hands."

Anthony went out and closed the door. It reopened immediately and MacMorran was surprised to see Anthony's head come round it.

"Not after the manner of a certain governor of Judaea!" Anthony closed the door again.

2

On his way to his bedroom, a thought occurred to him. He retraced his steps and walked quickly back to the telephone. He picked up the receiver and asked for a number. The time, he thought, shouldn't be too inconvenient. To his intense satisfaction, he got the reply he wanted.

"Is that you, Roger? Oh—good man! Anthony Bathurst this end. I was very much afraid I shouldn't be able to get you. Thought the time might be wrong tor you. I know what riotous living means. What?—No—that was your point of view. Listen—I want your help. You're still at the 'War House,' I take it."

Anthony waited for the terms of confirmation. "Oh—that's definitely good," he went on, "just what the doctor ordered. I'll tell you what I want you to do for me. It goes back to the Dark Ages a bit, but on the other hand it shouldn't be too bad as there's the chance it's still on the pension files. In my opinion it should be. But I can't be sure. Why not? Lack of data, old chap. Serious lack of data. Crippling. That's why I'm linking forces with you. Shows how hard up I am.

Well—here goes. I want all the 'gen' you can obtain for me concerning a certain 'Richard Atherton.' If there's a second Christian name it may be Manners. But that's a shot in the dark. He was killed in action, I should think—again I'm not sure, in 1917. On the Somme. Or perhaps in 1918—somewhere else. But certainly in France. What? No—sorry—can't supply any details with regard to either rank or regiment. What? Sorry again—but that's the way it is."

He stopped again to listen to what Roger Holt had to say.

"Well—it may sound a lot," was Anthony's eventual reply—"but I'd like to have everything that you can possibly get for me. With regard to that question of rank you mention, I'd have a stab at Second Lieutenant. Oh—that reminds me—I can let you have his approximate age. Circa 20. Might be a year less. Probably infantry. What? Yes—P.B.I. That's another shot in the dark. But I am confident. When? Oh—as soon as you possibly can. Mighty events hang therefrom—believe me. Where am I? At a really comfortable country pub, my lad—'Horse and Groom,' Greenhurst. What's that?"

Anthony listened again and grinned at Roger Holt's remarks. "Another nine o'clock walk for somebody? Shame! Just as though I should! What? O.K.! Bung-ho and bags of thanks. Yes—I'll do the same for you one day. What? You don't want it? The nine o'clock joke? Don't suppose you do—though I expect you deserve it."

Anthony hung up and walked thoughtfully up to his bedroom. As he ascended the stairs, he wondered whether he had done the right thing—whether he was troubling Roger Holt frivolously and with little real reason for so doing. It had always been his practice, however, to explore every avenue which presented itself to him, no matter how uninviting that avenue might appear to be, and more than once this procedure had meant all the difference between success and failure. Who was he to say that on this occasion he wasn't justified? Nothing venture—nothing have—and if Roger Holt turned the earth fruitlessly—well—he wouldn't be in any degree worse off.

Anthony put on a pair of grey flannel bags and made his way to the bathroom of the "Horse and Groom."

3

MacMorran chaffed him at dinner. "Who was the blonde? Or should it be brunette?"

Anthony looked puzzled at the inspector's questions. He knitted his brows. "How come, Andrew? Don't get."

"Well—you had a long enough spell with her in all conscience."

"I did? What's biting you, Andrew?"

"Nothing's biting me. I had the idea, though, that the entire telephonic system of the county was likely to be held up. Fat chance I had to speak to the missus."

"Oh! I see the drift. My light shines. No, Andrew—you're on another 'stumer'—neither blonde nor brunette. Neither blue-eyed nor brown. Neither siren nor houri. Just a highly intelligent and elegantly apparelled civil servant."

"Don't say income tax."

"Shouldn't think of it. Far removed. War Office."

MacMorran screwed up his face. "What's cooking? Were the uniforms used in the war cleaned by contract?"

"How do you mean?"

MacMorran grinned at his own sally. "How about 'Courtenay's Cleeno?' That's what I meant. I thought that was what you were tilting at."

"No. Atherton. The Rev. G.M.A. to you."

"Why? Was he a chaplain or something? Man's far too old surely?"

"There have been wars before this last one, Andrew. I can think of quite a number. Crécy, Agincourt, Waterloo. Snappy affairs."

"Oh—I see. Going back a bit—eh? What happened?"

"My esteemed inquiry will receive attention. Yours faithfully."

"Like that? Might have guessed as much. How long do you give 'em?"

"Oh—a day or so. Mustn't be unreasonable. After all—we can't criticize—we're taking our time on this job *we're* on."

"You're telling me." MacMorran embraced gloom again at Anthony's reminder.

"Cheer up, Andrew! As I said the other day—it may never happen. Actually—when all is said and done—I really think were making progress. Just a little. I can detect at least three reasonable rays of light shedding their effulgence through the clerestory."

MacMorran refused to be comforted. "All I can say is, then, that your eyes are better than mine. Since when has this happy state of affairs prevailed? Since you contacted the civil service side of the War Office?"

"No. Before then. I feel that out of this welter of mystery and plethora of 'phony' clues, I am at last beginning to do a bit of sorting out which may soon get me somewhere. At any rate—I'm hoping so. Your prayers and best wishes will doubtless add weight and influence to my own hopes. So release them, Andrew."

MacMorran recognized this mood of Anthony's. He knew it of old. Usually—it betokened that Anthony was very definitely "getting to grips." His eyes searched Anthony's face for further clarification.

"Is that all you're telling me? Is that the way it goes?"

Anthony shook his head. "No, Andrew—you're wrong. It's not like that. Actually—I haven't anything concrete to lay out in front of you. If I had you should have it. Merely surmises! I'm very much in the surmise stage. But—I'll be perfectly candid—I'm attracted by *one* of my surmises immensely. I'm pretty certain that I know why Field's clothes were divided as they were. That really was my jumping-off point. I don't know yet though, why Field was killed. Not even a completely satisfying surmise there—not more than seventy-five per cent of a nebulous one. There's this to it, though, my pal Roger Holt, within the next few days, may help me turn that three-quarter's surmise into a whole one."

"Who's Roger Holt?"

"War Office, aforesaid. Highly intelligent and elegantly apparelled. Don't you remember?"

MacMorran grunted. "The Rev. Atherton you said, didn't you?"

"That's the idea, Andrew."

"Can't see it myself. Vain hope! Although I suppose—"

MacMorran rubbed the ridge of his jaw—"it would explain the matter of the body in the porch. *His* church porch."

"It certainly would that."

MacMorran shook his head. "On second thoughts, though, it becomes rather incredible. In the first place, the vicar's an elderly man—seventy-ish, I should say, if he's a day—and in the second place, he'd hardly be likely to call attention to himself so sensationally. No—I'm afraid you're barking up the wrong tree."

"Maybe, Andrew. Maybe not. It all depends on what Roger Holt puts across. Till then—" Anthony broke off and shrugged his shoulders.

MacMorran came in again. "If Sir Austin Kemble comes through late to-night—he hinted that he might when I was last on to the 'Yard'—shall I tell him anything? You know—shall I paint the picture a bit rosier? Can I possibly? Last time he got through he tore me off several strips and I'm not particularly anxious for a second helping—I can tell you."

Anthony considered the inspector's question. "Well—if you do sound a slightly more optimistic note for his august ear—only do so in general terms. Don't in any way particularize. Mark time a bit. If he kicks at all and begins to throw the furniture about—shove it all on to me."

"Yes. I know. That's all very well. You haven't got your living to get. I'd like you to hear the old man lead off when he's in the mood. Once is more than enough for me."

"How long have you to go, Andrew?"

"Before I pack up? Just on five years. Four years and ten months."

"Well—I think you'll be able to hold the job down for that length of time. I think you'll just be able to manage it." Anthony's eyes twinkled. "Especially," he added, "if I make a special point of holding your hand on every possible occasion." MacMorran sat back in his chair, drew a deep breath—and charged to the attack.

Chapter XVII

1

Days passed. More days—as a period—than Anthony considered either comfortable or reassuring. Bernays and MacMorran, assisted by the indefatigable Sergeant Bland, followed up unsuccessfully almost every conceivable line of inquiry—no matter how unpromising it looked at the outset. The only news Bernays got came from Claudia Field. According to her Julian Field had carried the key of the surgery with him. Nothing whatever came through from the War House via the agency of Roger Holt, and Anthony, unwilling to prod the memory of one who was doing him a service, kicked his heels impatiently both in the "Horse and Groom" and its proximity.

Meanwhile the morning came of the day on which Ernest Courtenay had arranged his next meeting with his attractive cousin, Claudia Field. He drove to Twickenham from King's Winkworth and allowed himself ample time for the journey. He knew what the traffic on the road would be like. It was a typical December afternoon, and typical, too, of the afternoons devoted to the 'Varsity Rugger match. Mist hung about the ground, the air was chill and unfriendly, but the ground was just sufficiently holding for a fast game in which the ball wouldn't be too greasy for quick and accurate handling by the backs.

Ernest Courtenay had been so engrossed in his own thoughts that he had been entirely unaware of the car which had tailed him all the way from King's Winkworth. Had he known that Anthony Bathurst was at the driving-wheel, with Chief Det.-Inspector MacMorran at his side, he would not have looked forward to the afternoon with such keen anticipation. From the shelter of Anthony's car and a multitude of others, MacMorran saw Claudia Field join Courtenay. She had evidently arrived first and been waiting for him and her car seemed to be parked right over on the farther side of the enclosure.

MacMorran plucked at the sleeve of Anthony's big overcoat because he saw Courtenay and Claudia making their way in their direction.

"Satisfied now, Andrew?" said Anthony—"or is it just natural smoke from a purely utilitarian fire?"

"You mean—they're cousins? Which makes a certain amount of difference?"

"H'm—partly. Although, Andrew—in the words of the poet—*je ne le pense pas*! And after all—cousins need an alibi on certain momentous occasions equally with any other member of society. But come along—we'll see if we can get in their portion of the stand. Also, Andrew—I must warn you! I shall be rooting for Oxford. So I may not appear at my best. No man can under those conditions." Anthony looked at his watch. "We've tons of time and there they go—look! Making for the centre of the big stand. That's where we'll make for." Anthony slid off quickly and MacMorran followed him. Twickenham on a Tuesday in December was a new experience for him. Anthony watched to see which row Ernest Courtenay headed for and they were fortunate enough to secure seats rather conveniently and comfortably, two rows behind. "The Yard" has a way with it.

"How's this, Andrew? Suit you?"

"Admirably. And if only I were going to see some real football—"

Anthony jerked his head towards where Courtenay and Claudia Field were sitting. "There are your birds, Andrew. Sitting birds at that. We couldn't have worked things out any better if we'd known what seats they had beforehand."

MacMorran turned his attention to the two people of Anthony's conversation. It was obvious to the most unobservant that Ernest Courtenay at least, was finding something closely akin to delight in his lady's company. His eyes showed it, his face radiated it and his whole manner was similarly eloquent. Claudia, too, without exhibiting, perhaps, the same degree of enthusiasm, showed that she was pleased to be where she was. Anthony watched MacMorran gazing at the two of them with the eyes of a hawk.

"There's a game on as well, you know, Andrew. Or at any rate there will be—in a few minutes' time."

MacMorran smiled—but it was a grim smile. "I don't suppose I shall get much kick out of it."

As he spoke, a roar heralded the advent of the Light Blue fifteen. Anthony took out his field-glasses in order to obtain a better view of the men in the blue and white rings. Before he could bring the glasses to the appropriate condition of focus, a second roar welcomed Oxford.

"That's just reminded me, Andrew," he said, "while we're here, I want to have a look at young Stanhope. I feel a kind of semi-avuncular interest in him. With at the same time a devout wish that he won't play too much of a blinder."

Play started and Anthony picked out the Cambridge scrum-half. Oxford for a time did the major part of the attacking, but the Dark Blues met an eminently sound defence. Then Dudley Stanhope was penalized for not putting the ball in straight and almost immediately following the Oxford pack were similarly served for the use of the near-side foot in the scrum. MacMorran sat silently censorious. In the first half the referee awarded five penalties and from the last of these the Cambridge stand-off, a clever player with a tricky run and a beautiful pair of hands, kicked a goal to give Cambridge a three points lead at the interval.

Anthony turned to MacMorran. "Well, sternest of all stern critics—what's the verdict?"

"Lousy," replied MacMorran, "I'd as soon attend a Nonconformist tea-meeting."

Anthony laughed. MacMorran was certainly a last-ditcher. "It's not a good game, I admit. The referee's a pedant, rather. Still—there's a second half yet. It may be better."

"More likely worse," returned MacMorran.

"What did you think of young Stanhope?"

"He's collected plenty of mud on his jersey—that's about all I saw him do."

"One of the signs of a good player, Andrew. How are the birds? I fancy they've interested you more than the game."

"They're enjoying it all right. But it strikes me they're in the frame of mind to enjoy anything—even to a bucket of cold water down their necks. Love—Mr. Bathurst! Not only makes the world go round—but also earns the hangman many a fee." MacMorran glanced down towards Courtenay.

"Andrew," said Anthony, "your fingers are itching to arrest him, I do believe."

"Ay—and I'm not denyin' it! When I think what happened to that girl's lawful wedded husband a few nights back. Look at 'em now—gloryin' in their sin."

"Have patience—Andrew—and we'll see what we can do for you. Here come the teams again."

To Anthony's disappointment and—it is feared to MacMorran's intense satisfaction—the second half proved to be as dull as the first had been and the whistle of the referee dominated the proceedings. Groans came in regular procession from MacMorran.

"I have only myself to blame," he announced—"why do I listen to other people? It's been my biggest mistake in life. I might have shut some doors this afternoon or opened some windows, or even cleaned up a mess somewhere."

Anthony bore the stream of sarcasm in silence—hoping against hope almost that Oxford would yet manage to pull the game out of the fire. A few minutes from time his hopes were rewarded. The Oxford "three's" got away and the right wing crossed the Cambridge line near the corner. Three points all! The full back came up to take the place kick. The big New Zealander carefully wiped the mud from his boots and then gave the ball similar treatment. The kick was difficult and fell short. No flag was hoisted from behind the posts. A few minutes later the whistle went for "no side" and the game ended in a draw.

MacMorran looked at Anthony with disgust written plainly on his face. He tossed his head.

"Words fails me," he said.

"Spare me, Andrew," said Anthony laughingly, "the next game I bring you to may be a real snorter. I've seen some pretty filthy soccer matches. Still—as I told you—I didn't bring you for the game. You know why I asked you to come along. You've seen what I wanted you to see."

MacMorran looked at the crowd filing out of the stands and enclosures. "Yes," he acknowledged—"and I'm still seeing it. Look!"

He pointed away to the left. Ernest Courtenay was piloting Claudia Field through the swaying masses of the crowd. His right arm encircled her waist. Anthony didn't hear what the inspector said, although he fancied he was able to catch two words. They sounded to his ear like "cold" and "grave."

2

On the morning that followed the 'Varsity Rugger match at Twickenham, Anthony's personal stock rose several points. The reason for this sudden ascent in spirits was the receipt of a letter from Roger Holt. The gist of it was as follows.

My dear Bathurst.—Your inquiry turned out to be a trifle on the stubborn side. The result was that it took me rather longer than I had anticipated at the onset. And, of course, you will realize I had to go back a matter of nearly thirty years. However, I think I've got what you wanted. Second-Lieut. (one to you) Richard Manners (two to you) Atherton was attached to the 67th Fusiliers and was killed at Loos in September, 1917. He was within a few months of his twentieth birthday (three to you). He appears to have been married on his last leave—a week or so before he rejoined his regiment and went up the line. In June, 1918, he became the father of a son (posthumously—of course). The widow is still alive—but I don't know about the son—he may still be serving somewhere. You didn't ask about that side of it so I didn't take the trouble to pursue it. Her present address is "The Copper Beeches," Lavencourt, Suffolk. The name of the baby—according to the records I've been able to turn up—was Godfrey Manners Atherton. Well—there's the "gen" you wanted and I hope it chokes you. What's more likely, I suppose, is that it'll choke somebody else. Gertcher—you cold-blooded sleuth. Well—bung-ho.—Always yours, Roger L. Holt.

Anthony read the letter through twice—as carefully as he had ever read anything. Then he folded it up and placed it in his wallet.

Godfrey Manners Atherton—eh? Grandson of your grandfather? Was that the reason why the vicar's face had clouded over when Anthony had given him the three initials? What was behind it all? What had Courtenay said?

Anthony thought hard. The vital clue was there with Courtenay all right. And this young Atherton would be about twenty-eight. Very possibly just demobbed. It would be interesting to know his exact whereabouts on the evening of 27th October. Anthony thrust his hands into his pockets and walked to the window of the smoking-room of the "Horse and Groom." What should be his next step? What would be best? The Vicar of Fullafold again? Perhaps not. It might mean running things a little close, coming so quickly after his previous visit. On the other hand—what was the alternative? The more obvious one wasn't the easier. The less evident was comparatively simple in execution, but were the results anything like guaranteed?

Anthony decided that they were not. As he debated the issue in his mind, MacMorran came in. He held a newspaper in his hand and his face was flushed with triumph.

"Read that," he exclaimed, his finger stabbing at a paragraph. "Read that, my lad—and then eat a substantial portion of humble pie."

Anthony took the newspaper and wondered as he did so, what this new development was which afforded Andrew MacMorran such a measure of unalloyed satisfaction. Something to do with Courtenay? Or had the elusive "Mary" come forward at last. His eyes went to the paragraph of MacMorran's indication. Anthony smiled as he read. Its full purport was that in the 'Varsity Rugger match of the previous afternoon, the ball had been either in touch or in the scrum for 71 per cent. of the allotted time.

"What did I tell you!" almost shouted MacMorran, "now with the 'Spurs'—or the Rangers—"

3

Anthony heard the storm out patiently. When MacMorran had subsided, more breathless, if anything, than short of words, he changed the point of attack.

"From the ridiculous, Andrew—to the sublime. In one stride. Read that—and live again."

He handed the inspector the letter he had just received from Roger Holt. MacMorran, a little surprised at the sudden change of atmosphere, read the letter carefully and punctuated the exercise with a series of grunts. He then handed it back to Anthony.

"Interesting," he commented—"no doubt. Ve-ry interesting. It's nice to know all those things about the young fellow—his rank and his age and his Christian names—but I'm hanged if I see what it's got to do with us. Or how its going to bring us any nearer to Field's murderer. Especially considering that it all took place getting on for thirty years ago. But, of course, I'm always ready to live and learn."

Anthony grinned at him. "May I remind you of the initials of the son? Unless my memory be at fault—I rather fancy they go down to posterity as 'G.M.A.' Am I right, Andrew?"

MacMorran rubbed the side of his nose. "Well—what of it? They must be something or the other. You couldn't expect 'em to be X.Y.Z.?"

"Same like his own father's. Son's as grandfather's!"

MacMorran fidgeted. Anthony struck again. "Same like some to do with Doctor Julian Field."

"I still don't get it," said MacMorran a trifle impatiently. Anthony's hand went to his wallet. He took out a sheet of paper, gave it a cursory glance and pushed it over towards the inspector. "Look, Andrew—they're the notes I made out of that little interview I had with Ernest Courtenay the other day. Read 'em. You admitted yesterday afternoon at Twickenham that you were sweating on the top line with regard to that young gentleman. Well—look at these notes. Seems to me there's something there."

MacMorran read Anthony's notes and shook his head. "Yes—I think I see what you mean. But must you be so ruddy cryptic? Can't you draw the straight line for me and then tell me to travel along it? I admit frankly you were right with regard to that little bitch Claudia— but Bernays agreed with me—and at that time I hadn't visualized this Courtenay bloke on the scene at all. You must concede that he's an entirely new factor which has made a considerable difference."

"My dear Andrew," said Anthony—"I'd love to do all the things you say. I'd positively revel in leading you to the water and letting you emulate the example of the stag at eve. But—my very best of Andrews—I haven't the slightest vestige of proof. It's not the least use my taking you up to Courtenay, for example and saying 'Chief Det.-Inspector MacMorran, of Scotland Yard—meet Mr. Murderer,' if all the reception you're going to get from him is a cocked snook and a triumphant grin spreading all over his dial. And that's my trouble, Andrew MacMorran. What makes it worse—it's yours too."

Anthony took a cigarette and lit it. MacMorran shook his head solemnly.

"You can't get away from it," he said—"your words just now have set me thinking. Man—but Sir Walter Scott was a gr-rand poet—and no mistake."

Chapter 18

1

Anthony was still pondering over his problem when he went into the bar just before lunch for an appetizer. This information which he had been fortunate enough to obtain from Roger Holt, although highly valuable, had placed him in somewhat of a quandary. He was still uncertain as to which would be the best step for him to take next. What line could he possibly take if he made the journey to Lavencourt? In addition to which, he was by no means certain of his ground. The pattern of the crime was there and it was daily becoming less and less amorphous, but despite this fact, the actual design was as yet too nebulous to give Anthony the confidence necessary in order to take direct action.

"A nice half tankard of your best bitter, please, Beatrice," he said to the tall, rosy-cheeked barmaid, "so that I can get the real frame of mind to slaughter my lunch."

"You'll do," replied the barmaid—"from what I've been told, your appetite doesn't need much encouragin'. There you are—there's your beer."

She pushed the tankard towards him. As Anthony took it a tall, fair young man, standing at his side, grinned appreciatively at the barmaid's remark.

"Sounds pretty good that. You must be a man after my own heart. My trouble's not the disposal—but the acquisition."

"I'm afraid you're one of many," responded Anthony.

The fair young man nodded. "Nice little pub, this. I can't remember ever having used it before. It's on my own ground, too. Funny I've missed it."

Anthony thought his companion must be "on the road" in some way. "Well," he said, "if this is your ground, you're lucky. It's a lovely part of England—this, the West Country and Shropshire take an immense amount of beating."

The fair young man knocked back a tankard and shrugged his shoulders. "That's only one consideration. And it's a consideration which doesn't put the joint for the Sunday dinner on the table for you. The people down here are very sturdy and very independent-minded. Old yeoman stock, most of 'em. And besides their sturdiness and independence, there's a tidy basinful of ruddy obstinacy in 'em, believe me. They'll always listen respectfully to any suggestions you make—but will they act on them? No—sir. Not on your life! You think they will—they make you think it—but that's as far as it ever goes. They'll go their own ruddy road because their fathers did and their grandfathers before them. Dyed-in-the-wool stick-in-the-muds. Have one with me."

The fair young man smiled and pointed to the tankards.

"Thank you," said Anthony.

The barmaid filled and set them up. "You will be hungry," she said with a grimace to Anthony, "there won't be enough food in Greenhurst to satisfy you."

"I'll do my best, Beatrice. I'll try not to let the house down."

The fair young man grinned his infectious grin again. "All right," he said, "I'll have lunch here myself. *That'll* tax the commissariat." He turned to Anthony. "Going back to what we were talking about. I happen to be a Press photographer. Not in quite what we'll call the ordinary way. I don't work for one of the 'dailies.' I'm with the *Photographic and Illustrated Press* people. You probably know some of their stuff. No doubt you've seen it. Well—I'm attached to their big monthly show—*Eden*. Do you know it?"

Anthony nodded. "Oh—yes. Very well indeed. I constantly see it. Good show."

"Thanks. Not so bad. In the old days it was even better than it is now. Well—you can quite understand—you don't want me to tell you—most of the circulation's in the better-class country districts. People in the East End of London wouldn't buy it. Not down their street at all."

It was Anthony's turn to point to the tankards. "Drink up," he said.

"Thanks," said the fair young man—"damn good beer—this. Best I've tasted for some considerable time. Thank you, Beatrice. Don't forget to back 'Dante' next time out. Just your cup of tea. What? Oh, is that a fact? See you later then. Well—as I was saying before you made your welcome interruption—*Eden*'s a pretty 'posh' magazine. Now—we're just commencing a new feature. And they've shoved me in on it. 'Famous Farms of Southshire.' I'm telling you this to illustrate my point that you can never be sure where you stand with the Southshire people. The *real* Southshire breed."

The fair young man drank. He drank with artistry and satisfaction. The movement of the throat muscles was superb. Placing his tankard on the counter, he turned to Anthony again.

"One of our main features with regard to our 'Famous Farms' series is a number of photographs of each farm that forms the subject of the article. You know what I mean. There's nothing new about it. We usually show the exterior and a couple of really attractive interiors. Sometimes—the garden—if it's a bit over the average. You get the general idea—don't you?"

Anthony, who was keeping one eye on the clock, because he was hungry and wanted his lunch, and who was also getting a wee bit bored with the representative of *Eden*, nodded and said that he did.

"Well," went on the young man, "one of our future 'farm' articles has for its subject matter the well-known farm—'Gifford's' at Stoke Pelly. Belongs to a man by the name of Stanhope. You may have heard of him."

Eden drank again—and Anthony threw his clock-watching to the four winds of heaven, sat up—and took notice!

2

The fair young man continued: "My editor had, of course, been in correspondence with Stanhope—weeks and weeks ago, no doubt—early in the summer, I fancy—and Stanhope had agreed to allow his farm to be the subject of one of our series of articles. He seemed a very decent bloke in every way and didn't demur at all with regard to anything. Agreed to three photographs and to the complete bundle just as our people wanted it No reason on earth why he shouldn't—of course. Puts something on the value of his farm—no two ways of thinking about that. Any form of publicity or advertisement must do. People see the article and the photos which illustrate it and they talk about it. Stands to reason. Sometimes even—quite a well-known artist'll roll up and ask to be allowed to paint it. I say—how about another beer?"

"Thank you. As you say—it's good beer—this."

"I'll say it is. Hi! Beatrice!"

"All right, Herbert Morrison. I'm coming. You're not the only customer in the bar."

"No—but I bet you wish I was." He winked at Anthony as he spoke. "Well—to go on with my story. I blew down to 'Gifford's' one day—a week or so ago—end of October I fancy it was. Yes—that's right—October 27th—saw Stanhope and took the three photographs I wanted. One of the old dining-room with its oaken beams, one of the lounge and one of the garden. I had to wait for the outdoor one for some time to get the light right. But it's a really lovely garden—I don't know a better and that's a fact—and the photo was well worth waiting for. Still—I pulled it off—everything was O.K. and I was finished long before lunch-time. And—sir—I don't know your name—I got three smashing photos. I'll say I did. I've been in the game a good many years now and although I say it that shouldn't, I never did better work in the whole of my professional career. They were three real beauties! My editor was pleased, the photography expert was delighted—and all that was required to complete the picture was Stanhope's final O.K. to the photos before publication. They're wanted for our February number and we always submit them to the owner before they're sent to the printer."

The *Eden* photographer drank again. Anthony was listening carefully to every word. The date of the photographer's visit had been coincident with Field's. Just as he (Anthony) had made his mind up, too. And now this to come along! Still—he was running on too far ahead—there might be nothing to interest him in it whatever. Why on earth should he imagine there might be? Just because Stanhope's name had been mentioned. Again the tankard was replaced on the counter.

"Well—that's where I've been this morning. *Avec* photos. 'Gifford's,' Stoke Pelly, in the county of Southshire. The ancient farmhouse full of historical tradition owned by Philip Stanhope, Esq. Oh—yes. See February number of *Eden*—Britain's most artistic magazine. See February number—my foot! No—believe me—when he sees the three photos I shove in front of him for final approval— and were they good—oh boy—my lord Stanhope shakes his ruddy head and calmly says, 'Sorry—nothing doing.' Now beat that! I ask you—beat that! For cryin' out loud—I stood there flabbergasted. 'Why?' bleat I, when I get back to consciousness and open my eyes again, 'why?' What's the matter with 'em? They look O.K. to me.' 'I just don't care for them,' says he—'that's all there is to it! After all—it's my farm isn't it—and if I don't choose to have these photos published—surely that's all right? I'm within my rights—aren't I?' Well—I looked at him—I hadn't got two pennorth of wind left in the whole of my sails—and I said 'Have a heart, Mr. Stanhope. Don't forget I've been runnin' round on this ruddy job since about June last—when the correspondence started. If you persist in this line that you've just projected—it's been all dead waste of time to me! And there's no taste, you know, in nothing.' 'I'm sorry and all that,' he answers, 'but that's hardly my fault, is it? After all—I didn't ask for it. It all emanated from your people now—didn't it? When it was first mooted—I simply thought I'd oblige them. Now—I happen to have changed my mind. There's no occasion to make a fuss about it.' 'O.K.,' I said, 'O.K.—if that's how you feel! Sorry to have wasted your time—I won't mention my own!' And I just walked to my car and drove away. So you see what I mean when I say you can never be sure where you stand with these dyed-in-the-wool Southshire people. Just because old man Stanhope didn't like the position of one of his ruddy chairs in one of my photos—to hell with my newspaper, yours truly, and all that we wanted."

The *Eden* photographer looked moodily across the bar and even the seductive eye of Beatrice failed to dissipate his gloom. Anthony realized what he had to do. For the reason that it would be wilfully negligent to refused what the gods in their bounty threw at you. Philip Stanhope's reason for altering his mind with regard to the description of his farm in the February issue of *Eden* might be based on any one of a hundred reasons—all of them good, justifiable and innocent. But there was always the hundred and first chance and it would be criminally negligent on Anthony's part to pass it by on the other side. Open goals and full tosses on the leg side should never be allowed to get by. Such had been always Anthony's creed. He motioned towards the clock in the bar.

"Good lord—I didn't realize it was so late. I say—what about that lunch we're both going to have? Come along into the dining-room and have it with me. I can knock it back, I tell you. That beer's given me a most majestic appetite."

"That goes for me, too," said his companion—"I'll just see a man about a dog and then I'll join you in a brace of shakes."

"O.K.," replied Anthony—"there's plenty of room at my table."

3

Anthony just had time to say half a word to MacMorran. "For the time being, Andrew, you're reverting to civilian rank. So that when I introduce you—don't look surprised or even pained. There may be absolutely nothing in any of it—but I'm interested. You start with a spot of listening. You'll soon get the gist of it all—if you keep your eyes and ears open. Here he comes—the tall, fair chap."

Anthony beckoned the photographer to their table. "Here you are—take that seat over there and make yourself comfortable. I don't know your name—but mine's Bathurst, and this is my friend, Mr. MacMorran. I told him we'd make room for you."

"Pleased to meet you—Guy Knapp me—usually known to intimates and special cronies—I regret to say—as 'Shut-eye.' What do we eat?"

"Roast lamb," replied Anthony—"and it won't be too bad—either. If previous experience goes for anything. Do you know," he went on, "I've been thinking a lot about that yarn you just threw at me—about Stanhope, the farm and the photographs. It's jolly interesting—you know. Psychologically—I mean—more than anything else. I'll tell you why I just can't get the hang of it. You say—and it's your job—so you know, presumably what you're talking about all the way from A to Z—that the three photos are excellent that you took of the place."

"More than that," interrupted Knapp—"they're wizard! You couldn't better 'em in a day's march—for what they are."

"Right you are, then. Strengthens my point. Hallo—here's the grub."

Anthony waited for the meal to be set out and then went on again. "Your photos are as good as you say they are—and yet Stanhope—when they're dished up to him—shakes his head and says, 'Sorry—and all that—but positively nothing doing.' That's the point which puzzles me. I don't get it at all. *Why* did he take such a dim view of them? What was the reason behind it? Can't you, as a photographer, *find* that reason? Or at least something akin to it?"

"That's just it," said Knapp—"there isn't any reason. It was just sheer ruddy obstinacy."

Anthony pretended to think—and then suddenly, as it were, told MacMorran the bare outlines of what the discussion was about.

"Very strange," commented MacMorran—"but there you are—there's no accounting for taste. You do run across people who behave like that."

Anthony looked across the table at Knapp. "Do you happen to have them with you? I feel that I'd like to have a glance at them. You've whetted my curiosity."

"With pleasure, my dear chap. They're in my case. Outside in the car. As a matter of fact, I'd like you to look at 'em. Just in justice to myself. You'd sympathize with my point of view. I'll get 'em for you between the courses."

"Hear that, Andrew," mocked Anthony, "we've run into a super-optimist."

Knapp grinned. "Well then—before the girl brings the sweet."

"That's a lot better," said MacMorran.

"Not 'better,' Andrew," interposed Anthony—"merely 'truer.'"

4

The moment the plates and accessories of the main dish had been cleared away, Knapp rose from his chair and dashed out.

"It's a long shot, Andrew," said Anthony—"I wonder if we shall pick up anything."

"Of course you won't. Can't understand why you even consider the possibility. Why the hell should you? Just because a bloke changes his mind. That's happening every day. Probably—if you only knew it—in this case—because his missus gave the orders. Nagged him about it for weeks, I expect. Gave him no peace."

"You surprise me, Andrew—why should you imagine that every husband's as weak-willed and poor-spirited as you are? There are men, you know—and mice." Anthony's eyes twinkled.

"I like that, I must say," expostulated MacMorran—"if you want to know—"

"Cave," said Anthony—"here comes Knapp."

Knapp sat down, put his leather case on his lap and unstrapped it. "Here we are, Mr. Bathurst—here are the offending photographs." Anthony raised his hand.

"Before you show them to us, Mr. Knapp, answer me one question—please. Do you think you know, from what you may have seen or noticed, when you were discussing the matter with Mr. Stanhope, which one of the photographs influenced his decision?"

Knapp's eyes narrowed. "He made no specific complaint about any particular one of them."

"No—I realize that. I understood that much from what you told me in the bar before lunch. No—what I meant was this. Did you spot anything as Stanhope looked at 'em when you first showed them to him, for example? Were you watching him?"

"I see your point. O.K. then. Here's the first one I took. The lounge at 'Gifford's.' Nice little outfit, isn't it?"

It certainly was. Anthony scrutinized it with the utmost care. He also turned it over and looked at the back of it. He took in the furniture, the tables, the curtains, the ceiling with the hanging lights, the carpet—every article, no matter how small, which the photograph showed. And drew a blank. The grandfather of all blanks. Without the slightest comment, he passed the photograph to Andrew MacMorran. Knapp finished his sweet course, pushed away his plate, wiped his fingers on his table napkin and carefully took photograph number two from his leather case.

"Here we are—this is the second one I took. The old dining-room at 'Gifford's.' Also—very comfy—thank you!"

He passed it over to Anthony. The latter recognized the room where he and MacMorran had so recently sat at tea.

"See the old beams there," said Knapp—"according to one account of the house I've read in a book on English farmhouses—they go back to the fifteenth century—Richard the Second's time. Real old English oak. There's no doubt about it. 'Gifford's' is a grand old place and if Stanhope ever puts it in the market it'll fetch a pretty penny. I don't know a farm in Southshire to equal it."

Anthony concentrated on the photo of the dining-room. With the same infinite care and scrupulous attention to detail that he had bestowed on its predecessor. To draw his second blank of the day. The great-grandfather of all blanks—this time. Again he passed the photograph to the inspector with no comment. Knapp opened his case and took out the third photograph.

"Number three," he remarked, "and the last of the Mohicans. The gardens at 'Gifford's,' Stoke Pelly. And some gardens they are, too. I've never seen their equal. Honestly—I haven't. And my job takes me round a bit. I've seen a few in my time. The roses—for example—for the time of year—were really marvellous."

He handed the third photograph to Anthony. The latter accepted it—hoping against hope. It certainly was a lovely photograph of a beautiful scene.

"Gorgeous, isn't it?" demanded Knapp enthusiastically. "Could anybody ever want anything better?"

Anthony began to concentrate on the details of the picture. But if he had been anticipating finding anything in any way sensational or extraordinary, he was doomed to disappointment. Suddenly, however, he did notice something for which he had been unprepared. He knitted his brows in thought. Knapp was quick to notice the fact.

"What's the trouble?" he said—"don't tell me you've found a flaw in my photography."

Anthony smiled at his eagerness and shook his head. "Don't worry. Nothing at all like that. But tell me—does this happen to be the ugly duckling? This photograph of the garden."

"The ugly duckling? I must work that one out. I don't—oh, I see what you mean. No—it doesn't. The one I think Stanhope sniffed at was the photo of the dining-room. But—question for question—what is it you've found? I'm blest if I can see anything wrong."

Anthony shook his head again. "I haven't found anything wrong. Or anything like wrong. Don't think that. The point that did strike me was something quite different." He handed the photograph to MacMorran. "How do you like this, Andrew?" he asked.

MacMorran accepted the photograph and inspected it carefully. Anthony turned to Knapp again.

"I'll tell you all about it in a minute. But before then, why did you think the dining-room photo was the wrong 'un? That's what I'd be interested to hear."

"Merely this," replied Guy Knapp—"that when I first gave it to Stanhope to look at, I *think* I noticed him shake his head. That's all I was going on."

Anthony thought. "Can you remember—it's a small thing really and I'm quite prepared to hear that you can't—the order in which you handed them to Stanhope? When you showed them to him for his approval?"

Knapp showed signs of being puzzled. "I think I can. My memory's not too bad. Let me see now. Yes—I can. First the gardens—second the dining-room—and last of all—the lounge."

"I see. That's interesting. Now I'll tell you why I looked as I did. Who are the three ladies in the garden photograph? Do you happen to know?"

"Can I have the photo," said Knapp—"then perhaps I can show you? Do you mind, sir?"

MacMorran returned the photo of the garden at "Gifford's." Knapp held it up so that the two others could more readily see.

"This is Mrs. Stanhope—I'm pretty certain of that—and these two—this side—by the rose garden are presumably her daughters. But—I'm sorry if I seem to be dense—I really fail to grasp your point. Am I missing something?"

Anthony laughed. "No—not for a moment. There's no magic about it and I assure you there's nothing up my sleeve. What occurred to me was that the three ladies appear to be dressed in absolutely identical clothes. You spotted that, surely, when you took the photograph?"

"Oh—yes." Knapp nodded his head emphatically. "Very attractive, too, I thought they were. They were made of that striped material. You know—like the girl in the famous 'Kodak' advert. The stripes were a very pleasing shade of red. I tell you—they caught my eye. Of course, Mrs. Stanhope looks absurdly young. To be Stanhope's wife, I mean. She and her two daughters, in my opinion, would have no difficulty whatever in passing for sisters." He grinned. "And do you mean to tell me," he added, in mock anger, "that you've been making all this fuss just because three girls in a photo are wearing similar frocks? Gertcher!"

Knapp packed the three photographs together and replaced them in his case. Anthony laughed.

"Well—it's the only reason I can think of as to why Stanhope turned you down. Andrew—" Anthony looked across at the "Yard" inspector—"the stone which the builders refused, may yet become the headstone of the corner."

Knapp looked up. "You can pull my leg as much as you like—with regard to those three dresses—and I'll say I don't agree with you. Stanhope sniffed at the one of the dining-room. Nothing will convince me to the contrary."

"You may be right," said Anthony—"but somehow, I don't think so. What do you think, Andrew?"

MacMorran frowned at the question. "I'm hanged if I know," he replied, "what the hell you're talking about."

Guy Knapp threw back his head and burst into a roar of laughter.

Chapter XIX

1

Knapp drove away from Greenhurst almost immediately after lunch. Directly he had gone, MacMorran came at Anthony.

"I may be a mug," he said, "they tell me there's one born every minute—but what the blazes was all that about? What the hell does it matter to you, to me or to the old dog in his ruddy kennel, whether three women wore the same coloured frocks or not—I thought for a time that you were ripe for the nut-house. In fact I don't know that I'm not still thinking so."

Anthony laughed loud and long. "Andrew—I grieve for you. I shall sing sad songs for you and plant at your feet a cypress tree. Listen—and understand. The date that Knapp took his three now famous photographs was the twenty-seventh day of October! I thought I had made that much clear to you before we sat down to lunch. And the twenty-seventh day of October was the day which saw Doctor Julian Field gathered to his fathers. That's why I evinced such a morbid and apparently imbecile interest in Stanhope's strange refusals of the aforesaid Knapp's photographic art."

MacMorran whistled. "It's my fault. I didn't take in the significance of the date. But—just a minute! Are you absolutely certain the date's right? You know what the majority of people are like when it comes to remembering a date accurately. How many have you known that you could really rely on?"

"Don't worry, Andrew. I checked up on Knapp's memory. I intended to all along if I got half a chance. The date was on the back of all three photos. Every one showed the twenty-seventh of October. So I think we're justified in accepting that as established. Don't you?"

"In that case, I suppose we can. Not that it matters as far as I can see. The photos gave us nothing. I never thought they would. How *could* they? Field didn't arrive at 'Gifford's' until long after that fellow Knapp had gone and he left at seven o'clock—say. In addition, he was alive until round about ten. There's another three hours for you."

"O.K. and again O.K.! I'll take all you've said, go away, come back, and take it again. All the same—what is there in one of those three photographs which so completely influenced Stanhope that he changed his mind—and—mind you—deliberately went back on a promise. That doesn't fit in with the character of Stanhope as I've pictured him. A *business* promise, too, which meant financial loss to somebody?"

"Search me! I couldn't see anything. They all looked pretty good to me. Your academic lecture on the three striped frocks amused me though—I'll say that about it. I tumbled pretty quickly to the fact that you were pulling the poor bloke's leg." Anthony smiled at MacMorran's expression of opinion. "That was very nice of you, Andrew—and all that. But I wasn't!"

"You weren't? Do you mean to tell me that you were serious?"

"Never more serious in my life. In the photograph which our friend Knapp took of the gardens at 'Gifford's' there are three ladies. And they are all dressed alike. Forget the sartorial coincidence, Andrew, for a moment—why three? That's the first part of my problem."

"You mean—we met only two?"

"That's exactly what I do mean—where's the third turned up from?"

"There's nothing in that, man! The third girl is no doubt another daughter. We didn't know there was a second son—but we found there was—didn't we?"

"Did you look closely at the photo, Andrew?"

"I did."

"Were the three ladies like one another?"

"Yes. I should say they were."

"Almost absurdly alike—would you say?"

"I don't know about that. I'm thinking of your word 'absurdly.' Very much alike—I'll concede that."

"Good. We're making progress. Sorting them out, then, into two what I'll call 'age-groups,' were there two young and one senior, or one junior and two older? You say you examined the photograph closely?"

MacMorran thought he saw where Anthony was shepherding him. He began to shift his ground. "Ages are by no means easy to gauge in photographs. You'll admit that, I suppose?"

"To a degree. But I'm still waiting for you to answer my question."

"Well—with all sorts of reservations—I'd say two of the ladies were older than the third."

"So would I, Andrew. And that's my point. And it's a point against your solution of the two daughters."

"Well—at the cost of reiteration—what's it matter, anyway?"

"Just you wait a minute and get it firmly fixed in your head that Stanhope turned the photos down."

"Not *that* one! Knapp made that clear to you. It was one of the others he shook his head at."

"That we don't *know*. Stanhope may have foxed him. So that Knapp's opinion can't be treated as much more than surmise. Suppose, Andrew, those three ladies were all dressed in the same way deliberately. As part of a definite design?"

"Mother and daughters often dress alike. Especially when there's a strong, physical likeness between them."

"I'm not so sure, Andrew. When I said 'design'—I was thinking of something pretty big—something pretty staggering."

"What the hell are you getting at?"

Anthony thoughtfully caressed the ridge of his jaw. "I don't know, Andrew. Before this photo business came along and prodded me in the ribs, I'd more or less come to a definite conclusion as to why Field had been murdered and his clothes divided. It was in my mind to take certain steps to clinch matters. Now—I'm wondering again."

"Why? On account of those wretched photographs?"

"Yes. Just that, Andrew. I feel in my bones that Stanhope took that step he did—refused publication—for some obscure reason to do with the death of Julian Field. But for the time being, I just can't see 'why.'"

"And I can't see either why you should think so. I can't see the tiniest peg for you to hang that on."

"It's out of Stanhope's pattern, Andrew, to break that agreement with the newspaper people. Therefore, it interests me psychologically. Think of that marvellous piece of work by Marlowe in 'Trent's Last Case.' He heard his employer, Manderson *tell a lie*. But he *knew* that Manderson was essentially a truthful man. That lie worried Marlowe and he gnawed at it as a dog with a bone. Through gnawing at it—he saved his own neck. Now that's just how Stanhope's conduct strikes me in this instance. What did he see in any one of those three photographs which Knapp took on the morning of the day that Field was killed—which caused him to go back on his word? It's that third woman that worries me, Andrew—that third girl—if you prefer to call her that—in the striped frock. If it were possible—to—oh curse it—why has this contingency turned up when I thought I had the case nicely in hand and almost ready for tying up?"

Anthony stopped abruptly. MacMorran noticed the sudden pause. "What's the matter?" he queried jocularly. "Another contingency turned up? Worse than the three failure photos?"

"No—no, Andrew. But I *think*—I'm on to something."

"What, again?" grinned the inspector.

2

Anthony put another telephone-call through to London. The first of two that he intended to make that evening. This time to Sir Roderick Hope, one of the Crown pathologists. They had worked together on cases on several occasions in the past and had become firm and fast friends. Each had a sincere regard for the ability and integrity of the other. Anthony made the call on Sir Roderick's private telephone number and he deliberately chose the time. When he heard Sir Roderick's deep-toned voice at the other end, he felt gratified that his judgment had been sound.

"Hallo—Bathurst," exclaimed Sir Roderick—"do you know—this is rather strange your ringing me. I saw the Commissioner a couple of evenings ago—we were both dining at Murillo's—what? no—separate tables—and I asked after you when I ran into him in the foyer. Actually—he told me where you were and what you were on. And now—I'm blest if you don't jump on my telephone wire. Well—well, it's a small world. How are things? Got the rope ready yet?"

Anthony answered. "No. Not so good! I expect you let me down lightly. I know you of old. If I know Sir Austin, too, he probably gave you a basinful of my sins of omission. Andrew MacMorran's down here with me. No—what I wanted to ask you, Sir Roderick, was this. First of all—right up the medicine street—did you know anything about the dead man—Julian Race Field? You'll probably remember where he practised—King's Winkworth—in case it's slipped you. You've read the case, I take it?"

Anthony listened for Sir Roderick's reply. What he heard pleased him. "That's quite right," he returned, "you've got it. And as it happens, that's the particular point about which I'm inquiring. What's that?"

Anthony waited again. "Three to four years ago," was his eventual reply—"certainly not much more than that. Yes—that's right—you do—oh, good! Now what I really want is this. With regard to that matter of reputation that you just mentioned—can you, do you think, lay your hands on anything concrete? Something a conscientious 'busy' could get his teeth into? Usually where there's smoke, there's a certain amount of fire—*n'est-ce pas*?"

Again—a wait for Anthony. He heard Sir Roderick Hope out. Then he cut in again. "Oh—I know there was. And in more ways than one. I quite agree. Well—do what you can for me, sir—will you? You *may* land on something. Anyhow—I'm pretty well convinced by now that the solution to this mystery lies somewhere in the direction I've indicated. When? Oh—as soon as you conveniently can. Without putting yourself out. Thanks very much. Yes—here. I can't see myself getting away for a few days—at least. What's that? O.K. Perhaps that would be better."

3

Anthony spoke again to Roger Holt. "Hallo!" said the latter, as he picked up the telephone receiver. "What you again? Did you get my screed? Good! And you could read it? You could? Well—that's the best news I've heard for a long spell. From henceforward, I shall regard you as a really class detective. I shall number you amongst the sleuths immortal. What?" Holt pretended to groan. "You actually want more? Oh—all right—who is it this time?"

Anthony told him. When he had presented the full details to Holt, he added a question—"That won't be too difficult—will it?"

"No-o. I shouldn't think so. May mean contacting a somewhat obscure area—but they're more or less all tabulated and it merely becomes a sort of routine inquiry—when it all comes to be boiled down. The only thing is—"

Anthony sensed the hesitation. But he made no interruption and waited for Roger Holt to continue.

"Look here," came Holt again—"I presume you'll be wanting this before Wenceslas looks out, won't you? Before the mistletoe hangs in the old oak hall? Am I right in that brilliant conjecture?"

"You are, old son. You've arrived at that conclusion with your invariable and unerring accuracy. Why?"

"Well—I happen to be sliding off somewhere for Ye Jolly Olde Christ-e-mass—and also for the Feast of St. Stephen. That was the headache. I'm leaving town actually on the 22nd."

"Well—I'd like it to be before then—no good my saying I wouldn't."

"O.K.," said Holt, with a sudden snap of decision—"you shall have it. One marine never lets another marine down."

"Thanks for the unexpected promotion," said Anthony.

"Don't thank me," retorted Roger Holt—"you've deserved it for years—you can't keep a good man down."

4

As it happened, Anthony kicked his heels in the "Horse and Groom" at Greenhurst for another week. MacMorran had many consultations and conferences with Inspector Bernays at Four Bridges. Sir Austin Kemble, the Commissioner of Police, together with the Chief Constable of Southshire and Major Farrell-Knox, the A.C., met the two professionals and the meeting produced a wealth of criticism, plain speaking and a less amount of recrimination. But beyond the three conditions just described, its productivity was barren. Anthony purposely absented himself from this series of conference and consultation. For one thing, his mind was full of misgivings, and for another he was afraid. As things had gone and were going, he had solemn occasion for his fear. He knew—none better—that there is no way of escape if you are followed into a cul-de-sac.

MacMorran returned from the meeting which had been attended by his own personal bosses in a frame of mind which might be somewhat euphemistically described as "not the best of tempers."

"Well, Andrew?" remarked Anthony when the "Yard" inspector returned from the conference—"how did it go?" MacMorran shook his head in gloomy despondency. "It didn't. It just stayed put. The old man sat up in his chair, drew a deep breath, and made me his wash-pot."

"And over me, I suppose he tossed his boot?"

"He didn't refer to you by name—but it's 'mud,' all right!" Anthony grinned. "Dear, dear! And he's going to feel worse, I'm afraid, before he feels better. Poor old Sir Austin."

"Yes—I know. But, unfortunately, I can't feel quite so detached about it as you. You don't feel so clever when you're called to a conference of 'Big Bugs' and when you're asked what you've got for them—you say 'a lovely large lump of nothing.' That sort of thing has a knack of removing the spare liquid from a man. You try it yourself and see."

"Never mind, Andrew. Bear up! We all have our bad days—and our bad cases. The old man must learn to take the rough with the smooth. If clever criminals stage an unusually clever crime and cover their tracks as cleverly as they commit the crime—well—I'm not carrying the can back for the old man—and neither are you, Andrew—if we play our cards right."

MacMorran shook his head. "Those sentiments are all right, just as talk between you and me. Unfortunately, as I said before—the old man expects results from me. And he tears me off a strip when he doesn't get 'em."

"Andrew," said Anthony, "this is defeatist talk! What we need is a drink. How about tottering into the bar for a couple of tankards of the old and filthy?"

"I don't mind if I do," said the inspector.

Chapter XX

1

IT WAS on the 20th of December that Anthony was able to make a move. By one of those coincidences which Destiny has a theatrical knack of staging, the two letters for which he had been waiting so patiently arrived by the same morning post. He regarded the letter from Sir Roderick Hope as being the more important. He therefore opened it first. He began to read.

Dear Bathurst,—My apologies if I've taken rather longer over your inquiry than possibly you anticipated. You will understand that I had to be the soul of discretion, seeing the rather delicate nature of the affair generally—and you will understand, too, the reason why I have omitted all names—identifiable names—from this letter you are reading now. I shall therefore refer to the subject matter of your inquiry as "X." Putting the whole thing in a nutshell, as I am sure you would wish me to, there is little doubt that the 'reputation' at the time of decease was getting just a little—well—you can guess what I mean. Whispers here—mutterings there—and nearly all of them behind the raised hand. The cloud was there—although it may not have been bigger than a man's hand. There is no telling, of course, what size it might well have become. And I should say— from the hints that have been dropped to me—that your surmise is in all probability, the right one. There was any amount of that sort of thing going on—though God forgive me for both thinking and writing such a thing. Unhappily, though, it was all too true. What I don't see is where and how the "legacy" came to be picked up. If your conclusions are right—and knowing you as I do I've no doubt they are—I could bear with a spot of further enlightenment after the execution notice has been posted outside the precincts of one of His Majesty's prisons. Don't forget—you old scoundrel! Yours always, and delighted to have been of service to you—Roderick Hope.

Anthony read the letter through twice with the utmost care.

"Good," he said to himself—"that gives me step number one. Now let's see what Roger Holt has to say."

Anthony open the second letter. It was terse and to the point.

Dear Bathurst,—Have managed to pull off your little job with a few days to spare. So don't worry me any more with any of your stunts until well into the New Year, do you hear? Herewith the "gen." The man you inquired about saw no service at all. He was turned down on medical grounds. T.B. I rather fancy or something of that nature. Rather strange, don't you think, when you review all the circumstances? So there ain't no war service record to give you! Short and sweet that, isn't it? Well—cheery-bye until after Wassail—I leave for Market Harborough on the 22nd as I told you. I understand our host there—Colonel Enderby—runs a lavish table and rumour has it there's a bag of peanuts on the menu—purchased at an exorbitant price, I believe. Bung-ho and the compliments of the festive season.—Roger Holt.

Anthony slipped the two letters into his pocket. He rather fancied that his case was complete—but there was still the blank wall. Curse everything—he was beginning to wish he'd never come near the wretched business! It was heads he lost and tails the other fellow won. Which was a state of affairs that had no attraction at all for Anthony Lotherington Bathurst.

2

Anthony drove fast and fiercely. But the road was good—and better still—there was comparatively little traffic on it. The sun shone with the crystal clearness of a fine December and the road was dry. He had got away from Greenhurst like greased lightning after an early breakfast. He had told MacMorran that he had certain business to transact which might—or on the other hand might not—have some bearing on the Field case.

Anthony came to the Blackwall Tunnel in excellent time and turned east. He was making for the coast road through Colchester. There were now only four days to Christmas and he wanted this case dry on the hooks before Christmas Day dawned. But all the way along he shook his head with the same misgivings. The same doubt which had haunted him in the "Horse and Groom" at Greenhurst still reared its ugly head. No matter how Anthony sought a way out from the intricacy of his problem, this devil doubt remained in his path and persisted. Anthony drove for two hours. It was a quarter to twelve when he reached the sign-post for which he had been watching for the better part of half an hour. He halted the car by the grass verge so that he could read its directions. "Ipswich, Felixstowe—ah—here we are—Lavencourt—miles."

"Not so bad!" Anthony swung the car round again in the direction the sign-post indicated and after a time, when the road improved, pushed the speedometer needle up to fifty. He entered the village of Lavencourt just after twelve o'clock. He heard the church clock tell its twelve strokes when he caught his first glimpse of the yellow A.A. sign.

The little railway station with its quaint be-gardened platform was on his right as he entered and he soon realized that Lavencourt was a charming little place and in the direct lineage of Friar's Woodburn and Stoke Pelly.

The "Red Cock" caught his eye and Anthony was soon getting outside a pint of Suffolk ale and two extremely businesslike cheese rolls. A red bill in the saloon bar of the "Cock" of the same colour arrested his attention. It announced that the "Lavencourt Players would present 'George and Margaret' at the Church Hall on the nth day of January on behalf of the Church Organ Fund" and gave the names of the cast. Anthony read them with more than ordinary interest.

"All these miles from Fullafold," he said to himself—whimsically. As he drained his beer, he turned casually to the man behind the bar who had served him and said, "Could you direct me to a house in Lavencourt. I think it's called 'The Copper Beeches.'"

"I could that, sir," said the barman, "but you've got a tidy walk in front of you."

"I've a car outside."

The man shook his head. "Won't be no good, sir—leastways not all the way. I'll tell you. Go straight up the main Ipswich road till you come to a field with half a dozen caravans in it. That'll be as far as you can take a car, sir. Leave it just outside the big white gate. You'll find it open. It's always kept open. You'll then have to cross a field—bear left all the time—pass through a five-barred gate, cut through the spinney you'll find yourself in, keep to the left of what we call the broad-bean field and you'll see the chimneys of 'The Copper Beeches' right in front of you."

"H'm. Bad as that, is it? How long will it take me—after I leave the car?"

"How long, sir? Well—now—let me think. Best part of a quarter of an hour I should think. The pity it is the car's no good. A push-bike's the best thing for that journey. That's what most people use to get up there."

"Ah—well—it can't be helped. I'll make it all right. Many thanks."

Anthony waved and started out. He ran the car along the Ipswich road until he came to the field which contained the array of caravans. The white gate was open as mine host (perhaps) of the "Red Cock" had stated that it would be. Anthony parked the car behind another which was already parked there and started on his walk. As he began to stride out, he looked at his wrist-watch. Best part of a quarter of an hour so he had been told. He would see if the estimate were reasonably accurate. He crossed a wide field, bore left all the time, went through the five-barred gate and found himself in the spinney, thanking his lucky stars all the time that the weather for some days now had been cold and dry. The field had been hard-rutted. With rain, he guessed, it would be a sea of mud.

Anthony traversed the spinney and came to what he supposed was the broad-bean field. Much of the crop was still there, lack and dried—he presumed they had been grown for cattle and not all of them gathered. As the path by the side of the hedge bent round a little he could see the smoke ascending from a chimney. Shortly afterwards, he saw the house—about three hundred yards ahead of him. Thus it was that Anthony Bathurst came to "The Copper Beeches."

3

As he came out of the broad-bean field, he saw the garden gate of the house. It seemed that he was about to enter by the back entrance. Inasmuch as he saw no way clear which would take him to the front of the house, Anthony decided to carry on the way he was going. After all—it was in the country—and in the country the conventions rise to but a small stature. He put his hand on the latch of the garden gate. Before he could press it down enough to open the gate, a woman came round the side of the house and looked in his direction. What he saw administered to him a severe shock. For Anthony recognized her as Daphne Stanhope! But the dress she was wearing was not the striped frock that showed in Guy Knapp's photograph.

Anthony pressed down the latch of the gate and entered the garden. Daphne Stanhope walked rather wonderingly towards him.

4

Anthony raised his hat as gallantly as he had ever done.

"Good afternoon, Mrs. Stanhope. No doubt you remember me. It isn't so long after all, since we met. Although I'll admit I wasn't expecting to see you here."

The woman he addressed shook her head. "I'm sorry—but you've made a mistake, I think. I am not Mrs. Stanhope."

As she spoke, Anthony saw in a flash that he had and she wasn't. She was absurdly like Daphne Stanhope but there were subtle nuances of difference. Her face was a little thinner, for instance, and she moved her head more slowly.

"No—I ask your pardon," he said—"you took me rather unawares and I made my decision a trifle too quickly. Please forgive me."

She nodded—rather sharply he thought—and Anthony mentally castigated himself for having opened so shakily. "Actually," he went on, "I wanted Mrs. Atherton. I think you must be—"

"That's right," she cut in—"I am Mrs. Atherton. I take it that you know my—" She paused—a little too deliberately, he considered. "What is it you want?" she demanded—"it's not exactly warm out here—and if you would kindly let me know—"

"My name is Bathurst," he answered—"and I should be tremendously obliged if you'd be good enough to grant me a brief interview. In a way—you can regard me as—well—how shall we say—'unofficial Scotland Yard'."

Mrs. Atherton changed colour. There was no doubt about it. Her lips set and her fingers tautened. She looked searchingly at Anthony's face as though she were desirous of assessing his worth, his wit, his wisdom—have it how you will. Anthony knew quite well enough what she was doing. He wondered what answer she found to her questions. For she turned abruptly and said—"Please come inside the house, Mr. Bathurst. I've heard of you—an aunt of my husband was a second cousin of Sir Charles Considine."

"Oh—excellent," returned Anthony as he followed Mrs. Atherton into the house. "What a small world it is to be sure."

Chapter XXI

1

Anthony found himself in a cosy dining-room which had a noble fire blazing on an open hearth.

"I'm sorry the time is inconvenient, Mrs. Atherton," he said, "but I've come a long way across country and I had no really effective means of gauging how long the journey would take me."

"If it's my lunch you're disturbed about—you need have no qualms. I'm not lunching to-day until half-past one. My son is out and won't be back until just before then."

"Ah," said Anthony—"your son, Godfrey Manners Atherton. Yes, of course."

She shot him a startled glance. He nodded. "I'm delighted to find that you're an intelligent woman, Mrs. Atherton. I take it you were a Miss Bartlett—like your sister, Mrs. Stanhope?"

"That is so."

"Do you know?" Anthony went on, "I've been all sorts of a congenital idiot. I deserve to be kicked from Dan to Beersheba." A half-smile flickered over her face. "May I talk?" he said.

"Please do. For if you don't—I shan't."

This time it was Anthony who half-smiled. "Mrs. Atherton," he said, "I know how Julian Field died."

She paled.

"I know too why Julian Field died." Her pallor became ghastly. "By half-past one this afternoon—I shall know who killed him."

Mrs. Atherton rose from her chair—and then sat down again. "I don't think," she said—her voice trembled—"that you are bluffing me. But I must make sure. Because until I am sure I don't know what to do." She turned to him almost beseechingly—"Please—Mr. Bathurst."

Anthony began to talk. Mrs. Atherton punctuated his narrative with many nods and an occasional shake of the head. When he had reached his conclusion she sat perfectly still in her chair and as silent as she was still. Anthony waited for her to speak. He considered that he had said enough. Eventually, as was inevitable, Mrs. Atherton broke her silence.

"You said, Mr. Bathurst, when you came into the garden, that you represented 'unofficial' Scotland Yard. They were your words, were they not?"

"They were."

"Well, then, I don't know what to say. I don't know whether the more important part of that description you applied to yourself is 'unofficial' or 'Scotland Yard.' If I knew that, I can quite understand that it would make a tremendous difference. Not 'would'—'might.'"

Anthony made no move to help her. After all—there were so many considerations apart from both hers and his own. Mrs. Atherton shook her head again. There was helplessness in the gesture.

"My husband," she said, "gave his life for his country. And I gave my husband for the same cause. The years between haven't exactly meant roses and rapture for me."

"I know that," said Anthony gently—"that is, perhaps, one of the reasons why I'm here as I am to-day."

"I take courage when I hear you say that."

"I don't know that you should. There always remains the Assyrian."

Mrs. Atherton raised her eyebrows in a question. "The Assyrian?"

"Yes. The Assyrian who came down like a wolf on the fold."

She started convulsively at the allusion.

"Yes—I see. I was slow. But I haven't always been. I wasn't when Richard courted and married me."

Again there came a long period of silence. It was broken by the ring of a bicycle bell. Mrs. Atherton looked up. "Here is Godfrey," she said—"is it your intention to tell him what you've told me?"

"I don't think so, Mrs. Atherton. Introduce me as a friend of your people at Stoke Pelly. When I have seen him, I shall make up my mind. What you care to tell your son after my departure is nobody's business beyond your own."

"Thank you," she returned with a mixture of candour and simplicity.

2

The door of the dining-room opened and a young fellow entered. He was tall, thin and pale. His hair was long and it fell rather untidily on his forehead. But his face was a good face, taking it all in all, for it showed unmistakable signs of intelligence well in advance of the average and even, too, of intellect. The brow was the brow of a thinker who might turn out to be a scholar. There was much of his grandfather in him. His mouth opened rather loosely when he saw that his mother was not alone.

"I'm sorry, mother," he said jerkily—"I didn't know you had company."

Mrs. Atherton rose to the occasion. "This is Mr. Bathurst," she said, "he's a friend of Uncle Philip's—this is my son, Godfrey, Mr. Bathurst."

The young man nodded to Anthony rather curtly. Anthony thought that he knew the reason which had produced such a nod. Godfrey Atherton turned towards his mother. His eyes held a multitude of queries. But, if they did, no answer was forthcoming for them. His mother went on in purely conventional strain.

"Mr. Bathurst happened to be motoring in the district," she said, "and he remembered that Uncle Philip had mentioned to him that we lived out here. So he paid us a call. That was nice of him, wasn't it?"

Godfrey muttered something which Anthony wasn't able to distinguish.

"Have you lunched?" asked Mrs. Atherton.

"Oh—yes—thank you! I did myself rather well at the 'Red Cock'—the pub near the station. And if you're due for your lunch now—I think I'll be getting along."

"You're sure you won't stay and have lunch with us?"

"Quite. I should be more than trespassing on your hospitality. Well—good-bye."

Anthony spoke to Godfrey Atherton. "No sooner it seems do we meet—than we part again."

"Good-bye," replied the son of the house. There was relief in his face.

"I'll walk with you to the gate," said Mrs. Atherton.

"Thank you."

Mrs. Atherton piloted Anthony from the dining-room and out of the house. "Well?" she queried as they walked down the garden, "you've seen him." She paused.

Anthony filled in the gap. "Yes—I've seen him."

"He is very like his father—but you wouldn't know that."

"He is very like his grandfather—which I do know."

"And—er"—it was evident that she found the question excessively difficult to ask—"you have made up your mind?"

"Yes, Mrs. Atherton—I have made up my mind." Anthony's tone was grave.

They came to the gate. "Will you be here for Christmas?" he asked suddenly. She looked afraid at the question.

"No. We shall be at Stoke Pelly. Godfrey and I. We always spend our Christmas there. Just the family—nobody else. Peace on earth—goodwill to all men. Please remember that, Mr. Bathurst."

He shook his head. "Or—rather peace on earth—to all men of goodwill."

"I accept the correction." She leant forward impulsively and placed her hand on his sleeve. "Don't forget one thing, Mr. Bathurst. To me—Julian Field was—"

Anthony cut into her. "But there was always Claudia Field. No matter what you say. Claudia was his wife and was therefore always *somewhere* in the picture. You can't just relegate her to oblivion."

"What did we care about Claudia? How could we? We were only human. But there—argument's useless and mere talking will lead us nowhere. It's just waste of time. Why did you ask where Godfrey and I would be at Christmas?"

Anthony half-smiled at her. "If I told you—I wonder what you'd say."

"Tell me and see."

Anthony told her. Mrs. Atherton achieved some dignity when she replied. "I do not think," she replied, "that there need be any difficulty whatever. As I visualize the situation. And, of course, I am in your hands. Thank you, at least, for giving me Christmas. I'll arrange everything for you. Shall I explain all the circumstances—or do you think it will do, if I just—"

Anthony shook his head. "I leave it entirely to you yourself, Mrs. Atherton—but from what I know of the 'Gifford's' ménage—they'll add the two and two together satisfactorily and come to the correct total. There is one stipulation, though, which I would make. No word of this must reach the ears of the Vicar of Fullafold."

Her eyes looked strange as she turned away. "I promise you that. Mince-pies and mistletoe—snap-dragon and handcuffs! I don't see that anybody in his right senses could add those up."

3

Anthony made his way slowly back to his car. By field, spinney, gate, field and gate. As he walked, he took off his hat and let the wind buffet his head. He felt that after the interview he had just brought off, he must have air. For his feeling of satisfaction that he had successfully worked out the pattern of the case and the full design of the crime, was strongly tinged by the disconcerting knowledge that he had been so hopelessly wrong in his deductions with regard to the identity of the murderer of Julian Field. It would be a salutary lesson to him for all time. What a far cry it had been, to be sure, from the church-porch at Fullafold to "The Copper Beeches" at Lavencourt in the county of Suffolk. And the drama was not yet played out! Anthony started the car and began his journey back—the victim of conflicting thoughts and emotions. Certain words of an Old Testament lesson which had impressed and which always would impress him, rioted through his brain. After a time, he found himself reciting some of them aloud for the magic of the Old Testament prose held him in its grip. "And there stood a watchman on the tower in Jezreel; and he spied the company of Jehu as he came; and he said 'I see a company.' And Joram said: 'Take a horseman, and send to meet them, and let him say "Is it peace?"' And Jehu said 'What hast thou to do with peace? Turn thee behind me.' And the watchman told, saying: 'The messenger came to them but he cometh not again. Then he sent out a second on horseback which came to them and said: "Thus saith the King. 'Is it peace?'"' and Jehu answered, 'What hast thou to do with peace? Turn thee behind me.' And the watchman told, saying: 'He came even unto them and cometh not again, and the driving is like the driving of Jehu, the son of Nimshi, for he driveth furiously.'"

Anthony repeated the phrase to himself—"Is it peace? What hast thou to do with peace?" Anthony shook his head. In time he came to the tunnel under the river again and later—to Southshire and Greenhurst.

The dinner which the "Horse and Groom" would provide for him that evening would be very welcome. For Anthony was hungry—really hungry—and when that happened—

4

He dined with MacMorran. MacMorran's eyes were on him all the time. They searched and re-searched his face. The inspector noticed that he was unusually silent.

"I presume," said MacMorran, "from the disinclination to talk, that the day has not been exactly a day of triumph."

"Oh—I don't know. Comme ci, comme ça."

MacMorran continued in his previous vein. "I find no exultant enthusiasm. No—how shall I put it—no 'cock-a-hoop.'"

"No," replied Anthony—"none of those things. This is our first case together when the killer is going to give us such a run for our money that we shall wish the winning-post a good deal nearer than it is."

"You're tellin' me! I've thought on those lines for a long time." MacMorran sprinkled salt on his potatoes. "The gist of all this is, of course, that you've drawn a blank?"

"I don't know that I'd call it a blank, Andrew. More like a non-runner."

"From my point of view—they're much the same."

"You don't lose on a non-runner—that's the difference."

"Oh, yes, you do—if it's drawn in a sweepstake or you back it ante-post. Now argue that one off."

Anthony grinned. "Well—we didn't come into the Fullafold murder ante-post. Call it post-post and I'm with you."

"This isn't getting us anywhere," declared the inspector. "Too true, Andrew. And for another thing—there's Christmas right in front of us. And much as I like Sir Austin Kemble and the jobs he finds for me—and your own charming and congenial company—well—I don't propose to spend my festive Yuletide at the 'Horse and Groom,' Greenhurst. In fact, I can't—I've been booked up already."

"I'm not blaming you for that. If I were in your shoes, I'd say the same myself." MacMorran arranged his now empty plate. "Until we are able to fill in what happened to Field between leaving the 'Ram' and coming to the church-porch at Fullafold, we're just ploughing the sands. And we're no nearer to doing that than when we started."

"I entirely agree with you, Andrew."

The inspector shook his head with the gloom of despondency.

Chapter XXII

1

ANTHONY sat down and wrote two letters. Each letter was composed by him with scrupulous care. Each in a way, was a corollary and complementary to the other. The first was addressed to Ernest Courtenay, Esq., and the second to Mrs. Claudia M. Field—both of King's Winkworth.

When he had completed them, he read and re-read them. There was no loop-hole as far as he could see and he had emphasized the time-factor in such a manner that it would be almost impossible for either of them to ignore it. Anthony walked to the village post office and posted the letters himself. He looked at the collection timeplate with interest and satisfaction. If his calculations were worth anything—the letters would arrive just in time. With this thought uppermost in his mind, Anthony returned to the inn.

2

Anthony came again to King's Winkworth. Although the morrow was Christmas Eve, the little village looked much the same to him as it had on previous occasions. "Bulmer's" evidently were still dispensing morning coffee and the dispensation was in the hands of the same girl. Anthony, who had chosen the ground deliberately, knocked on the door of the house which had been inhabited by the late Dr. Julian Field. Before his summons was answered, he looked at the time by his wrist-watch. To his satisfaction, he saw that he was within two minutes of the time he had named in his letters. Claudia Field came to the door. He saw at once that the lady looked anxious, sad and worried. The lines of her pretty mouth had hardened with apprehension and Anthony guessed that for some little time, perhaps, she hadn't slept o' nights.

"Please come in," she said.

Anthony thanked her and followed her into a lounge. A man was seated there—in a low, extremely comfortable-looking armchair. The man rose as Claudia Field opened the door. Anthony saw that it was Ernest Courtenay. The birds had responded to the crumbs he had thrown to them.

3

"Good morning," said Courtenay—"I suppose I should add—this is an unexpected pleasure. Decent people, they say, should always observe the conventions."

Courtenay smiled. But the smile was forced and his face didn't live with it. They were as two things apart.

"Good morning," said Anthony, "and thank you. After all—you could have refused to grant me this interview." Anthony took the chair towards which Ernest Courtenay had gestured him. Claudia spoke as Anthony sat down.

"If he hadn't spurned my advice," she said, "we would have done." She spoke with asperity. "You might as well know that at the start of the interview, as at the finish."

Courtenay stood with his back to the fire and looked at them. "My dear Claudia," he said a trifle coldly, "when I'm standing on the wrong side of the fence, I flatter myself that I have the sense to know it. Bathurst here is top dog. He's top dog whether we like it or not." Courtenay turned to Anthony. "You see," he remarked, with a touch of something that sounded suspiciously like bitterness, "I've decided to come clean."

He looked at Claudia. It was evident that he harboured certain anxiety with regard to her reception of his last statement. Anthony saw that Claudia looked away from him and shrugged her shoulders. Anthony felt that he must begin to do a spot of sorting out.

"When I came in," he said, "I thanked you. I thanked you for your acceptance of my suggestion. As I said—you would have been entirely within your rights had you refused to discuss the matter with me. But as I see things—if I charge you (both of you) with the murder of Julian Field—you might feel that you were in an extremely awkward position."

Anthony paused—to let his words sink in. He watched the faces of the man and the woman. Claudia Field paled perceptibly and Courtenay for a brief second looked something like a haggard old man.

"Your charge, Bathurst, would be absurd. We were never within twenty miles of Fullafold."

Anthony shook his head. "That, my dear Courtenay, is your story. Mine would be that you were. That you have been illicit lovers for some time (most British juries would be ready to hang you for that at sight—before your trial for murder even began), that you were together on the night of the murder, that Julian Field accidentally ran into you in a place where you never dreamed there was an infinitesimal chance of meeting him, that there ensued the inevitable quarrel and that between you you killed him."

Claudia Field blazed at him with fire in her eyes. "That's untrue," she cried, "every word of it."

Anthony shrugged his shoulders. "Can you prove it?" Claudia Field came back at him "It's for the Crown to prove guilt—not for us to prove our innocence."

"Very true, Mrs. Field. But it's not an easier path for you, if you can't prove that innocence! You can leave the Crown, I suggest, to look after its own case."

There was an ominous silence. Courtenay tried another tack.

"This is hopelessly irregular, you know, Bathurst—"

"Oh—I agree. I agree cheerfully. But that doesn't alter the fact that you're in a nasty hole. I'll prove it to you. Not that it really needs proving. You know it yourself. Apart from what I may tell you. You admitted as much in an early part of this interview when you said you were the wrong side of the fence. But it can all come to a question of alibi. And alibis, when you haven't got 'em, can be nasty things as the Irishman said. You're shrewd enough to know that, Courtenay. Where were you, Mr. Courtenay, on the night that Julian Field was murdered? Not within twenty miles of Fullafold—say you. Very good! Can you prove that, Mr. Courtenay? Have you witnesses whose credit is beyond dispute? Have you witnesses like Caesar's wife? You haven't! Nary a one. Your only witness is not *Caesar's* wife—but *Julian Field's wife*! Because she was with you."

Courtenay bit his lip. Anthony turned his attention to the indignant Claudia. "Where were you, Claudia Field, on that night that your husband, Julian Field, was murdered? What can you say? Your answer would be the same as your cousin's. Can you prove that, Mrs. Field? Are your witnesses all good men and true? No—your one and only witness is the man who stands accused with you of murder. So of what value becomes the word of either of you? I may be wrong, of course," added Anthony—"jurors are proverbially 'kittle cattle'—but I wouldn't give a row of beans for your chance. You'd swing—both of you! Like Edith Thompson and Freddy Bywaters."

He looked at them and saw differences now. Claudia twisted her square of handkerchief round her fingers and a vein in Courtenay's forehead was beating fiercely. Anthony struck. But the blow was more merciful than they had anticipated. Because they hadn't called the bluff he had dangled in front of them.

"I wonder whether you feel now that you'd be ready to answer certain questions? Which will not be used in evidence against you! As you pointed out—this is completely irregular and an entirely unofficial interview."

Courtenay looked up quickly and caught Anthony's eye. "Yes," he said firmly—"I'll answer any questions you care to ask. And Claudia will too."

Before she could expostulate, Courtenay asserted himself. "For once, Claudia—be guided by me. You won't regret it, I assure you."

Claudia made no answer. Both Anthony and Courtenay took her silence for acceptance of Courtenay's request. Anthony waited for a moment and then spoke to Claudia.

"How long, Mrs. Field, had you been in the house on the evening your husband was killed when your telephone rang?" Claudia looked across at her cousin. Courtenay nodded.

"About ten minutes," she answered—"scarcely any more."

"So that you didn't get home until past eleven o'clock?"

"No."

"Even though your husband was expected home about nine o'clock?"

"Yes."

"Why was that, Mrs. Field? Why did you run such a risk?" Claudia looked at Courtenay interrogatively. Again he nodded to her. "We had trouble with the car," she said. "I wasn't late intentionally. I intended to be home before my husband got in. I don't know what the actual trouble was. Ernest, no doubt, will tell you."

"Carburettor," said Ernest laconically—"and unfortunately—doubly so now—there was no garage handy. I had to see to it myself and it took me a hell of a long time."

Claudia came in again. "I could say, Mr. Bathurst, that I was indoors all the evening."

"You could, Mrs. Field—but then Courtenay would have no witness as to where he was."

Anthony had been prepared for that—and had his reply ready. Claudia was silent.

"Where—actually—did you go?" asked Anthony. "Tunbridge Wells," answered Ernest Courtenay, "and again unfortunately, we didn't stop on the road anywhere. Not even for a drink. We hadn't a lot of time. Claudia didn't meet me till past six and you know the time we wanted to be back by." He paused—to continue again almost immediately. "There's something else I'd like to say."

"Go on," said Anthony, "there's nothing like the truth for clearing the air and removing all misunderstanding."

"That evening jaunt was entirely my affair—from the point of view of any censure. I prevailed on Claudia to come with me. I'd badgered and pestered her for some time. That's one thing off my chest. Now—here's another. Claudia has always been faithful to Field. That may or may not interest you. But it does me. And in justice to her—I've told you. Claudia's my cousin—don't forget that. I knew her before she met Field. We've always been tremendous pals—on my side it's always been something stronger than that. That evening was the first time we'd been out together for years—and we were damned unlucky. But I give you my word of honour that neither of us knows the first thing about the murder of Julian Field. If you don't believe that—well—I can't help it—and it's just too bad."

Anthony rose from the chair he had been occupying. "Thank you, Courtenay. As it happens—I do believe it. If I hadn't believed it, I shouldn't have come here to-day as I have. But I had to clear the matter up. I'm thanking you for being frank with me."

He held out his hand to Claudia Field. "Good-bye, Mrs. Field. Thank you, too. There's not much point in my remaining any longer—so I'll be getting back."

Claudia smiled and shook hands. Courtenay did likewise. Anthony lingered for a moment by the door. "I don't know whether I should tell you this. But I think I will. As you know—it has been well and truly said that there isn't much difference between the best of the worst of us and the worst of the best. Be that as it may—I'm going to say this." He looked straight at Claudia Field. "You need reproach yourself but little, Mrs. Field. *De mortuis, nil nisi bonum est*—I know all about that—but all the same, if you *should* decide to marry again, your second husband'll be a better man than your first."

Anthony opened the door as Claudia came forward to see him out. "And that comes," he added, "from a man who is seldom given to prophecy. Good luck to both of you."

When Anthony got back to Greenhurst, MacMorran said what Anthony thought was a surprising thing.

"Do you know," said the "Yard" inspector, "I've a good mind to chance my arm."

"How come, Andrew?"

"Have a smack at Ernest Courtenay. I've been thinking things over very carefully while you've been out and I've had two more long talks with Bernays at Four Bridges. I've a damned good mind to go for a warrant for Courtenay. The old eternal triangle makes a thunderin' good motive nineteen times out of twenty. I wonder if he could give a satisfactory account of his movements for the evening of October 27th?"

"Well, Andrew," said. Anthony, "it's your pigeon and I'm a mere tyro compared with a man who's had your experience at this game. But if you take my advice—you'll lay off Courtenay. For one thing he's not Field's murderer—I'll make you a present of that piece of information—and for another—you'd have a herculean job making anything like a case against him."

"I'm not so sure," replied MacMorran, "seems to me, he might give himself away if he were suddenly jumped on. I've known that happen before now."

Anthony shook his head. "Well—as I said, Andrew, you know your own business best—but in my opinion, you've nothing like enough to pin on Ernest Courtenay. If you move, you'll make a mistake—and you don't want that to happen."

MacMorran walked to the window and looked out. "I'd never have believed," he said, "that when I took this case, I was walking into a failure. Not even if you had told me. There seemed so much to work on. It wasn't as though no clues came to us. Take that note from 'Mary,' for instance. Who'd have thought that would lead absolutely nowhere? Why couldn't Field have met a girl named Petronella—or something like that? No—it had to be Mary." MacMorran muttered under his breath.

"That's right, Andrew, let yourself go properly. Say it! Invoke your favourite queen!"

MacMorran stared. "How do you mean?" he queried. "Didn't I hear you say 'Bloody Mary'?"

The inspector glared—and said it again.

Chapter XXIII

1

The sky had looked grey and sullenly angry for some time. More than once Anthony had given it an anxious glance. When he had completed about half his journey his fears were realized. The snow began to fall. The temperature was such, too, that it lay where it fell. "Thick and heavy," said Anthony to himself, "and everybody bar a champion mug spending Christmas indoors." His wind-screen wiper was hard put to it to clear his vision.

Anthony trod on the juice. When he came to Stoke Pelly, it looked like a village of a Christmas card. Comfortable and friendly lights peeped through from cosy interiors and told Anthony that the inhabitants of Stoke Pelly were spending their Christmas in the warmth and glow of the fire. The car came to the cross-roads and Anthony swung left at "The Old Oak." He remembered that "Gifford's" was only about half a mile ahead. The gate was open as it had been when he had come before and the car purred up the drive. As Anthony brought it to a halt, a clock away in the distance struck five. Five o'clock on Christmas night. "Mince-pies and mistletoe" quoted Anthony, "snapdragon and handcuffs. Mine is an errand strange and bizarre—Kaspar, Melchior, Balthasar."

A door opened somewhere and Philip Stanhope stood at his side. His face was lined with care and when he spoke his voice was heavy with anxiety.

"Good evening, Bathurst," he said—"you're on time—despite the filthy weather."

"Yes. I suppose I haven't done too badly—considering everything. Oh—and by the way—thanks for the invitation. It was very decent of you."

Stanhope made no reply. He stared at Anthony questioningly. Then, with an abrupt turn of the head, he said, "Come on inside. We're all in here. We've been waiting for you."

"How many?" asked Anthony.

"Seven of us," said Philip Stanhope.

"Thanks," said Anthony.

2

Philip Stanhope escorted Anthony into an almost perfect room. It was beautifully decorated in honour of the season and there was a fire on the hearth which was the full epitome of comfort and joy. The Stanhope family and their Christmas guests were grouped round the fire.

"Anthony Bathurst," said the host.

"Sit down, everybody," said Anthony. "For one thing you look too comfortable to move and I can see that I've met every one of you before so that there's no need for any special introduction."

"I don't think so," said Philip Stanhope—"have you met Dudley? I don't think he was here when you came before."

"Sorry—my mistake. I met him though at Twickenham the other day—in the distance." Anthony turned to Dudley. "Pleased to meet you, Stanhope."

Dudley Stanhope grinned back. "Oxford, weren't you?"

"Yes. Uppingham and Oxford. Way back in the Stone Age. Or at least—that's what it seems like."

"Don't you believe it. From your appearance—it might have been only yesterday."

There ensued an ominous silence. Philip broke it. "Drink, Bathurst? What shall it be?"

Before Anthony could reply, Daphne jumped up. "No, Philip. We were just going to have tea. I'm sure that after that terrible journey Mr. Bathurst would prefer tea now. I remember what an enormous meal he ate when he was here before."

There was a slight laugh at this—but the two Athertons remained silent.

"If you were about to have tea," said Anthony, "please have it. Don't let me disturb you in any way. If you do—I shall be sorry I came. But I'll promise Mrs. Stanhope one thing—I'll tone down my enormous appetite."

"You shall have tea," said Daphne, "thin bread and butter and real Christmas cake. That's quite enough for anybody after a Christmas dinner. Come with me, Nancy, and we can help in the kitchen."

The two sisters went out. Elinor grimaced. "For some reason," she said, "I'm being let off. Wonders will never cease. But I'll bet there'll be a day of reckoning."

Anthony switched back to Twickenham and when the tea-wagons came in, the conversation was doing very nicely and the general atmosphere approximating to the normal. When tea was finished, Anthony looked up at his host.

"What's the weather like now, Mr. Stanhope? Is it holding up at all?"

"It's stopped snowing—but there's a pretty thick carpet everywhere."

Anthony looked at his watch. "I mustn't leave it too late, then. What about a billiard foursome before I stagger forth again? Dudley and I, say, against you and Howard? I'm only a moderate player myself—so you needn't worry."

Philip Stanhope looked at him critically. "Yes—good idea. We usually have a game about this time in the evening. Howard—would you pop along and get the table ready?"

Anthony looked round. "We'll make it a stag party. Perhaps Atherton would come along and act as marker for us? Would you mind?"

Godfrey Atherton got out of his armchair. "Certainly," he said—but his face was pale and his hands not as steady as they should have been.

3

Anthony prepared to play his first stroke. "As you know," he said, "I've been engaged for some little time now on an investigation into the murder of a doctor named Julian Field."

Anthony potted the red and all through the game which followed he went on talking. The others merely listened. Not one of them spoke. The only noise came from the impact of the balls.

"For the first time in my career," went on Anthony, "I must confess myself beaten."

There was a slight stir from Godfrey Atherton's corner of the board.

"Beaten," said Anthony, "but, to employ a cliché—not disgraced. I'll try to explain exactly what I mean. Let's begin with Field himself. And you must remember that I'm trying to give you, from my imagination, a picture of the genesis of the crime and of the manner in which it *might* have been carried out. Oh—good shot, sir."

Anthony watched the roll of the balls. "Field was a doctor who purchased a practice at King's Winkworth from the executors of a Doctor Louis Wolff who, with his wife, had died very suddenly as the result of a motoring accident. When he took over, I suggest that Field came across a number of very interesting documents in the nature of case papers. His predecessor had been a specialist in T.B. and kindred diseases of the lungs and chest. During the war Wolff had dabbled in dirt. Made a lot of money out of his dabbling. Operations to do with the evasion of military and other similar service. One, in particular, which achieved, so I've been told, a considerable measure of popularity. There was something approaching certainty about it. I refer, as you have probably guessed, to the creation of an artificial pneumo-thorax. This is an operation which collapses the lung and is usually performed on a select case of active pulmonary tuberculosis of one lung. Or, of course, on a perfectly healthy lung. And the beauty of this operation, from the point of view of the gentlemen who desired above all things to evade combative military service, is that it is impossible to tell by either X-ray treatment, or by any other method, if the lung so treated were tubercular or not. Wolff did a number of these operations and collected no doubt thereby a considerable amount of cash. But his sudden death and the disposal of his practice put certain information in the hands of his unscrupulous successor, Julian Field.

"Certain case papers were found by Field in Wolff's surgery and Field rubbed his hands. 'There was gold in them thar 'ills.' In the language of the criminal class, Field dug into the details and commenced 'to put on the black.' Quite a number of people were threatened with exposure and made to toe the line. Field took quarterly payments and these foolish people, frightened for themselves and frightened in some cases for the sons who had been operated on, and who might have been called upon to face a serious charge, were bled white. The initials of one of these gentlemen were G.M.A. They might have stood for George Murray Atkinson—on the other hand they might signify initials much more familiar to you. I can visualize a condition where a loving mother, widowed in comparative girlhood by the cruelty of a previous war, a son born to her after the death of a gallant husband, vows to herself passionately that she will keep at all costs the only thing she was left in the world to love. That son, too, might be affected, conceivably, by pre-natal fears and inhibitions and feel that he must fall in with his mother's wishes. But—of course—all that is mere conjecture on my part. To know all is to understand all."

Anthony stopped to make a stroke. The silence was almost uncanny. He missed. "I can now imagine the position," he went on, "of a woman, bled white by an avaricious blackmailer, almost at the end of her mental and moral tether, going in sheer desperation to a member of her family, confessing her secret and begging for help. It might have been to a sister—or even to a brother-in-law—and I can sense the burning indignation which that relative would feel. Steps must be taken. No—more than that—steps will be taken! She is promised that the problem will be faced and tackled. And failing all attempts at what we will call persuasion, no mercy will be shown to this possibly most loathsome of all human creatures, the blackmailer. Cigarette, anybody?"

Anthony passed round his case. He continued: "It became obvious that contact must be made with Field. The question was how? What method would be the best—and in the event of the worst happening—the least likely to excite suspicion? This question was no doubt talked over and discussed for some time. The answer to the query became clearer. What could possibly be better, from all angles, than to approach Field in the most normal and natural way? He was a medical man, with a growing local reputation in respect of chest and lung complaints—why not then, lure him into the circle of action with the bait of a patient? It was obvious that he must be looked over, as it were, first of all. This was important, certainly, from a physical standpoint. How would the conspirators stand with him—if it came to a rough house? They must find that out. Which looked like two visits from the doctor fellow at least. Well—the patient was produced and all arrangements made for the first and preliminary visit. The telephone was employed and the message based on the traditional reputation of the late Doctor Wolff. The first appointment was made and the stage prepared for what I'll term—Act One. And then I suggest," Anthony began to speak more slowly, "that the initial snag began to poke its head out. A healthy woman doesn't need a second medical examination within a few weeks. If the patient is examined in September, say, and she's found to be perfectly fit, which was a pretty safe bet in this particular instance—what need would there be for the doctor's second visit in October? A possible solution to this difficulty would be to play the card, when Field arrived, of what I will call, for want of a better description, 'the reluctant lady.' Apologies would be tendered—you know doctor, what women are—prostrate with nervousness—you've had your journey, I'm afraid for nothing, but there you are, the lady refuses to see you—you'll have to come down again—say in a month or so's time—in the meantime I'll talk her round and get her to be sensible. That's a much better plan than trying to force the issue now. Now—what about some tea, doctor, and you can come along again—well suppose—we fix it for October 27th. Would that fit in with you all right?"

Anthony changed his tone. "Of course, these are all conjectures on my part and I may be, in parts, wide of the mark. On the other hand, I may not. It is my shot? Sorry. I think I can pull that one off with just enough top-side. Thought so! Well now—where was I? Oh—I know. Field's first visit. The conspirators size him up. Nothing to worry about from the physical standpoint. They can deal with him all right—if the necessity should ever arise. I *think*, though, they discovered in some way that Field carried a revolver. It's a habit of blackmailers. Their consciences are like crowned heads. The gun may have been in his overcoat and he *might* have been sitting down to tea when his overcoat was frisked. I can now assert, I think, that the stage is set for Act Two. Always, the most important and crucial act of any drama. In this play, it might be given the title of the showdown. The cards are all going on the table.

"As before, the medical gentleman, whose bluff is to be so well and truly called, is met at the railway station and I feel confident, his appearance and general externals are impressed upon—well—let us say—the stationmaster. And Field is a splendid subject for this exercise. In one respect, it would be almost impossible for him to be bettered—he wears a trimly kept pointed beard! Now, when he arrives at the house of his patient, on this second occasion, Field soon becomes acquainted with the truth. There is no delay now in letting him know where he stands. Only the most commendable promptitude. In some manner, at which I can only hazard a guess, he is confronted with the sight of his blackmailed victim, no less than three times. Three ladies, all bearing an extraordinary physical resemblance to each other which is quite natural and understandable, seeing that they could be—shall we say—sisters and a daughter and all dressed exactly alike—stand perhaps, at three different doors. *And when he sees them* in their triple array, Field knows, with a nasty feeling somewhat round the pit of his stomach that the fly has walked very sweetly into the spider's parlour."

There came a harsh clattering noise from one end of the billiard-room. Philip Stanhope stooped and picked up his cue.

"I am forced, of course," continued Anthony, "to draw almost entirely upon my imagination for the details of what transpired after that. Field, realizing now the true purpose behind his visit, may have turned nasty, like a cornered beast at bay. I shall assume both now and later that this is what actually did happen. He may even have attempted to use his gun—and, possibly, after that, a struggle ensued, where conceivably all the odds were against him. I should put them at three to one in actual mathematical figures and two of those three were young men, one on special leave from an historic university and each physically fit to a degree considerably above the average. On the outer hand, it may have been a man to man struggle. The life was choked out of Field—a mode of death probably much too good for him, and with which, speaking purely as an individual, I have no quarrel at all. Is it my shot again? I thought so—and a pretty filthy leave at that. Pity—not legs enough."

Anthony re-chalked his cue. "Well—there we are—and a dead body is not the most pleasant object to have lying on the family hearth-rug. From the council of war which followed there emerged, I fancy, a most ingenious plot, conceived and carried out with consummate skill and audacity. The main planks of the plot were constructed in such a manner, that no real, provable suspicion could be directed against the family escutcheon. In the first place, Field must obviously seem to leave the house alive. He must be produced, seen, recognized and identified by more than one person. The more—the better! Now—how could this best be achieved? If one of those three main actors were roughly of Field's physique—you for example, Mr. Stanhope—would have filled the bill excellently had you been implicated—" Anthony nodded to Dudley Stanhope—"and worn certain of Field's clothes—plus the pointed beard—well—it would be darkish about seven o'clock (the time of Field's train back to King's Winkworth)—and the created identity would have every chance of passing muster. The clothes which would be required to be worn would be those, naturally, which anybody would recognize who had seen Field arrive. The station-master, for example, at Stoke Pelly railway station. They would consist of what I'll call the externals—hat, overcoat, scarf, tie, shirt and collar, shoes and gloves—plus such things as ring, wrist-watch, and other accessories which would help to fill in the complete visible picture of the returning doctor. The strange separation of the dead man's clothes, at first so seemingly inexplicable, at once attains reasonableness when one remembers that the second clothes parcel from the font of the church at Friar's Woodburn contained all those articles of clothing which a man need wear if he wanted, to look like Field! With the possible exception of the jacket—and then a small part only of that would be showing. So the jacket was chanced! I was a long time understanding the clothes problem—but when I did—I felt that I was really beginning to make progress."

The silence in the billiard-room was now more intense than ever. It hung over the room like a huge cloud—ominous of an approaching storm. Anthony had paused in his narrative to take another stroke. He kept himself in play and went on talking. "I'll now just sketch the next series of incidents in the order in which, I think, they took place. The first point was a masterstroke. Something to clinch Field's identity acceptance. Something extra! Something which everybody would see when they encountered him anywhere between Stoke Pelly and his destination—which, as Field, hadn't yet been decided. What should this extra emblem be? Of course—a red rose from the garden! That would catch the eye splendidly. What did it matter if Field hadn't worn it on his journey down? He could wear it on his journey back—and the police would be told about it! There were several ways in which this could be effected. So there we have the first picture of the first complete dénouement. Dudley—I'll call him Dudley—just for simplicity—attiring himself as Field. For which he had bags of time. Clothes—rose in coat—but the rather awkward problem of the beard. The beard which was absolutely *essential*! Now, you can't grow a beard in a couple of hours so the only alternative was a false one. Which, in the absence of the wherewithal, or the perruquier, was something in the nature of a headache. Now—I don't pretend to know how this gulf was bridged. All I'll do is to offer, very naturally, an intelligent suggestion."

Dudley Stanhope struck a match—but his fingers shook—and the flame went out.

4

"It may have been," continued Anthony, "that Mrs. Atherton—I'll name the cast now—had come by car to take her part in the early shock due to be administered to Julian Field, known as 'the three victims.' It may have been that her son, who takes part in amateur stage-work, had his make-up box in the car. It may have been that the box contained crêpe hair. I'll say no more—but there is no doubt that the beard was made and that the initial stage of the plot had been successfully accomplished. Apart, too, from the possibility that it had been made in advance and was being held in readiness. Now let us look carefully at what our three musketeers had to do. Their complete programme consisted of (a) disposing of the body, (b) destroying any evidence at Field's surgery, which would implicate them and at the same time supply a motive for the murder, and (c) the provision of what I'll call certain sadistic embroidery to the crime. With regard to (a) of these three contingencies the church-porch at Fullafold was selected. It was known to them—I think there had been a wedding in the family there some years before—and whichever way you looked at it, it was an ideal spot. Dark, lonely and save for a few people who cut through the churchyard at very odd intervals, usually given a very cold shoulder at night by the majority. The place where the church lantern hung would hold the body admirably and if everything were got ready beforehand, the whole job could be done in a few minutes.

"Item (b) could then be taken in stride, providing they could make sure in advance that the surgery would be empty when they arrived there. A bogus telephone call might well be the means of ensuring this condition and it could be sent from the Fullafold area when the body had been disposed of. The embroidery, or the embellishments, if you like, became the next matter of consideration. 'Field' would leave the train at Greenhurst (the nearest station to Fullafold) where he would surrender the return half of the authentic ticket, advertise himself well and then meet the others at the church. The intervening time could very well be filled in for further advertisement purposes in the saloon bar of a pub, not too far away from the church of their design."

Anthony stopped and looked at the marker's score-board. Godfrey Atherton, evidently, had ceased to mark. The others, too, seemed to have stopped playing. They were listening to Anthony's recital now with an utter disregard for anything else that might be happening. Anthony accepted the situation philosophically and went on.

"Our conspirators were determined, however, to leave nothing whatever to chance. If the pseudo 'Field' left the train at Greenhurst, a reason must be furnished for this deviation from the normal. What could this reason be? How could it be suggested? By a really brilliant brain-wave (at least I regard it as such), an illicit love-affair was manufactured for the train-leaving 'doctor.' A note suggestive and indicative of an amorous assignation and signed with perhaps the most popular of all girls' names would serve the purpose admirably. There could be nothing better calculated to put the cat among the pigeons. The note was written—I fancy that three hands held the pen in rotation for each successive word,—signed 'Mary'—and a well-known lovers' rendezvous near Friar's Woodburn, known as the Cornelius Stones, was nominated for the trysting place. The note then went into Field's wallet which was placed in his overcoat pocket. And if the bogus 'Field,' when he left the railway station at Greenhurst, should inquire of the ticket collector for the Cornelius Stones, so much the more confusing and an ever bigger headache for the police authorities. So there we are, gentlemen, with the stage set once again for the next act in this amazing drama. The time, we'll say, is five minutes to seven. Mrs. Atherton and her son have already departed. It is well that they should be off the stage. They may have driven to town or taken the journey back to Suffolk. It makes no odds. We have Field's nude body in a big travelling trunk or maybe wrapped between large blankets in the back of a car. Round his neck are the rope and two hooks, one extra in case of need. Dudley—I feel certain it was Dudley—is dressed in those of Field's clothes which he needs to establish his 'identity' plus the red rose from the garden—the remaining garments are in the car. The conspirators have the key of Field's surgery. The car sets off—for Stoke Pelly railway station, to be *just in time* to catch the 7.3." Anthony stopped again, and for the first time there came an intervention.

"Get Bathurst a whisky and soda," said Philip Stanhope to his younger son, "we'll all have one—on second thoughts," he added.

"I thank you," replied Anthony, "I don't mind if I do."

5

"I give you my word," said Philip Stanhope, as he handed Anthony the glass, "that it's free from all poison or 'deleterious' substance."

"Thank you. I don't doubt that. Well—here's the compliments of the season." Anthony drained his glass. "That's 'White Horse'—that was. Let me see now. Ah—just in time for the 7.3, and to be vouched for by the excellent Plummer, the station-master. Good. Twenty-five for none—and a good sight of the ball. Messieurs Philip and Howard drive eventually to the edge of the slope at Fullafold. Dudley gets out at Greenhurst, does his 'Cornelius Steps' at the station (a further deliberate touch of confusion), goes to the 'Ram,' drinks with a blonde (who in all probability, judging by her subsequent silence, was supposed to be somewhere else), and then when the pub shuts and 'Field' has been well 'seen' in Fullafold and Greenhurst, meets the car with his father and brother at the foot of the slope to the church-porch. The time, I should think, would be about half-past ten.

"I was a comparatively easy matter to park the car well away from the road and carry the body to the porch and fix it up. To hang it nude would give a sensational touch to the crime which would still more mystify the police. Two could work while the third watched—to keep 'cave.' The job was done and the parcel of unwanted clothes placed in the font—when Mary Whitley began to walk up the slope. She was, I think, neither seen nor heard by the three principal actors. But she heard them. But what about Field's gun? How about dumping it? How about, too, firing a shot? That might look better and fortify the suggestion of dirty work somewhere. How about 'Mary's' husband? How about 'Mary's' lover? Field might easily have supplanted somebody. Right! Now for the telephone to Mrs. Field. And then the quick run to Field's surgery at King's Winkworth, in order to destroy the documents there which contained the incriminating evidence. That something of the kind was there was well known, from information in the possession of Mrs. Atherton." Anthony took a cigarette and lit up.

"Here something happened which I find rather unaccountable. In fact it bothered me for an appreciable time. I refer to the entry to Field's premises brought about by breaking in at the back of the house. Why break in—I said to myself many times—when you have already obtained possession of the key of the front door? I can only think that the key must have been mislaid in some way. Possibly lost—or possibly dropped somewhere. On the floor of the car, perhaps. That is the only conclusion to which I have been able to come. It may not be entirely satisfactory, but like one or two other minor matters connected with the case, it can more or less be taken as read. The search for the incriminating papers and their inevitable indication of the Atherton family, which if found by the police would have quickly, of course, led in turn to the Stanhope implication, proved successful. I think, too, that certain other files which contained evidence of Field's similar nefarious activities in relation to other of Wolff's 'patients' were also discovered, removed and, doubtless, subsequently destroyed. I commend this exercise in altruism. And somewhere about the time that all this was going on"—Anthony altered his rate of speech and began to speak very slowly again so that the full moment of his words should sink in and be thoroughly understood—"one of the Field homicide squad, in attempting a distinctly clever piece of elaboration, made an appalling mistake. It was this mistake which first put my fingers round what I feel must be the truth."

The silence was so intense now that Anthony could hear the others breathing.

6

"This mistake to which I allude was occasioned by a quite understandable trick of memory failure. In other words the person responsible fell into the pit which he himself had dug for another. Or, if you prefer it another way—he was 'hoist with his own petard.' At any rate—he overreached himself. Purely as a matter of academic interest, I'll tell you what that mistake was. Let us, first of all, refer to the 'love-note' which had been prepared for Field's wallet in the name of 'Mary.' *Inter alia* it stated this: 'Will meet you, etc., etc., same time but *different place*. The other side of Cornelius Stones.' And then at the end of the message 'anybody will direct you to Cornelius Stones if you ask.' Now that meant, gentlemen, if the note were genuine, only one thing. That Field was *unacquainted* with this new rendez-vous. That's unarguable! We will now, however, return to Field's surgery. I suggest that the three principal actors in the drama are on the point of departure. One of them notices Field's engagement diary

217 | THE SWINGING DEATH

on the desk table in front of them. He sees, too, the entry relating to the Stoke Pelly visit and he realizes that here is something to which the police will undoubtedly devote serious attention. He sees other entries to do with their own case. Field, remembering, doubtless, the lady's refusal to meet him on his first visit, had scrawled against the October date 'query meet Me.' Quite a natural thing for him to write in the light of the previous circumstances. The man examining the diary turns back to the pregnant date in September. He finds an appropriate entry and also the word 'refusal.' All in order. And at that moment a brilliant idea is born within his brain. He sees how he can absolutely strengthen the subtle suggestion that Field was running an illicit love affair with this non-existent 'Mary.' He takes a pencil and right down in the corner of the space devoted to the day in question he scrawls, in a handwriting as much like the other writing in the diary as he can make it, the damning phrase 'saw M.C.S.' What would be the police reaction when they discovered this? There would be one—and one only. Here would be undoubted confirmation that Field was meeting a woman named 'Mary' when he visited Stoke Pelly in a professional capacity. 'M' would be at once interpreted as 'Mary' and from there it would be an easy stage to travel to identify the letters 'C.S.' as 'Cornelius Stones.' I don't think that there can be much argument with regard to both those contentions. But therein lay the appalling mistake of which I made mention just now. Field, on the 22nd of September, according to the note, purporting to have been penned to him, *did not know where Cornelius Stones were*! He had never been there before! He wasn't aware of their existence in all probability. What happened, exactly, I think was this. When our gentleman decided to add the embellishment to Field's diary, he made a mental miscalculation. His mind was full of the fictitious 'Mary' whose existence belonged only to his imagination and the imagination of his confederates and of her meeting Field at the Cornelius Stones, the place *they* had also named for the false assignation. In his haste he forgot the exact terms of the note they had jointly written and in the heat, excitement and impulse of the moment, put the damning letters 'M.C.S.' *under the wrong date in Field's diary*. For some few seconds, I was deceived by the entry myself. Eager to interpret the 'M' and the 'C.S.' into the terms with which my mind was busy,

I failed to realize the significance of the error. When I did—and it came to me in a flash—out of nowhere as it were—I began to see for the first time, the pattern of, and the design behind, the crime. The entry was *not* in Field's writing, I decided. It had been deliberately added to the engagement diary by the man or men who had entered the surgery to destroy the files—and 'Mary' and her love-letter were false clues cunningly inserted into the case to lead the police astray. When all our subsequent inquiries and investigations failed to elicit any evidence as to the existence of the amorous lady, anywhere in the district where she might have been expected to live, I felt more than ever certain that my view was the correct one."

Anthony walked up to the stand which held the billiard cues and replaced the cue he had been using.

"There you are, gentlemen. I hope that I haven't wearied you and that you aren't sick of the sound of my voice. I have endeavoured to give you a picture of the murder of Julian Field and of the reasons which led up to it, as I think it *might* have happened. If you like—call it an intelligent reconstruction of how the crime *could* have been committed. What do you think of it, Mr. Stanhope?"

Anthony addressed his question to the head of the household. There came a period of silence. Philip Stanhope's voice was dry and harsh when he replied.

"I consider it remarkable. Really remarkable! As a piece of imagination."

The emphasis was placed on the last word.

"How about you?" Anthony spoke to Howard Stanhope, habitually a man of few words.

"It's been—er—interesting—to listen—to."

Anthony looked toward Dudley. "And what says the Cambridge scrum-half?"

Dudley Stanhope laughed—but there was a certain grimness in the laugh.

"My dear Bathurst," he said—"I think you're another Edgar Wallace—and also the greatest investigator of all time—but the latter, as my father said, 'only in the imagination.'"

Anthony smiled. "Thank you, gentlemen. I assure you that I shall value your tributes until the end of time." He looked round the room.

"I realize, that even if I desired to, it would be an almost impossible task for me to prove my story in a court of justice. There would be the stationmaster—who saw Field alive at 7.3 p.m.—there would be the gentleman who saw him in the Ram Inn at Fullafold between nine and ten o'clock—and, of course, Doctor Wolff, too, is dead and therefore couldn't be called—"

Anthony paused. "I said 'if I desired to.' I meant that. I have no wish to attempt to send a decent bloke to the gallows just because he removed from the world a vile creature who, by his despicable behaviour, had forfeited most, at least, of his right to live. There is scarcely a country in the world where decent people don't regard the blackmailer as something like a slug upon which you should stamp your foot."

Anthony turned suddenly to Godfrey Atherton. "By the way, Atherton—I didn't ask you. What did you think of that piece of imagination I put over to you just now?"

Godfrey Atherton came slowly from the corner where he had been sitting by the marker's board. He walked unsteadily. His eyes were strained and glassy-looking. A vein in his forehead was beating incessantly. He opened his mouth as though he were about to speak—but no words came. He looked anxiously, almost imploringly at his uncle and his two cousins. His eyes searched their respective faces, one by one. But they gave him no answer—neither help nor suggestion of help. When he saw their blank and stony acceptance of the looks he had given them, he pivoted suddenly on his heel and rushed out of the billiard-room. Anthony shrugged his shoulders.

"So that's that," he declared quietly. He glanced at his watch. "Well—I really must be saying good-bye. I'm later now than I intended to be. And I'll ask you to pay my respects to the ladies. I'm sure they'll be happier if they don't see me any more. Birds of ill omen cannot expect popularity."

He extended his hand to Philip Stanhope. The latter took it and shook it warmly. "Good-bye, Bathurst. And—er thank you! For—er—coming."

Howard Stanhope shook hands. "So long," he said laconically.

It came to Dudley's turn. "Cheerio, Bathurst. It's been both a pleasure and an education to meet you. Personally I wouldn't have missed it for worlds." He held Anthony's hand. "You must have one for the road. I'll mix it for you, myself."

Dudley brought the drink to Anthony as he stood in the drive by the car. He grinned. "Just between our two selves," he said, "and as one decent bloke to another *very* decent bloke—there'd be a third witness for you to reckon with. There was a chap in the train with 'Field' on his way back. You should have heard him on roses and rose growing. What he didn't know about it would have gone into a small ice-cream glass and then you'd have got an ice-cream on top."

He grinned again as he waved Anthony off.

Chapter XXIV

Letter from Anthony Lotherington Bathurst to Chief Detective-Inspector Andrew MacMorran, dated 28th December, 194—.

My dear Andrew,

Since I left you down at Greenhurst, the festive season has come and gone. No hot news about that—you'll say! But here is an item of news for you. I have had another gnaw at our little problem of the Fullafold murder and I am convinced that we are no "forrarder." I have to-day written to Sir Austin Kemble at the "Yard" and presented him with the same morsel of information. I have also informed him that in my opinion, too, we shan't get any "forrarder." That is to say, from the point of view of the twelve good men and true and the old black cap.

You, who have worked with me before on so many of our investigations, know me, I think, well enough to realize that I should never back out of a case, if I thought there were any reasonable chance of bringing it to a successful conclusion. Frankly, Andrew, I can't see that happening—hence these tears!

As you know, in these affairs, one of my first rules is always to sort out the false clues from the true. In this case from Fullafold, they're nearly all false—in fact the whole show is wall-eyed from the beginning to the end. Instead of having to search for the wrong 'uns they rise from their little nests and whisper in your receptive ears from all points of the compass. Also—and this is by no means a negligible point, the investigations I have made, which I feel I can rely on, have led me to the almost certain conclusion that our friend Doctor Julian Race Field was a damned bad hat and that the world probably smells a good deal sweeter by reason of his sudden translation and precipitation across the Styx. Be that as it may, Andrew—that's the position as I've come to see it. Incidentally, I've put in a word for you with the "old man"—so I don't think you'll have any real cause to worry.

Yours very sincerely,

Anthony L. Bathurst.

P.S.—How about a thrill for you on the third, Saturday in January? If you like, I'll book a couple of seats—England and Wales at Twickenham! What could be better?

P.P.S.—One day—when you've retired—and you're living down at Hogsnorton or Sheepwash-on-the-Snurge—I'll whisper in your ear the name of the man who killed Julian Field! S'right!

P.P.S. (2).—That made you blink—didn't it?

THE END

KINDRED SPIRITS . . .

Why not join the
DEAN STREET PRESS FACEBOOK GROUP

for lively bookish chat and more

Scan the QR code below

Or follow this link
www.facebook.com/groups/ deanstreetpress

CPSIA information can be obtained
at www.ICGtesting.com
Printed in the USA
LVHW030411150922
728386LV00004B/56

9 781915 393401